P9-CLS-198

We the People ...

Pamela Ackerson

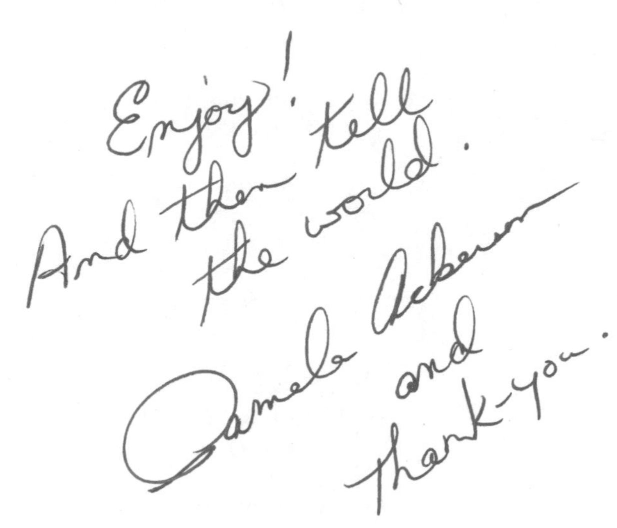

Austin, Texas

We the People ...

By Pamela Ackerson

© 2006 Pamela Ackerson

1st World Library
8305 Arboles Circle
Austin, TX 78737
512-657-8780
www.1stworldlibrary.com

Library of Congress Control Number: 2006900685
ISBN: 0-9765821-9-8

First Edition

Senior Editor
Barbara Foley

Editors
Bob Mahoney
Brad Fregger

Book Design & Production
Pamela Ackerson
Brad Fregger

Cover Design & Production
M. Kevin Ford

Original Cover Image
Roland Dempsey

All rights reserved. No part of this book may be reproduced or utilized in any form by any means, electronic or mechanical, including photocopying or recording, or by any information storage and retrieval system, without permission in writing from the publisher.

This is a work of fiction. Any relation to real people, living or dead, are creations of the author's imagination.

We the people of the United States, in order to form a more perfect union, establish justice, insure domestic tranquility, provide for the common defense, promote the general welfare and secure the blessings of liberty ...

Acknowledgments

First and foremost, my deepest appreciation goes to **my family** for understanding the intricacies of an author getting lost in a story. Without their encouragement, this book would never have been completed. They sat at the dinner table night after night listening to me talk about my characters as if they were real people, involving themselves in the story with much enthusiasm.

A special thank-you to **Junior** for having the utmost patience with me, tolerating my constant interruptions of his day, answering my questions about South Dakota and the Lakota people, as well as gently guiding me in the right direction.

And finally, I'd like to thank Bob Mahoney, Barbara Foley, and Brad Fregger of 1st World Library for helping this book be the best that it could be.

Wakan Tanka nici un.

To help you follow the characters in my story:

Karen	Spirit of the Mountain
Matthew	Gentle Raccoon
Andrew	Little Red Hawk
Christine	Little Owl
Devry	Floating Flower
Bonnie	Sings to the Wind

Prologue

Matthew, Jennifer, and Karen sat at the kitchen table, the stereo playing Jen's favorite Marc Anthony CD. Matthew added honey to his coffee while his mother cut the pastries and served them.

The three were silent for a few moments, the air heavy with anticipation.

"Are you ready, Son?"

"Yes." Matthew Standing Deer was ready to live his dreams. "I have waited a long time for this gift from you."

"You must be prepared," Karen emphasized. "For years, you and your sister have worked toward time traveling. When you were younger, you traveled under the strict rules of guidance. Those strict rules must continue. First rule …"

"I know. 'Don't attempt to change the past by interfering with recorded history.' I understand. I remember how irate you were with Bonnie."

Karen's friend Bonnie, known to the Lakota as Sings to the Wind, had journeyed back in time with Karen many years before. "By trying to prevent a battle that was meant to be, she altered history. Little Big Horn happened anyway," Karen shrugged. "Her interference not only changed what occurred in the past, it also altered the present. When I returned to the 20th century, the Lakota were in a worse situation than before I had left."

The elaborately carved four-poster bed sat in the spare bedroom, the door locked. It waited, waited patiently to give them the mystical gift of time. This precious blessing, sacred in its use, would honor them with the celestial gifts from the Creator.

His mother time-traveled on occasion to visit her friends in South Dakota. His parents had decided to wait until after he finished college before allowing him to seek the gift of the mystical bed. He had postponed the journey another two years to work as a firefighter. Jennifer, his sister, would have to wait another two years.

As he was growing up, he had heard the stories of his mother's paranormal experiences. She had found herself in a whirlwind of events beyond her control. Karen Anderson had been a modern-day surgeon, living life where it led and always playing it safe. Her life had changed the day she purchased the antique four-poster bed in an estate sale from an elderly woman named Bea.

Lying down for a nap, she had awoken in the past. Unsuitable for survival in a wilderness where only the strongest survive, the Creator bestowed precious, paranormal gifts. There in the past, she had finally surrendered to the inevitable and allowed herself to be spirited away in the arms of Matthew's father, Standing Deer.

Combining her modern life with the serenity of the plains, she had learned the ways of the Sioux and battled by their side over the span of time. His mother had lived the adventure of one of the most controversial battles of all times. Having raised her guns in the Battle of Little Big Horn, Custer's Last Stand, she saw, felt, and breathed the historical life of the great Sioux, joining the People as they fought their battle for freedom, for the promise of tomorrow.

Matthew responded. "I understand that I cannot change history. I know that would have ramifications in our world." They may have been born in the 20th century, but time travel had put them in both worlds. "I will be careful."

"No one uses the bed without my consent." She raised her eyebrows and looked directly at Jen. "We still do not understand everything about it. We cannot take the chance of something happening that would be irreversible. We do not control the bed; it decides your destiny. Once destiny's path is determined, you need to learn how to use the gift it has entrusted to you. The celestial power of the bed decides where you belong."

"We understand that, Mother."

Karen sighed. "I'm just making sure, Jennifer."

"I know where my destiny is." Matthew spoke with confidence. He had used the bed without permission, to transport himself to the past. Expecting to find his own adventure, he had awoken in Sitting Bull's tent. Jen had time-traveled without permission, also. She had found herself in 17th century New England during the witch-hunt. Their jaunts had put them both in deep trouble with their parents.

"Matthew, you believe you know where your destiny lies. You were young when you traveled on the bed without me. What if there is a different destiny waiting for you now?"

"But, *you* can control where you go," Jen pointed out.

"Not entirely. Through trial and error, I learned what I could and could not control. I can determine where, as in township or camp. However, I cannot determine a particular day, or even a particular year."

Matthew bit the inside of his cheek. "The bed is picky. It has been selective about who was able to travel and when.

What if it doesn't take me anywhere? I remember when Dad tried to take us to the past with him. He returned to his world but Jennifer and I remained here. What if it determines a time and place for my destiny and then doesn't let me return, when I want?"

"I don't know," Karen raised her hands. "However, *what ifs* are not the way to live your life. If it doesn't take you anywhere, then, doesn't that tell you that your destiny lies here in the present? I don't even want to think about you not being able to return."

"Maybe it won't take him anywhere because he isn't ready." Jennifer bit into a jelly donut, a smirk crinkling her eyes as Matthew shot her a glare.

"There are many unanswered questions. That is why you must be careful, Matthew, be prepared."

"I am prepared for whatever destiny hands me."

"We will not attach the canopy to the bed until we are comfortable with the situation."

"That must have been freaky when they figured out the canopy stopped the time traveling." Jennifer shivered.

"I imagine it was." Karen tapped her finger on her coffee cup, "However, Bea had warned me about the canopy when she handed it to me. At least, I was prepared to test the canopy to see if it prevented traveling."

"Do you think that there were people who owned the bed and never knew what it could do?" Matthew wondered, "How many … just hung the canopy and never knew the gifts it had to offer?"

"Really," Jen frowned. "I never even thought of that."

Karen sighed. "Let's stay on track here. We've gotten off the subject I wanted to discuss." Jennifer lit a cigarette and Matthew eyed her in disgust. "You cannot assume that you will journey to the Lakota. However, that is what we shall prepare ourselves for." Karen paused.

"The bed will determine where you go. If your destination is different from what we expect, we will do our research on that era. You are going to be, basically, living two separate lives. If it gets to be too much, you will discontinue. Do you understand? I will stop you."

"Okay."

"When you are ready, I will go first and wait for you. Before you fall asleep, you must concentrate and focus on your destination. If it works the way we expect, you will be in South Dakota with me, in 1890; and it will give us better knowledge of controlling the bed. That way, when it is Jennifer's turn to travel, we will have that much more understanding."

Matthew nodded.

Handing him the key, his mother smiled. "When you are ready."

The Breath of Heaven whispered quietly in his ears. The Elk River, singing its song, orchestrated the music of the land. He stood alone, overlooking the valley. His heart was ready for anything. Pine Ridge Reservation beckoned in the distance. Mother Earth was speaking to him, whispering tales of the past and blessing the future.

The trees sang a gentle song of welcome and a mournful goodbye. His time had finally arrived; he could feel the change in the wind. Nothing would block his path to the past and to his future. His soul was strong, and he knew he possessed the faith to face the challenges.

He had enjoyed the holiday with his Uncle Jim and his family from the Pine Ridge Reservation. He would miss them terribly. His mother had traveled ahead to South Dakota, to the year 1890. She waited for him now. Her second husband, John Black Elk, refused to sleep on the bed. He understood his wife's needs but preferred to keep grounded in the present world.

John had suggested the move from Pine Ridge and their subsequent return to Florida. Matthew had resented John for years until he had returned a few months ago and stayed with his uncle. Uncle Jim had given him immense insight regarding his stepfather's position on life.

His flight home to Florida would depart in three hours. A part of him would remain. He would leave this modern world, perhaps a final farewell, and seek his destiny. Though it was not in his plans to stay in the past, he heeded John's words well. *Men plan, God laughs.* He would be prepared for whatever and wherever the road led.

Matthew anticipated sharing tales with old friends he had not seen in more than ten years. He would travel to the town that developed near his mother's cave house. The cave house and ranch, an endeavor for new beginnings, now represented a heartrending symbol of the ravages of defeat.

The Lakota elders would teach him well. He would grasp this moment of a lifetime with an open heart. Matthew would cherish his time with Sitting Bull, Black Elk, and Gall.

His mother had forewarned him. He knew he would not see a thriving reservation. The government had confined a majority of the Indians to reservations where the land was poor, the meat scarce, and starvation was common. The treaties promised food and supplies; if the supplies arrived, they were of poor quality. An appeal for volunteers to aid the Indians brought Quakers and ministers of many denominations to the reservation. Their efforts to convert the Indians to Christianity caused more problems.

Matthew was heading into a powder keg, and he knew it. The Indians were ready to rebel. The government had attempted to purchase land from the Sioux Nation. Before they could obtain the land, a minimum of seventy-five percent of the warriors had to sign the contract.

Matthew smiled to himself. Sitting Bull had outright refused to sell any of his People's land or their future inheritance. He had informed the officials that no one had the right to sell his portion of tribal lands. He had never signed a treaty selling his lands, and he never would.

Animosity and corruption filled the Indian Bureau, creating disdain among the People. Coercion and deception were rampant. Minor children were encouraged to sign, as well as non-Indian males who had married Sioux women. Officials summoned the Indians to the agency and refused to permit their return home until they had placed their signatures on the documents.

A few conscientious souls strived to help the Sioux Nation, searching for proof of inaccurate census records and illegally obtained signatures. Despite their determination, the government eventually took nine million acres from the Sioux.

Loss of the land was not the only mockery that derived from this horrendous greed. The reservation had now been scattered into six smaller areas. It essentially created a prison, requiring the Indians to obtain written permission to leave the reservations. It was no wonder the Ghost Dance had become so popular. Repression causes rebellion.

Matthew knew he would be walking into a roaring fire pit. By comparison, he had until now lived an uncomplicated life with mere pebbles tripping him now and again. However, his parents had taught him well. He was ready for the road ahead. He knew it would be a long hard walk.

He lived in the white man's world with the beliefs of the Lakota burning in his heart and soul. It was his time to spread his fledgling wings. He could hear the winds of change blowing from afar.

No one would deter him from his intended path. His heart and soul would lead him; the faith in his heart would keep him strong. His mother's gentle wisdom whispered in his ear. *You must have faith to believe you can do anything.*

Chapter One

The playful scurrying of squirrels and chirping of birds filled the air in the tranquil woods as the young boy waited for his twin brother to find him. Jeremy Little Red Hawk's right foot was falling asleep and he desperately wanted to move it so it would stop tingling. Leaning against the tree, he adjusted his weight to his left side. He wiggled his toes and flinched at the dull pain. This would not do at all. He was aghast at the humiliation. A brave warrior's foot did not fall asleep while he waited silently for the enemy.

He was fortunate today. The wind was silent, allowing him to hear any unnatural sounds in the woods surrounding him. There were no rustling leaves or falling branches to mask footsteps. Jeremy listened intently, the way his father had taught him, and became one with the forest. He waited diligently for the sound of crushed leaves, for the telltale footstep or the snap of a twig underfoot. The rules were strict. He had to keep his position unless he heard his brother's approach, and then he would search for another hiding spot.

The two boys played in the woods behind their home. To be a Lakota brave, one must be able to creep up without a sound and touch one's enemy on the shoulder. Thus, his brother Emanuel could proudly declare that in the year

1890, upon his 7th winter count, he had become a true Lakota brave.

Emanuel was improving immensely. Jeremy had not heard the stealth approach of his brother's vulpine steps. The sudden deafening betrayal of silence in the forest alerted him to the persistent vigilance of the enemy. The creatures in the area were holding their breaths in anticipation, alerting him with their finely honed senses. He could hear his father's wise words whispering in the silence. *Become a part of Mother Earth. Become one with nature and you will become a true and proud warrior.*

Jeremy slowly moved his head left and then right. Which way should he go? Which way was his brother? The trail was ten feet behind him. He would go there and then retrace his steps to this same spot. Wiggling his toes, he bit his lip against the pain as his foot popped back to life.

Crouching, he silently inched his way to the trail and the open copse. The snap of a branch rang loud in his ears as his brother emerged from the shadows of the trees. Jeremy ran onto the trail, his new moccasins dulling his sounds of retreat. He circled to an open area of the woods where he found himself staring at a saddled thoroughbred beside a man sitting against a tree. The man appeared to be asleep; his head leaned back, mouth open and eyes closed.

The young boy rounded silently and walked into his brother Emanuel.

"Ha!"

"Not fair! Look." Jeremy pointed to the sleeping man. "Isn't that Mr. Burke?"

"Looks like him. Why's he sleeping in the woods?"

Mr. Burke's hat was sitting askew, shading his eyes, a bottle of whiskey clenched tightly in his right hand. His clothing was crisp and starched, pristine as always. Nothing appeared unusual except, of course, a man of Mr. Burke's status would not be sleeping in the woods. His well-trained horse stood gallantly by his side.

Jeremy frowned as Emanuel soundlessly walked over to the man and shook him gently. "Mr. Burke … Mr. Burke? Are you well?"

The man slumped backward, dried blood crusted under his nose, his limbs rigid. Thickened blood trickled from his mouth as the body descended to the ground. The boys jumped and screamed in terror, running blindly home. Attaining the dream of a warrior's first coup was far from their minds.

The boys' father, Andrew Little Red Hawk, and Karen Black Elk were sitting quietly in the morning room, drinking excessively sweetened coffee and enjoying freshly made pastries.

"It has been a while since your last visit."

Karen Anderson Black Elk, known to the Lakota as Spirit of the Mountain, rarely traveled the long road to his world. Her second husband, John Black Elk, never traveled to the home and lands she had once shared with her first husband, Standing Deer.

"I miss my friends and this town. I am happy I found this peaceful corner of South Dakota."

"If not for you … you encouraged us to build the town. It is a menagerie of the world, a rainbow of cultures."

"The only other choice available was the reservations," Karen added. "Many felt as you did. They would rather have died than become dependent on the government. It was depressing, watching the ranch burn; watching the death of such a well-placed safe haven. I cried for many days."

"I am glad you did not lose faith."

The vision of the hot fingers of blackened smoke slashing the skies burned in her memory. "It was not easy. We have lived through many tragic and happy times together. Of course, I prefer to remember the happy."

"Well, here's to another celebration."

Andrew's dark Lakota features brightened as he lifted his cup of coffee in cheer. Karen laughed and clinked her own cup against his.

Although Andrew lived in the white man's world now, he had never deserted his Lakota heritage. He kept his raven-black hair long, tied back with a leather strap. While he was in town, he would don the white man's clothes, but when he worked on his ranch, buckskins and moccasins prevailed. He easily moved between cultures, blending them in a way unique to him.

He taught the ways of the Lakota to his children, a legacy of a life he had once known. They learned to live and thrive in both worlds. He cleverly combined the teachings of the Christian religion with the spiritual beliefs of the Lakota. All of his children knew how to live off the land. His attitude of taking care of Mother Earth helped his ranch thrive, making him a wealthy man. If it had not been for his life-long friend, where would he and his family be now?

On her last visit, he had requested Karen's assistance. She had readily agreed to take his oldest daughter Devry to Standing Rock to visit Sitting Bull. It would be a year of good memories, happy times, and celebrations.

He had heard the tales of how she had come from a different world, a world filled with incomparable magic. He had listened to stories around the fire of how she had resisted what life had planned for her, how she had fought destiny. She had refused to accept her fate until she took the lessons of the Lakota into her heart. Once she had opened her soul to the breath of the Great Spirit, her life had changed. She had found an incredible love for eternity.

When he had first encountered Karen, he had instantly understood why the Lakotas had named her Spirit of the Mountain. Green eyes imitated the grass and leaves of the trees. Her hair radiated the colors of autumn, streaking rays of sun-kissed yellow and gold. Even now with age painting its colors in her hair, the silver strands glittered in the sun's rays, brightening the aura that surrounded her.

After the Battle of the Little Big Horn and Standing Deer's death, her family had stopped returning to the Dakota Territory. Only on a few occasions had Karen come to their home or gone to visit Sitting Bull and her Lakota friends at the Standing Rock Reservation. She was one of the strongest-willed women who had ever crossed his path. Their mutual respect and deep friendship would last until the end of their days.

Andrew smiled. "When is Matthew …" He was startled at the sound of the rear door slamming against the wall, followed by the distinct sound of glass breaking as a vase was knocked to the floor.

The boys charged through the house. The shrill screams of terror interrupted their comfortable table banter. Karen and Andrew ran from the room and found the boys running down the hallway toward the morning room, revulsion etching their angelic faces.

"What is it?"

"What has happened?"

Jeremy's eyes were full of fear, tears streaming down his dirty face. Emanuel bounced, stuttering in a high-pitched squeal. "The … woods … Mr. … Burke … dead … blood … horse …"

Jeremy gripped Karen's skirt as she bent down to hold him. Andrew calmed Emanuel with soothing words.

"Now Son, tell me slowly. Take a deep breath. Try to stay calm and tell me from the beginning …"

Chapter Two

Lydia Wetmore Williams, otherwise known as The Widow, sat in the coach for a lengthy minute after it had stopped rocking. She gradually pulled herself out of the cushioned seat she had been resigned to for the last four hours. The trip across country from her uncle's estate, Chateau-Sur-Mer, in Newport, Rhode Island, had been an arduous one. For the second year in a row, she had taken her holiday in the spring instead of the usual autumn excursion.

With a deep sigh, she glanced to the right. In an unhurried manner, she straightened the tousled skirt of her dark green traveling dress and disembarked from the coach, smiling. It felt good to be home.

Many looked upon the town and saw peace. At times, she wondered if it was truly a paradise hidden among this mountainous country. In the last year, Lydia sensed that paradise had grown its own entity, an evil serpent lurking somewhere, until its need to strike arose again.

As she approached the luggage, she navigated amongst the clusters of people. A tall man wearing the uniform of a Regulator was talking to a simply dressed woman whose face showed resignation to the man's unhappy news. A younger boy of ten or twelve, tears stinging his eyes, held the woman's hand.

Hearing her name, Lydia turned and smiled at Juan de Rivera, who had waited patiently for the coach to arrive. The warm afternoon sun beat on the two friends as he grabbed her hurriedly packed carpetbags. She watched, in amazement, as he placed the heavy cedar trunk into the carriage. He stood eye to eye with her, yet she could not move the trunk, let alone pick it up with the ease he had … putting it into the carriage as if it were light as a hat box.

Juan assisted The Widow as she struggled to step into the carriage. "Almost home, Lydia, just a few more minutes."

A high feminine, cultured voice greeted her. Catherine Miller, Juan's eldest daughter, sat smiling as she leaned over to give Lydia a hug. The Widow adjusted herself, glancing from Catherine to Juan, watching as the footman slowly shut the door and Juan tapped on the roof with his umbrella.

Though Catherine was a year older than Lydia, she had always seemed to be younger; or rather, The Widow felt ten years older. Because of that difference, she had become friends with Juan and his wife Domina during the Indian Wars, when life had become complicated and survival was the only reality.

The two girls had met at a very young age and had attended finishing school together. Lydia had returned to New York for a holiday before she traveled to the Chateau-Sur-Mer in Newport. Catherine had been visiting friends and had received a much-prized invitation to the exclusive, most-sought-after costume ball of the season.

Mrs. Alva Vanderbilt had thrown one of the most lavish and expensive costume balls in her newly built home on Fifth Avenue. A rumor elaborated Alva's extravagance of spending over $75,000 for the masquerade. It was a flagrant and extraordinary amount of money; Lydia wondered at the time if it would cause a competition of who could throw the most lavish and expensive parties.

Lydia had shocked the elite society by donning American Indian regalia. Most of the thousand guests wore costumes for the occasion. A few guests, like the former president, Ulysses Grant, had attended but had stayed with their usual conservative nature, wearing formal attire. Alva surpassed all imagination by outshining everyone with an elaborate costume she titled The Power of Electricity. Her husband William had dressed as the Duc de Guise, reigning supreme for the evening.

Carrie Astor, Catherine, and several young ladies had performed a waltz. The women had adorned their heads with shimmering stars and had pronounced themselves the Star Quadrille. All who attended reminisced for years about the event.

Catherine had been the wind impossible to hold, the sort of girl who either forgot her dance program or danced with any boy who pleased her. That had been seven years ago. She had collected suitors as trophies and her marriage had not seemed to settle the butterfly in her spirit.

Many believed she was far too egotistical and heedless of other people's feelings. At times, this was an accurate call. Unless Catherine liked you, you were insignificant. However, if you were in her heart, you had it all. Though the woman never did anything vindictive and would never intentionally hurt anyone, she craved attention … a lot of attention.

A lock of Catherine's dark chocolate hair strategically wrestled itself out from underneath her sunbonnet. Everything she did was intentional, all the way down to the hair out of place, the rip in her blouse, or the smudged dirt on her nose, depending on whom she might be attempting to entice at the time. The bright cotton dress and matching parasol, along with her perfect beauty, made her stand out regardless of where she was. Alas, Catherine would look exquisite in a gunnysack.

Juan appeared exhausted, as if he had been in battle. In the three months Lydia was away from home, three people had died and the good doctor, Glenn Carson, was suffering from kidney failure.

"How is the doctor?" Lydia inquired softly.

"My unmitigated apologies for cutting your holiday short. I am at a loss. I was hoping you would arrive without delay to be able to persuade Glenn not to do anything rash." Juan leaned forward and nodded. "Indeed Lydia, I was hoping that you would be able to persuade him to keep fighting this, not to give up hope."

"What do you mean by rash, Papa?" Catherine asked, clearly puzzled by his concern.

"You will soon begin to realize," Juan de Rivera opened both his gloved hands, "what news is waiting."

"Be so kind as to inform *me*, then." Lydia regretted her coarse and angry voice, always striving to keep her persona buoyant and congenial.

Her lungs felt as if they were bursting, as if she was submerged under water straining to break the surface. Juan struggled, delaying the news that he had no desire to render. His hard Spanish features contorted with reluctance, his mouth opened and closed with no words coming forth. The noises of the world outside magnified the silence within the carriage. She could hear the metal-rimmed wheels of a milk cart treading along the rock-strewn road, scraping her nerves.

"You will soon discover such matters for yourself. Glenn refuses to listen to anything I propose, making it quite difficult for his housekeeper to tend him. It has been an interesting quagmire, to say the least." Juan took another long silent break.

"I have not had any trouble," Catherine said indignantly.

Juan and Lydia laughed as he patted his daughter's hand. "That's because you could cajole a dead man to drink."

Catherine laughed, eyes twinkling with total awareness that she probably could.

"One thing, Lydia, I must tell you. He is fading fast, much faster than any of us could have imagined. I pray your convalescing him at your home will not pose too much of a burden."

Of course, she would care for him without any qualms or misgivings. The news of his illness was not a surprise, for she had been aware of the doctor's health problems before she had left for her holiday. The quickness of the disease shook her clear to her core. Lydia remained frozen in time for half a minute or more, vaguely aware of passing the homes of friends and neighbors. She stared at Juan, uncertain what to say, too anguished to express her emotions.

"What will we do without him?"

Lydia wondered if life's occurrences had become too comfortable in this modest town. Had she been walking around the last few years with blinders, too relaxed in her now uncomplicated life? They had known each other since her earliest memories. The Indian Wars had brought them together. When you had to trust your back and your life to someone, they became a part of you.

She could not recall a time when Juan and Glenn had not been in her life in some way. Glenn had convinced her to move here after the death of her husband. She had no regrets. Lydia's family name kept her in Society, but Society was not where her heart lived. Glenn had described it as a sleepy little town that wrapped you in a nice soft blanket. He could not have been more accurate.

The aura of paradise hung lightly over the peaceful town. Whenever tragedy struck, the townspeople would ease the burdens of their neighbors and work together to help. Celebrations gathered everyone to unite in happiness and good cheer.

The financially comfortable were far from ostentatious. They never flaunted their money and the residents of the town never worried about where their neighbors stood financially. Tokata's elders expected them to keep the town prosperous and the younger residents did not disappoint them. The town's atmosphere whispered prosperity, but if a family floundered, the town assembled as one.

However, like any large family there were disagreements, too. There were neighbors with eccentric quirks that irritated others, and secrets were whispered, never spoken aloud.

Tokata was a small bustling town shaped like a beaming star. The main road circled a luscious green park at its center, where benches sat, placed among the gardens and pathways to allow residents to converse. The residents kept the park pristine for the town picnics and they organized games for the children to play among themselves.

Like Chinese fireworks, the roads fingered out to their own individual section. One road led to the White River and the thriving wharfs, where pleasure boats floated leisurely and the shipping commerce sailed to the Missouri River. Another road led to the shimmering hot springs off the Cheyenne River and the lake where, during the warm days of summer, the townspeople would swim and the children would play.

The people of the town kept things simple. Rapid City Road led to Rapid City and the main train station. Lake Drive wound out to the lake, and Mission Road ran to the Old Mission that years before had also been used as a mill. Some old-timers still called it Mill Road.

Lydia would not have realized the carriage had reached the house if Catherine had not breathed a sigh of relief. She leaned forward in her seat, clasping Catherine's soft hands, watching her somber eyes as they radiated confusion. Though Catherine had become selfish because of personal needs, she was a very loving woman who did not understand the tragedies that life served.

Lydia walked toward the double-sized front doors and white-trimmed windows that shouted a happy welcome. The butler, awaiting her arrival, opened the doors. She entered the foyer, relieved that she was home. Juan followed, carrying one of her carpetbags as the footman brought in the trunk. Among the mild commotion, the housekeeper snapped quick orders to the house servants, sending them scurrying in several directions.

With a quick kiss on the hand, Juan bid her good day. "I promise to return to help you get the house ready for the doctor."

Chapter Three

Anyone and everyone who entered Lydia Wetmore Williams' home always felt as if they belonged and were part of the family. There was a room for everyone: a gentleman's library, a lady's sitting room, a quilting room, a small ballroom, and a smoking room. She even had a small medical office in the back for people who came to her for healing with herbs.

Lydia's sanctuary, however, was the gardens and backyard, artfully designed as a miniature park. The boathouse next to the half-acre pond was a miniature replica of the main house. She had animals of all varieties and every one of them believed you were there specifically to pet or feed them. Unless you had food, most of the geese and ducks frolicked around the large circular pond and were quite content to mind their own business. It was a blissful, heavenly sanctuary—except for Sir Elmer, as the neighbors and friends had dubbed him.

Sir Elmer … the most complimentary word one could use for Elmer was persnickety. There were a few, a handful of people, blessed with his acceptance that he would not chase or treat to an invidious greeting. He believed he was human with the misfortune of having feathers, acting like a grumpy old man with the regrettable ability to fly. He absolutely adored Lydia and followed her around the house and grounds like a love-struck puppy.

Sir Elmer had made multiple attempts to live in the house. Since he was human, where else should he lay his head? Finally, Glenn had made the suggestion to give Elmer his own private quarters in the back of the house. They arranged it so the door leading into the house locked when necessary, and the exit leading to the backyard remained ajar in the summer months.

This had pacified Elmer's persistence until the snows arrived. He had squawked and complained until a bed with warm blankets became a permanent addition to his room. It had made life more comfortable for those who were … Sir Elmer. The world revolved around him, and as soon as everyone accepted that, life would be much easier for him. As far as he was concerned, everyone *must* conform to the proper pecking order. He, of course, was at the top.

With the unexpected return of his most beloved Lydia, Elmer was exasperated. Too many raucous and uninvited people were coming in the house. It was utterly audacious! They were distracting Lydia, taking her away from him, moving packages around, and just causing utter chaos. Now that she was home, Elmer expected her exclusive attention. How was Lydia supposed to give him her undivided attention with all these transients and troublemakers coming in and out of *his* house? The neighbors down the street heard him squawking his obnoxious objections for hours.

His Lydia … gone for months and it had been utterly dreadful. Did the house have to be in such an uproar? He placed his wing dramatically on his forehead. All these people were giving him an abominable headache. Sir Elmer wished these inconvenient distracters would leave and attend to their own homes where they belonged.

Grumbling and stomping to the bedroom where most of the commotion seemed to originate, Elmer squeezed through the housekeeper's legs and clomped his feet as he made his way to the corner. Hopping atop the table, Sir Elmer perched as if he were on a throne. He eyed the inconvenient and unwelcome intruder lying in the bed. Once he recognized the doctor, the goose accepted his presence with a regal nod and sat down.

The town's only doctor lay sick, dying from kidney failure. Lydia took a cool cloth and lightly brushed his fevered forehead. Neither his modern medicine nor her herbal concoctions would save him now. He smiled in gratitude and winked when he heard the distant knock at the bedroom door.

Juan de Rivera was his good friend and confidant. They had come to this little town together after the Indian Wars and both had thrived. There was only one secret between them. Today, he would ask. Today was the day the box would open. They knew that soon the doctor would be in a coma and nothing would bring him back.

The Widow poured another cup of tea and held it out to Juan as he entered the bedroom. Elmer jumped up from his corner, alert as a seasoned soldier, ready to attack and defend the doctor and his mistress. Recognition penetrated his guard; he squawked a petulant greeting before he sat back down. Stretching his neck and rotating his shoulder, he relaxed into the soft cushions

With a quick peck on Lydia's cheek, Juan took the cup and sat next to his old friend. He looked around the frilly, feminine room. It had a peaceful and welcome atmosphere. Foregoing and ignoring the whispers of impropriety, she had opened her heart and home to a friend in need. It was warming to the soul to know, though one may have many acquaintances, there were a blessed few who had friends as special as these two.

The doctor pointed to Juan, his Scottish brogue trembling in his weakened state, making it difficult to understand him. "You will tell me. You cannot let me leave this life without telling me the truth. The Widow over there is as stubborn as you are and refuses to answer my questions; claims she has no idea what I am talking about."

Juan sighed. "Your brother-in-law arrived safely and is at this very moment unpacking his bags. How was Lydia to know this when we never told her we sent for him?"

"What are you two up to now?" she asked.

"That is not what I am talking about and you know it. You're trying to distract me."

"I would do no such thing," Juan replied indignantly.

"You would, too. Don't you be giving me any hogwash. I will come back and haunt you for the rest of your days if you don't answer my question."

"What are you talking about?" Lydia insisted again.

"My brother-in-law. We called him in to find out who is killing off all the club members. There have been too many unexplained deaths in the last year. There is someone eliminating the members of the Gentlemen's Club, one at a time." Glenn struggled to continue. "Now, granted, they deserved to be knocked off, but that is not for us to decide. That is what the good Lord is for." Glenn knew Juan was circumventing the actual question.

"Why your brother-in-law?"

"He's a Pinkerton man, or I should say, was a Pinkerton man. One of the best, of course, but he retired a few months back and has been traveling and sowing his wild oats, so to speak." Glenn had the grace to blush as he cleared his throat.

"Isn't that what the sheriff is for?" Lydia wiped Glenn's face with a cool cloth.

"Sowing his wild oats?" Juan intoned with a chuckle.

Lydia bit her lip to cover the smile.

"You're very conveniently changing the subject again, old man." Glenn pointed a shaky finger. Juan gave an elegant shrug, not willing to deny the accusation.

"The sheriff may have twisted a blind eye to the club members, but he wouldn't tolerate murder; never did. Unfortunately, if he does not die before me I will be surprised. He suspects one of the members. Maybe he was a little too close to discovering who it is and that is why they have gone after him. That's why we decided to send for my brother-in-law."

"I think someone is poisoning them." Juan scratched his forehead.

The Widow snorted. "Maybe it's all that opium they've been doing." She paused and pursed her lips. "The sheriff is dying? I was under the impression that it was just a minor cold."

"I thought so, too."

"That's why I sent his wife the cold remedy." Glenn cringed in pain. "But he is going just like the others; sick on and off for the past three months. I am not sure how the murderer will do it. You mark my words; it's to be a stroke, heart attack, or the lungs. The killer knows what he is doing."

Juan raised an eyebrow, "He is getting overconfident, too, killing Burke right out in the open like that, for those children to find him. Sly fellow that he is, I wonder how many people he killed before we realized they were murdered."

"The sheriff will be dead in less than a week. It's almost as if the murderer has my medical records and knows where their weaknesses are." Glenn closed his eyes, mulling over a mental list of who had access to his office files.

"You need to get some rest. Drink some more of your tea," Lydia quietly encouraged.

"No, I will not. You put laudanum in there to make me sleep. I want answers … thought I'd forget, did you?" Glenn yawned and glared at her.

"I did not put laudanum in your tea." Lydia glared back.

"Then you put some of your tricky witch herbs in there. I practically heard you cackling while you were brewing it." Glenn rubbed his hands together and started cackling in a high-pitched voice. "Do not argue with me, you will not win. I want answers and end this attempt to change the subject."

"I do not cackle." Lydia raised her chin and sniffed.

The doctor laughed. "It's good to know I can still ruffle your feathers."

Sir Elmer raised his head and lifted one eyebrow, apparently offended by the choice of wording. He cocked his head toward the doctor and tapped his foot with impatience, expecting an apology.

Glenn stared at the goose and piped, "I'm waiting, and not very patiently, mind you."

Juan and Lydia both sighed. Lydia shrugged and nodded her head.

"As you wish, my friend. Make your queries."

"I've waited five years for the answers to these questions." The doctor stared them down in his familiar way. "It was the two of you who saved my life, wasn't it? You were part of the snipers. Who knocked me out? Which one of you took the bullet for me? Whose safe house was I in when I was recovering from pneumonia? Why did you keep me blindfolded when I was one of you?"

"It was my home. We had to keep you tucked away and safe," Juan said quietly.

"I was the driver."

"Lydia's husband took the bullet. We had to get the Indians to the cabin." Juan looked down at his hands. "It was our fault you got pneumonia. We're the ones who left you in the storm."

"Tall Oak? I thought he was already in Montana. I thought he died there from a battle wound." Glenn was silent for a few minutes and drifted into a restless half-sleep, leaving the other two lost in their memories.

It had been a dangerous moment in their lives. Risks taken and lives lost from both sides. The snipers were handpicked, an elite group known for their deadly accuracy. They had joined a cause they believed was true and moral.

They recalled their involvement and clandestine actions in the Indian Wars. The gentlemen knew Lydia felt exposed. She gallantly repressed the loss of her husband as it threatened to bubble to the surface. The winds of memories flushed emotions they believed were peacefully at rest.

"Why the blindfold?" Glenn asked, making both Juan and Lydia jump in surprise.

"Come now, you would have wanted to join us," Juan intoned.

Glenn rubbed his throbbing head, trying to alleviate the pain. "Of course, I would have sought to join you; we worked together. Why would you even consider me a threat?"

"We did not consider you a threat. We were protecting you."

"I did not need protection. Tall Oak was supposed to be in Montana. What happened?"

"Lydia's husband was *Metis.* He could walk the woods unseen. He traveled and hid in the forest like the shadows. The story of him fighting in Canada and taking the Indians and Metis to Montana is true, but that day he was with us. We had to use that knowledge to keep suspicion away from us. We had to keep you out of it. You were the sawbones."

"I was already in it," The doctor proclaimed. "The day you asked me to meet you at the Canadian border put me in the middle of your battles. Once you had me taking care of the wounded, you involved me and I accepted it without question."

"That is true," Lydia answered. "We were taking a chance involving you. We had not finished getting the rebels across the border yet. Fighting Canadian forces and hiding the rebels was our main priority."

"Glenn," Juan interjected, "Tall Oak died a warrior's death. He was proud to fight and die for freedom. He believed his lifeblood would give a better life to the children of this country." Lydia's husband had fought with the famous buffalo hunter Gabriel Dumont. Fighting in western Canada, Tall Oak Williams, along with a group of Indians and the Saskatchewan Metis, fought several skirmishes with the Canadian forces.

When their headquarters had been captured, the defeated group of approximately three hundred rebels traveled to Montana to take refuge among the other Indian tribes. Juan, Lydia, and a small group of sympathizers had assisted their escape, aiding in the transfer of the rebels to safe houses until they had reached their destination.

"So you weren't part of the snipers?" the doctor raised his brow in disbelief.

"No, well, yes we were. The snipers watched our backs until we were safely away from the Canadians. Lydia's husband was the one who attacked you from behind and hid your body under the table. He had been alerted that the Canadians were going to rush the campsite."

"He knew he would be able to fight them, whereas I was unarmed." Glenn stared out the window. "He gave his life for me."

"Tall Oak gave his life for freedom," Lydia declared.

"Thank you. It was always a part of my life that had too many unanswered questions." The doctor sighed in relief. It had been troubling, not knowing what had happened. He understood their actions, had compassion for the extreme measures they had taken to protect him. He would never have voluntarily left the injured rebels.

"You're welcome," Juan and Lydia answered.

"It's about blessed time you two fessed up. When's that no good brother-in-law of mine going to show his shining face?"

Juan laughed. "Well, it shouldn't take Domina much more than a few days to fatten him up. I'm sure Lane will be over as soon as he is able."

"Don't know what is causing his delay." Glenn grumbled, "It's not like my house has been empty for more than a day."

"He has his work cut out for him. I believe he will want to ask questions of a lot of people."

"Starting with the sheriff, I imagine," Lydia piped in.

"So now we seek a murderer amongst us."

"Well, at the rate the killer is going, he will dispose of all the members," the doctor snapped back.

"They're ruining our town. Do we really want the killer caught then?" Juan inflicted.

"Juan!" Lydia looked at him in shock.

Juan did not look the least bit remorseful. "South Dakota's plate is full. We are dealing with the Indian Ghost Dance; South Dakota became a state last year. Add the drought and the depressed financial economy to all of that ... how much more can we tolerate?"

The doctor leaned forward. "The government pushed the majority of Sioux Indians onto the reservations and destroyed their lifestyles."

A faint frown marred Lydia's forehead. "It angers me when they make decisions that affect us, when they are thousands of miles away. Though it has not touched our hometown in the same way it has the rest of the Midwest, the corruption is unacceptable."

"Now, we have a murderer seeping his poison into our town." Juan grimaced.

Lydia assisted Glenn as he lay back; his eyelids drooped. He declared with a yawn, mumbling before he fell asleep, "Like I have a say in what happens in the world around us. Besides, Lane will be here soon to speak with me. He will be investigating the murders with the persistence of a hungry wolf. He will have the murderer behind bars in no time."

Chapter Four

The raised embroidered linen shades welcomed the morning breeze into the room, eerily billowing the net and Spanish lace curtains. Elegant fabrics of muted blue and peaches masterfully painted a picture of elegance. It was a room for a princess.

Oblivious to her outward beauty, the young girl tapped her fingers on the rosewood vanity and sat transfixed, staring at the reflection in the mirror. Regal and earthy, she was a contradiction of sexuality and innocence that intrigued all. Dark penetrating eyes radiated an inner beauty and wisdom beyond her years. Her voice had a smooth musical lilt with a mild caress of a mixed accent, creating a kaleidoscope of child-like illusion and exotic indolence.

Unlike most of the women of the Mid-west, her beauty was mysteriously exotic, even at the early age of thirteen; she carried a reserved countenance for one so young. She inherited her mother's Polynesian beauty and elegance. Her hair, never cut except to keep the length uniform, sparkled in the sunlight like the brilliant luster of polished hematite. Wrinkling her nose, Devry Little Red Hawk pulled the front of the dress higher to cover more of her all-too-soon generously proportioned breasts.

"Quit fiddling, Devry. I'll never get your hair finished before your dance instructor arrives."

Frowning at her maid in quiet frustration, she sighed heavily. "Why have I started my dance lessons so soon?"

"It is what your father wishes, Devry."

"I do not care for it."

Aghast, Anna's jaw dropped, incredulous at the girl's statement. "You do not like to dance? For the four months you have been taking lessons, you have not uttered one word of dissatisfaction." Anna squinted her eyes as if it would help see into Devry's mind.

"He is old." Devry looked toward the door to make certain no one was about. She whispered, "That man has clammy hands and mean eyes."

Anna laughed. "Why do you always refer to him as 'that man'? He has a name, Devry. He is certainly not old. He is but twenty-five years old. That man, as you call him, is also doing your father a great service by teaching you to dance. Mr. Taylor was not available." She sighed when she saw the pout on the girl's face.

"He is a friend of your father's and can teach you well. Come along. I am sure he has arrived and is awaiting you." Anna sighed again. "And stop wrinkling your nose, you're going to put wrinkles on your pretty face. It is going to stay that way if you keep doing that."

How could she explain to Anna how much she detested the dance instructor? She wrinkled her nose again. He was too … too everything: too smooth, too smart, too cunning. It was easier not to call him by name. He was not quite as real that way.

Devry smiled and changed the subject as they alighted the stairway. "Can you give me a hint of my birthday present?"

Anna grinned. "No, Devry. But I will tell you that you will be informed of the surprise after your lesson is completed."

The two quietly entered the gilded ballroom. Inviting the cool breeze, the opened French doors overlooked the formal gardens. The sun created a sparkling effect on the mirrored walls. Devry's father Andrew and the dance instructor stood near the fireplace, beside the Victorian rugs and black walnut furniture. To the side, a shadow darkened the carved arched alcove, where the band played when they entertained. Strategic placement of the tables and chairs allowed the center of the ballroom to accommodate approximately twenty-five couples.

Anna nodded to Devry and eased herself into the feather-filled cushion seat by the window. Devry smiled at her father and cautiously acknowledged the dance instructor.

"Sir, I hope you have not had an extensive wait."

"Ah, Devry Bonita, I would wait as long as it would take to see your beautiful face." He took her hand and kissed it. Hidden from Andrew's sight, he blatantly stared at her breasts.

Devry smiled and wondered if her smile was as spurious as his appeared to be. His smile did not reach his eyes. She was cautious and alert. The eyes, her mama had said, were the portals of truth.

After her father departed the room, Devry pleadingly looked toward Anna. Hopefully, she would not fall asleep again and Devry would not have to endure that man's odious pawing.

"We shall practice your turns today, Devry … *Bonita.*"

Devry averted her eyes downward as she hooked the train onto her middle finger. His instruction was extraordinary. She gave him homage for his endurance of her stepping on his feet, missing the rhythms and floundering like a fish. Her awkward steps did not seem to bother him, his patience remarkable.

Though she had told Anna otherwise, dancing *was* a pure pleasure, until she had to endure his supposed accidental touches of her breasts and backside with each turn. He would mumble his apologies but the sincerity was not in his eyes. The accidents happened too frequently. She might be naïve in the ways of coupling, but she knew the look of desire.

The man was an accomplished dancer. He could make the worst dancer in the ballroom appear as one of the best. Devry had to give him some credit for his expertise. His steps, seductive and polished, flowed with graceful rhythm, making her feel as if they were dancing on a cloud.

He was not an offensive-looking gentleman, for someone that old. Groomed to perfection, his pearl-blond hair always impeccable, he appeared the ever-efficient and meticulous gentleman. His voice was soothing to the ears and his laugh, if she had to be honest with herself, was contagious. The man was what The Widow described as smooth and charming.

Then, she heard Anna's little snore. The pleasure of the dance disappeared. As if on cue, she felt his hand on her backside as he turned her in a swirl of petticoats and silk. She stiffened, forced to cling tighter, lest she find herself in an undignified position on the floor. He praised her stance. Devry wanted to gag in his face.

Unfortunately, she giggled at the undignified image and he, the beast, took it as encouragement. Blushing, she focused her eyes across his right shoulder, unsuccessfully ignoring his endearments.

"I will wait patiently for your father to allow you to come out, Devry. You will be mine and I will show you another dance, one you will find much more pleasurable." He licked his lips and smiled, caressing her breast with his left thumb. "I will make you dance and sing with pleasure."

Devry lost count of the waltz and tripped. He slowed his pace and eased into a basic step so she could gather her wits before gliding across the floor. "I see I make you nervous with anticipation. That is good. The thought drives me to exacerbating pleasure."

"Time is up. Are you staying for tea?" Anna stood and stretched, ignoring Devry's heated glare.

"That will be my greatest delight." He nodded his consent to Anna.

The Morning Room was directly across from the music room and foyer, which opened onto the ballroom. The French doors were open, allowing a spectacular view of their rose garden. Sky-blue walls and carved moldings created a fresh atmosphere in the day and an intimate setting in the evenings.

They entered just as a knock sounded at the front door and the hall clock started to chime.

"Well, I see my timing is excellent." Andrew Little Red Hawk spoke in his usual cheerful voice as he entered the room. "Janice will be in with tea and cakes shortly. I believe the caller knocking is most likely our good friend arriving, late as usual. Eduard will bring her to us shortly. How did the lesson go?"

"Very well, Andrew. She has a natural talent with the dances."

The differences between the two men was stunning. Her dance instructor was sophisticated, a tall and muscular man with pearl hair and blue eyes. Her father had a quiet dignity, short and overweight with the dark coloring of his Sioux ancestry. Her instructor was reserved and stoic, her father congenial and good-natured. That man acted the gentleman, but only when eyes were upon him. Her father was always a gentleman.

Lydia Wetmore Williams entered the room with the wisp of fresh air that always seemed to follow wherever she went. Though it had been five years since her husband had died in battle, the townspeople still referred to her as The Widow. She had yet to remarry and became an enigma among their elite society. Lydia had left the high society of which she was born and, as far as 'the 400' were concerned (Mrs. Astor et al), The Widow lived with savages in the 'Wild West.'

Her eccentricities caused a much bigger stir, however, for she tended the poor with expert apothecary skills, knowledge she had learned from her late husband. Now that the doctor lay bedridden, with his help she had acquired his medical practice, at least to those willing to accept administrations by a woman.

There was also the gossip and stories of why she had to leave St. Augustine two years earlier and move to South Dakota. However, truth be told, she arrived in town like a swift, refreshing breeze. Juan and Domina sent several missives, trying to convince her to come for months, but it was not until Domina de Rivera Aquinaldo had written, pleading to The Widow to help their family, that she had responded in the only manner she knew. As a true friend, she came when needed.

She had such a gentle and kind spirit. Once people met her, they dismissed the rumors of scandal and considered them quite outrageous. How could someone so serene, face accusations of such atrocities? Despite the unofficial title, she rarely wore black and a day did not pass without a smile brightening her face. If someone needed help, she was there.

Devry watched as the petite woman greeted her father and instructor, apologizing to him for her tardiness. Devry noticed that The Widow barely acknowledged the dance instructor. *Interesting … Mrs. Williams does not care for that man, either.* She greeted him with just enough of an acknowledgement to be polite. *What could that man have possibly done to offend her?* Devry had never seen The Widow be anything but pleasant and generous.

Her dress was bright and cheery. The Widow was the epitome of etiquette, except for the lack of a hat. She had her golden-brown hair wrapped and uncovered like the Seminole Indian women, which of course always caused a stir among the elders. Devry sometimes wondered if The Widow did it to intentionally irritate the old biddies. Her retort to them would have been that she had a hat on; it was just made of her hair.

Devry smiled. *Mrs. Williams is definitely a feisty lady.*

"Devry, are you listening?"

Stunned out of her contemplation, she blinked. "I'm sorry, Father. What were you saying?"

"I was saying that your birthday is next week. It is also opening night of the season." Andrew Little Red Hawk looked at his daughter and smiled. "I am having a ball gown commissioned for your birthday. It will be whatever you choose." Andrew kissed his daughter on the cheek.

Looking at her dance instructor, Andrew added "Although my lovely wife Christine is in Washington, D.C. involved in the suffrage movement with Mrs. Stanton and Miss Anthony, we have decided to allow her to come out and attend the dance."

The maid placed the tea and cakes next to Devry and quickly departed the room. Devry's hands shook as she absorbed what her father had just announced. Anna stood in the back of the room, watching the young girl's reaction.

Grabbing the opportunity to calm herself, Devry served the tea and cakes to her father and their guests. She inhaled a slow deep breath. With a serenity that belayed her distress, she responded to the surprise. "Am I ready? Aren't I too young? I will only be fourteen next week. I am not supposed to come out until my sixteenth birthday."

"That is true, my pet. However, there was a town meeting a while back. With all that is happening, there are not enough young ladies at the usual age for a true season. There are only four, you must understand, who are at the proper age for coming out, so the parents have decided that it is necessary to push the required age back."

Devry nodded in consent. Her heart thundered in her chest; she bit back the overwhelming panic threatening within. How could she tell her father she did not want to come out yet? It would hurt him. He looked so excited.

This should please her and make her happy. This was her preparation for womanhood and marriage. However, Devry was terrified. The season … embraced by the elite and used to find the perfect spouse. *What if some ugly old man asks for my hand in marriage and I have to marry him?* She spied the look of fascination on the dance instructor's face, shivering in revulsion. *No, please, not him!*

"You will have the most beautiful gown. Your appointment is in an hour." Andrew's grin widened. "Choose whatever fabric and style you wish, my pet. Mrs. Anderson is prepared to have it ready for you by Friday. Mrs. Williams will escort us. You need not be so worried and distressed."

Devry walked over to her father and gave him a hug and kiss. "Thank you. I will make you proud of me."

"Now, my pet, go upstairs and Anna will help you get ready to leave. Do not take too long. We don't want to keep Mrs. Anderson waiting."

As she was leaving the room, Andrew whispered, "Oh, my pet, you already make me proud."

The Widow turned from looking out the window and watched the two gentlemen. What she saw sitting before her was a vulture and a deer. She mused to herself. Yes, he might be a deer but sometimes she forgot how deadly Andrew Little Red Hawk could be. The white man's world was where he lived but his heart remained Sioux. She wondered if, or possibly when, Andrew would send Devry to Sitting Bull for the ceremony of womanhood.

Lydia eyed the vulture. The Widow did not trust him. She would wait and watch before telling Andrew how she felt about this man. *Time.* She just needed a little bit more time, to find solid undeniable proof before she broke her silence and made any pronouncements.

"Gentlemen, I will go upstairs and assist Devry if neither one of you object?"

"If that pleases you." Andrew waved to a servant to escort The Widow.

Andrew looked at Devry's dance instructor. "I don't know if this is wise. She is still so young."

"Andrew, she will be ready. She is beautiful and will be the princess who rules the soiree. I will ensure no one harms her, protected as if she was the finest jewel in the world. I am sure you will be attending some of the dances. Besides," he pointed toward the door where Lydia had departed, "Do you really believe The Widow and the other old hags will allow anyone to compromise Devry?"

Pointing at the younger man, Andrew laughed. "Some of those old hags are younger than me. Seriously, you know whom she must avoid. The club members must not have my daughters. We have been lucky with Devry's cousin Catherine. Though Richard is a member of the club, it appears she has escaped the repercussions of being married to one of them.

"Attending one of their business meetings was enough for me. I still have the scars because I left early. I will kill the man who considers using either one of my daughters in their macabre and dishonorable activities."

His guest swallowed hard at the threat.

Andrew shook his head in disgust. "Did they really believe I would denounce their behavior publicly when the new sheriff was part of their corrupt clan? Look where the sheriff is now, fighting for his life."

"Andrew, I know you are unsure of your decision," his friend encouraged, "but you must trust me. None of those men will have her."

Chapter Five

The flames in the fireplace danced and popped a merry song as they slowly eased the chill from the Morning Room. The young ladies were silent while Janice placed the tea and finger sandwiches on the sideboard. Their sewing meeting had launched into a discussion of the Woman's Suffrage movement. Though none had actually ever done any sewing during the meetings, the politics they discussed had always refreshed and invigorated them.

Devry insisted that Janice could be trusted. Unlike Devry, the other ladies had not been encouraged to be independent. Not one of them was willing to take the chance of enduring their father's or husband's wrath for discussing a subject their little minds would never be able to comprehend. Women were not supposed to discuss anything but the weather and fashion.

Each waited for the click of the door to signal their freedom to speak. Excitement coursed through the room. They had been discussing Devry's mother Christine who had joined Elizabeth Cady Stanton's and Susan B. Anthony's outspoken struggle of national suffrage. Christine was an enigma among the elders. Still, they cheered her efforts.

A few weeks after Stanton and Anthony had announced they would unite, the National Woman Suffrage Association and the American Woman Suffrage Association merged into the National American Woman Suffrage Association. Christine traveled to the state capital after Mrs. Stanton's election as president of the Association, to help with the fight to gain a woman's right to vote.

"We should have had the right to vote when the constitution was written. There was absolutely no reason why women were excluded," Catherine insisted.

"Were women allowed to be landowners then?" Elizabeth asked.

"I believe everything became the husband's property," Devry answered.

"Well, anyway, even if that is true, when they wrote the 15th Amendment, women should have been included to receive the right to vote. I can't believe they allowed uneducated black slaves to make such crucial decisions with our country," Elizabeth scolded in her southern drawl.

"Ex-slaves," The Widow corrected.

"They were still uneducated."

"I won't deny that, dear. Whose fault is that? If it had not been illegal to educate them or the fact that they were bound to be servile to start with, we would not have been in the situation."

"If the North had minded their own business …" Elizabeth intoned acerbically, leaving the statement unfinished.

"I don't understand why you are so bitter about it," Arabella remarked. "You were not even alive during the War Between the States. America's shame is what I call it. How could they have fought against each other, brother against brother, father against son?"

"It also ended 25 years ago. Maybe we should discuss another subject. One not so heated?" Devry wondered if she would need to break up fisticuffs.

"An excellent suggestion!" Elizabeth commented. "Catherine, I am sure your husband feels quite relieved that the officer who was about to arrest him believed his story." Elizabeth relished any form of gossip.

"Yes, Richard claims he was walking down the street minding his own affairs when the men encircled him, forcing him to follow in the shuffle. I would say it put a bit of fear in him. I don't think he has yet calmed down about it."

"What was he doing in Deadwood again?" The Widow's eyebrows rose.

"It was business for his father. I just cannot picture him involved with people like that. Richard is so reserved and quiet."

"It amazes me that so many of them were arrested," Arabella chimed.

Catherine covered her mouth, a devilish gleam in her eyes. "Well, I will tell you what good it did do. He was so riled that he performed quite well, and in the afternoon, too. It was scandalous and exciting."

The room filled with girlish giggles. "That was a first for us." Raising her hand to her forehead, Catherine pretended she was fainting. "Which reminds me. I am almost out of my special herbs. I will stop by later this evening, if it is satisfactory with you, Mrs. Williams?"

"Of course, dear."

Jumping up, Catherine announced, "Well, I am off for now. I have promised to go down to the Quarters and give Memaw some old dresses of mine. I'll be back in a few."

Catherine gave kisses to the ladies and rolled her eyes at the last question she heard Elizabeth pose as she shut the door.

"So, how is a woman supposed to feel about her duties to her husband? Are we really supposed to enjoy it like Catherine says? I mean, is it normal to *like* it?" Elizabeth looked directly to Mrs. Williams while she nervously fiddled with her sampler.

"When we were discussing my possible upcoming betrothal, my mother informed me that it was something one must get accustomed to," Arabella nodded.

"I believe there must be a mutual desire for it to be enjoyable. It makes living with him that much more pleasant, if you enjoy all the aspects of marriage." Lydia smiled and winked at the girls.

"I'm not marrying unless I'm in love; no arranged marriage for me. Papa and Mama promised," Arabella replied.

"I am sure Papa will arrange my marriage to the perfect man for me," Devry added. "It would be grand to be in love. Just like you, Mrs. Williams."

"My father didn't choose my husband. He did not speak to me for almost a year because I ran off a week before my wedding. I certainly was not supposed to fall in love with the neighbor's half-breed son. But, that is a different story. I know your fathers well. You will have some say about who you marry. And love can grow over the years."

"Well, how will we know true love?" Elizabeth queried with a worried frown. "We are all coming out this year. How will we know we are choosing the right man?"

"Yes, how will we know?"

"Now, what makes you think I can tell you what love is when poets have tried for centuries?" The Widow's eyes twinkled above a coy smile.

Lydia looked at the three young ladies leaning toward her in anticipation. Elizabeth fought to tame tight blonde curls every day without success. Her blue eyes seemed to penetrate to a person's soul. An excellent catch, she was already in demand among the men.

Arabella, at sixteen, with auburn hair, mint-green eyes, and a fiery personality, would need a strong and independent man, a husband who would not feel threatened by her subliminal strength.

Then there was Devry. Lydia feared for this child. Not that Andrew would do her wrong; however, Devry was much too complacent, never wanting to make ripples with anything or anyone. She would need someone who did not take advantage of that.

"You ladies want to know about love?" She watched the three nod their heads enthusiastically.

"For me, it was a gradual thing. I met my husband after my betrothal to Robert, a gentleman my parents had chosen as a suitable husband. However, I felt a pull toward Tall Oak. He was intriguing. I would be busy with the accounting records and his face would come to mind. I started hearing his laugh and seeing his smile. When he came to deliver correspondence between our families, my heart would pound the whole time he was there.

"We would laugh and talk for hours. I am sure his parents wondered what kept him. After a while, Tall Oak was all I could think about. I became sullen and cranky. I felt guilty for desiring a man that was not my betrothed. It was quite an unpleasant feeling. I thought that I was just infatuated with him and it would pass. I was wrong."

"What happened?" they asked in unison.

"After months of platonic friendship, he had suggested a clandestine meeting. We arranged to meet near the Old Stone Mill. Tall Oak confessed his attraction to me."

"Oh! How exciting!" Elizabeth exclaimed as she flipped her fan open.

"And romantic," Arabella sighed.

"What did you do?" Devry gasped, as she stared at The Widow, seeing her for the first time.

The Widow laughed. "Why, I met him at the Old Stone Mill. We talked for over an hour. I sensed that he would never kiss me. He was the type of man who needed a boost, just a smidgeon of encouragement. Always the gentleman,

Tall Oak would never have attempted to kiss me if I had not taken the course into my own hands. So, I kissed him. That's when I knew he was the one I would marry."

"Because of a kiss? How?" Arabella asked.

"It stayed with me even after he stopped kissing me. I could feel the tingle on my lips. The heat from the gentle touch made me desire more. At the time I did not understand what more I yearned for." Lydia laughed at the pleasant memory. "I didn't understand what more there could be. I wanted him to keep kissing me until I couldn't stand it anymore."

"It's the kiss that lets you know?"

Lydia laughed. "The kiss is extremely important, but you have to understand there is a whole big picture to deal with." The Widow sighed as she returned to memories that seemed a lifetime passed.

"It's the watching of the door when you're at a dance and not realizing that you are looking for him until he arrives. It is the pounding of your heart in anticipation of him coming over to greet you. It is the desire of wanting him to be the only one you dance with; the thrill and complete awareness that you belong in his arms. And most unusual of all, it's being in a room full of people and he is the only one you are aware of."

All three girls sighed in unison.

"It is the way your heart flutters when he's near … the way it pounds in your chest when he touches you. It is all of that in one big package. It is knowing that no matter what, he'll always be at your side because that is where he belongs."

The girls flushed, romance illuminating their eyes, as they watched The Widow intently. Lydia cleared her throat and smoothed her dress. She did not need to be encouraging romanticism in these girls.

"Well, we should all be so lucky to get the perfect man. Sometimes I get carried away." Lydia took a deep breath and pushed aside an imaginary piece of hair.

There was a knock on the door and the butler entered. "Miss Elizabeth, your carriage is here."

"Thank you, Eduard." Arabella and Elizabeth gathered their samples and sewing baskets. The Widow excused herself and went to find Andrew, leaving Devry alone to absorb everything she had said.

Catherine licked her lips and wondered how she could still be thirsty. It was uncharacteristically warm for this time of year but if she drank any more water or tea, she would float away. Maybe she should consult The Widow about it. While she was at it, she would mention how she was always so tired.

Saying her goodbyes to Memaw, she left the cabins, heading southwest on her horse. Taking her time, she anticipated the extensive visit to the Quarters. The ladies' meeting would not be over for at least two hours. Lunch hour would be concluding soon for the first group.

Catherine was lonely, a woman with needs. Her husband had come to her bed twice in the two years they had been married. The first time was her wedding night, consummating the marriage. The second was just recently, when that fiasco in Deadwood had excited him. Odd that fear would increase his desire in such a way.

On her wedding night, she had been prepared to show her virgin's blood by using blood from a chicken. Nevertheless, luck was a friend that day; she had just the beginnings of her monthly, enough to give the appearance that he had taken her virginity. Richard had not known the difference. She should have realized something was wrong with the man; he had not attempted to kiss her while they were courting.

When they first married, she came to believe he did not care for her dark Spanish looks. Then she began to wonder if Richard did not desire women at all. Nevertheless, as their marriage continued, she noticed how he seemed to find light-skinned women attractive.

She had caught him several times lusting over their neighbor, Amanda Burke. He had attempted to hide his swollen discomfort when she came visiting. It was obvious to both women that Richard was having trouble controlling his desire. Catherine would flush with anger, and Amanda would flush with embarrassment.

His blatant desires changed dramatically when Amanda had become fat with child and her husband sent her to her sister's home to have the baby. She recalled one time that Richard's member had become so hard watching Amanda that he had to leave the room in haste.

Catherine's forehead had scrunched in frustration.

It was not until the last few months that he had started showing his desire for her. She could see his member pulse, tightening his trousers, but Richard would just turn and leave the room. She would be reading or sewing in the salon and he would join her for tea and swell while he spoke about the most menial things. Catherine would watch his eyes glaze with desire, but then Richard would just leave her sitting there wondering why he never made an attempt to bed her.

This change in behavior started about the time Amanda had left town. She recalled the very day Richard had come into the library and proceeded to inform her that his men's club voted and they were now hosting the meetings.

Richard had requested that she divest herself of all the petticoats she usually wore while she was a hostess for the club members. He claimed it was distracting to forage through petticoats to get to the honey. Of all the strange requests Catherine had ever heard from men, that one puzzled her the most. What did being a hostess for the club members have to do with how many petticoats she wore?

She rolled her eyes. As if he mounted her when he had desires to fulfill. She shook her head in disgust. When had Richard ever gone foraging through *her* petticoats?

Thank precious life for the men willing to serve her where her husband lacked, and for the herbs that prevented pregnancy. She could not possibly imagine herself tethered to one man for the rest of her life. Perhaps Richard should have waited a few years and married Devry. They could have deferred each other to boredom.

Catherine watched a group of Andrew's employees filing out of the Lunch House, the sunlight gleaming on their glistening, hardened, and muscular bodies. She guided her horse into the pied shadows, waiting for the men to walk by while her body shuddered with anticipation. Her nipples peaked as she hungrily stared at the bare chests.

Anthony stopped and looked toward the shadows. "Well, Miss Catherine, come to join us for a while?"

Catherine laughed as Anthony strolled over, putting his hands on her waist as he helped her dismount. Her body tingled from his touch.

"Why, thank you, Anthony. I have come to visit for a while."

A few men followed as Anthony guided Catherine to a hidden clearing.

Chapter Six

Devry stood and admired the transformation from the child, who just earlier that morning was digging with her hands in the garden, to the exquisite lady before her in the looking glass. It had taken a considerable amount of persistence to get the dirt from under her fingernails. Anna clucked her tongue the whole time, reprimanding her for the unladylike behavior. It was half-hearted, since Anna had been working in the garden beside her.

"You look beautiful, Devry."

"I wish Mama was here to see it." Devry sighed.

"She is, Devry. She is watching and with you always for she left her heart here. Do not forget, there is also the photograph taken yesterday. She'll be able to see how elegant and beautiful you look."

The gown, sophisticated and romantic, caressed her body. It flowed from her waist to the floor, creating a feminine and dreamy allure. The deep curved neckline, decorated with a floral overlay of Celtic gold and silver embroidered appliqués, covered the fitted bodice in the front and back. Pearls accented the embroidered appliqués, adding extra shimmer.

About the waist, the gathered skirt and train was a light-blue satin lining, layered with a full gathered crinoline skirt of sparkling lavender. A third layer of the skirt carried a ruffle, encircling the hemline with several bands of ruffles lifted in the back, creating a mountainous peak that increased the bustle.

Devry lifted the train and circled as she watched the fabric glitter in the lamplight. The dress sparkled as if distant stars danced about her.

"It's breathtaking. Mama would love this gown."

"Here Devry, put your gloves on. Everyone is downstairs in the foyer, waiting for you. You must make a spectacular entrance." Lifting her chin, Anna kissed her cheek. "Are you ready? Remember, do not dance more than twice with any man. Do you have your dance card? Where is your fan?"

Devry hugged Anna and laughed. "I believe you are more nervous than I am."

As they approached the staircase, Anna replied. "Yes, oh I certainly am. Do you remember the rules of the fan, Devry? We do not want you giving the wrong impression to anyone. Make sure you keep the fan up and to the side. Do not fan yourself slowly in front of your chest. You will be inviting the man for favors. And, please, do not forget to look straight at your host and hostess when announced. We must show them the respect of being chosen as hosts for the First Ball of the Season."

Anna inhaled slowly. "Oh, my baby, my Devry." Anna's eyes filled with unshed tears.

"Please do not cry, Anna."

"But you have grown so fast. You have become a lady right before my very eyes. It is all too soon."

Anna hugged her and watched as she made her entrance into the foyer. Devry descended the stairs into the open arms of her family. Catherine, Richard, Domina, and Juan stood waiting next to her father and The Widow.

Devry watched her cousin; her agitated antics and pale face caused Devry great concern. She was dressed in a simple ivory and peach satin gown, hemmed with deep coral rosettes. Normally, the ivory color would have accented her Spanish beauty, but lately Catherine appeared sallow. The dress drew attention to her lack of health.

Standing next to Catherine was her husband Richard, dressed impeccably as always in formal wear tailor-made to match his skin color and hair. The silk attire caressed his tall lean frame, accenting the gleam from his golden-brown cropped hair and deep brown eyes.

The Widow was wearing a bright yellow silk gown and train, her hair swept up in a cascade of curls. Her attention was on Catherine. Devry knew that Lydia was concerned with her cousin's health and behavior. Turning toward the stairs, she smiled as Devry descended.

Nervous and excited, Devry entered the ballroom on her father's arm. Chinese lanterns encircling the dance floor created a mysterious, mystical atmosphere, a fairy tale of glittering prisms. Shadows danced on the wall while the lanterns swayed in the breeze, sprinkling light onto the ceiling mural; angels and cherubs appeared to fly down to greet the guests. The dance card, shaped like butterflies, had Chinese lanterns drawn next to each dance, completing the theme.

Arabella and Devry relaxed in the cool evening breeze as they waited on the veranda. They hoped their dance cards were bursting with names as the band started tuning their instruments, preparing to strike the first waltz.

Catherine approached them in a huff. Stomping her feet as she strode toward the two young ladies, she crossed her arms, her voice as steely as her gaze. "Do you know what The Widow just told me? To be careful with the laudanum I have been taking. When I told her that I was not taking laudanum, she told me to leave the morphine alone!" The two girls stood dumbfounded as Catherine raged.

"The audacity of that woman. That witch has to be involved in everyone's life. If my life gets any more calm and serene, I will be dead! Of all the stupid tonics out there, I would not take morphine. Gracious!"

"She may just be concerned with your health. Maybe you should go see a doctor," Arabella said.

Catherine stomped her foot and shrieked, "I am not going all the way to Rapid City just to see a doctor to allay her delusional fears. What would make her think I am using calming tonics? Say something, Devry! Do not just stand there and stare at me!"

"Well," Devry stammered, "maybe you …"

"Ah, there you are, Catherine." Richard approached with two glasses. "I have been looking for you. Here, I have brought you some punch. I just had a word with The Widow. It appears she is concerned with your health. She said you look a bit peaked and tired."

The two ladies warily watched Catherine as she spun on her heel to look at her husband. They could see that she had nearly released her fury on him, but had stopped herself after looking into his concerned eyes.

Richard was always so calm, serene, and complacent. His charm and attentiveness was what had attracted Catherine when he was courting her; he was generous and nurturing.

When they were betrothed, Catherine had told Devry that he was what she wanted and needed. She had no idea that Catherine had been recently thinking just the opposite. She could see resentment clouding Catherine's eyes. Was she unhappy with her marriage?

Catherine sighed and took the cup of punch. "Thank you, Richard. Hopefully, it will get rid of my headache."

"Drink it up, love. It will help you relax. There now, that is good. You must be thirsty." Richard smiled to the other two ladies. "Take mine, then I will get us more."

They quickly realized they were gifted a reprieve and left the couple while Catherine was distracted. Catherine drank the punch thirstily. Finishing the second glass, she placed it on a tray near the door as Richard approached with another.

While Richard cooed and encouraged Catherine to drink the punch, Devry and Arabella gradually made their way to their table and joined The Widow and Arabella's mother. Handing them their dance cards, The Widow watched as Catherine and Richard glided onto the dance floor in anticipation of the first dance.

Catherine appeared to be quite relaxed and composed. The Widow squinted her eyes in anger, drumming her lips with her index finger. What magical gift had Richard given the woman to calm her so quickly? Would Richard put laudanum in her drink without her knowledge? Maybe Catherine was not aware she had been taking laudanum and morphine.

A solid muscular wall dressed in formal attire strategically blocked The Widow's field of vision. Her eyes slowly and methodically scanned upward, noting the hard muscular thighs as she gradually made her way to his face.

The snug fit of his trousers did not hide the muscular legs, or the generous bulge in his manly region. Lydia blinked as she noted the small waist and wide shoulders of the fortress before her. He was toned and hard; though the dress coat hid most of his build, the arms of the jacket strained against his bulk. The man's hair was a swath of mahogany, his eyes cerulean. His structured cheekbones made his straight Roman nose less prominent. The man had a boyish glint, yet carried the steel of inner strength.

His lips were kissable and intriguing. Caressing his body slowly with her eyes, she found herself aching to touch him.

The scent of sandalwood tickled her senses, invoking sensuous desires. As her heart pounded, Lydia's mouth went dry and she licked her lips. She looked into his eyes and caught the twinkle of humor. He slowly raised his eyebrow as if to say, 'Are you pleased with what you see?'

Aghast at her uncharacteristic thoughts, Lydia immediately felt the heat flushing a scarlet crimson from her neck to her face. *My goodness, how rude for him to point out … of all the blatant, ungentlemanly, and arrogant … oh but his voice was sensual and mellifluous.*

Juan stood next to the formidable icon that was blocking the view of the dance floor. As he introduced The Widow to Lane Parker, former Pinkerton man, she tried in vain to recover her dignity.

Lane Parker enjoyed The Widow's discomfort and sympathized. He had already filled his eyes with this intriguing lady from across the dance floor.

His investigations had prepared him for a widow, except for one major problem. Lane had mentally developed a picture of a plain-looking, elderly lady in her sixties, willing to mother every human being and animal in the town. Whoever had called this woman plain needed to visit the doctor and be fit for spectacles. He had pictured a gray-haired, overweight, tottering grandmother. She did not appear to be past the age of twenty-one.

The townspeople he had spoken to had placed her on a pedestal that practically made her a saint. When Juan had expressed his desire to introduce him to The Widow, Lane believed it would be to the older woman sitting beside Lydia. He had not one bit of desire to have a Grandma fluttering around distracting him while he scrutinized the murders. Resigning himself to the inevitable, Lane had been calculating how he would finagle his way into an introduction to the young lady, hoping she was unattached.

Her golden-brown hair, placed in ringlets atop her head, sparkled in the lamplight. Deep brown eyes seared through him, firing his blood. The iridescent yellow gown accented her coloring, making the lady appear as if the sun had kissed her. The gown was conservative but low enough to hint at the creamy, generous glory of her breasts.

Taking The Widow's hand, Lane kissed her fingers as he gently stroked the inside of her palm. Lane had to consciously restrain himself from licking his lips like a hungry wolf. Nevertheless, a wolf he was, desiring to corner her, preparing to pounce on the unsuspecting innocent.

This striking woman, this celestial Venus before him, was The Widow. She was intriguing and beautiful. He prayed that she was unaware of the impact she was having on him. She was an enigma. What person with any claim to normalcy would have a goose as a pet? Not only that, but also create a personal bedroom for the grumpy old codger! Eccentric, that was what it was, completely and utterly eccentric.

Lydia closed her eyes, opening them slowly. The moment became surreal. Everything and everyone appeared to be shadowy glimpses in a dream, as she saw and felt only him. Her initial reaction was to stand up and fall into his arms, which, of course, would not do at all!

Common sense told Lydia to bolt. She needed to run from Lane Parker as fast as her feet could carry her. Mr. Parker was a Pinkerton man, an ex-Pinkerton man. He was dangerous.

She could feel her whole being shake. She was no longer safe in her secure world if this man was in it. She knew things were going to change, drastically. He would be her undoing;

the earth underneath her feet seemed to rumble with forewarning.

The strings of the orchestra chimed and filtered lazily through her burble of chimera. Lydia felt herself helplessly pulled from the chair. She would never be able to fight this magnetic enticement. *Did she want to?*

The evening passed in pure illusory splendor as they danced all night, causing the whole town to flush and sputter.

"Look at The Widow," Richard whispered into Catherine's ear. "She never dances with potential suitors."

Catherine swept her drug-hazed eyes toward the center of the ballroom where The Widow and a gentleman danced, oblivious to those around them.

"Who is that man?" Catherine slurred and stumbled as she turned to watch the couple.

Lydia Williams had inadvertently created a whirlwind of intrigue and mystery. Those who had not already met the Pinkerton man whispered … "Who is that man? Why has The Widow accepted him so quickly?"

The answers flowed through the room and created more questions. Would he be able to identify the murderer?

Devry sat next to Domina and watched as Catherine and Richard left the dance. She had noticed that her cousin appeared a bit unsteady on her feet. Domina handed her the dance card and Devry cringed. "That man" was next. She bit her lower lip wondering if she could invent an excuse to sit out the last dance.

"What's wrong with Catherine?" Devry asked as she surreptitiously darted her eyes among the crowd searching for her dance instructor. She spotted him standing in the corner speaking quietly with her father. His pearl-blond hair shimmered in the rainbows of light cast from the Chinese lanterns.

"She looked under the weather. Richard wished to take her home. He said the night was exhausting her," Domina explained.

"Many of the older men are leaving early."

"Yes, I noticed. They are mostly club members. Ones whom you should not be interested in, Devry."

Mrs. Sally Barnes piped, "No lady is safe around the club members. I wish the sheriff would stop their behavior." Hands clasped tightly together, Mrs. Barnes leaned over and whispered to Domina. "The Widow better watch out. That Pinkerton man won't care she's a woman when he finds out she's the one murdering the club members."

Domina closed her eyes and gritted her teeth, seething. "The Widow heals people with her herbs. She is a healer, not a murderer."

"Well, that is not what they say in St. Augustine," Mrs. Barnes quipped.

"And how would you know?" Domina growled, "You have never been there."

"They say she was killing men with her herbs, punishing them by giving them the death sentence. Men who were abusing their wives; she felt she was avenging those who were wronged. She was escorted out of St. Augustine without even a 'by your leave' and told never to return. I heard she was nicknamed the Black Widow because unexplained deaths have followed wherever she has lived."

"They? Who are *they*?" Domina retorted indignantly. "Those are groundless, offensive, and very damaging rumors."

Mrs. Barnes stood in a huff. "Well, Domina, watch your back. Upset the Black Widow and you may be next."

"Ah, I see Mrs. Barnes is in a Sir Elmer mood." Devry's dance instructor approached as he watched the woman make a well-designed exit.

"I do believe she was acting the goose, Sir," Domina smiled as she watched Mrs. Barnes approach another table.

"Come, Devry, I believe we are to end the dance together."

His smile was cunning and self-assured, the way a hungry mountain lion eyes its feast after the kill. Devry was wary of his self-satisfied grin as he took her hand and led her to the dance floor. *What have he and Papa been discussing?*

Chapter Seven

Questioning the townspeople had become difficult; the replies appeared rehearsed. It was extremely exasperating. Was the whole town coordinating their answers? He was asking either the wrong questions or the wrong people. However, he would get down to the bottom of these murders. Surrendering and declaring defeat was not an option for Lane Parker.

The list of club members lay in his pocket awaiting his chance to review their actions and possibly be on guard for the next victim. The sheriff had taken the time to scrutinize the list of suspects and answer Lane's questions. He had scribbled notes next to their names, as well as reviewing their particular quirks.

Lane sat across from Mr. Davis. He must have finally started asking the correct questions. Mr. and Mrs. Davis seemed more than willing to provide information about everyone in Tokata that they possibly had met, could meet, and would meet in the near future.

When Mrs. Davis left to retrieve some cold drinks, Mr. Davis quietly informed Lane he had information that he would not discuss with Mrs. Davis in the room. Lane turned on the neighborly charm, leaving the air of an ex-Pinkerton man buried. Lane quickly ensnared Mr. Davis' confidence, and in return received the man's opinions willingly.

"It is horrendous what they do to their wives. The club members choose a host for the meetings," Mr. Davis watched the doorway, listening for his wife's footsteps. "The wife *entertains* ..." Hearing Mrs. Davis' approach, he quietly whispered, "We must discuss this later, around four, at the tavern down the street? I can give you more details about the club members and their indiscretions."

Lane nodded as Mrs. Davis handed him a glass of iced lemon water.

"Thank you."

"You are welcome, Mr. Parker. Now, let us get to the point of this visit, shall we?" She sat next to her husband. "What can we do for you?"

"As you know, I am here in Tokata to investigate the murders. It is frustrating." Lane dramatically sighed, taking advantage of his boyish features, playing on Mrs. Davis' sympathy.

She leaned forward and patted his hand. "Do not fret, Mr. Parker. We may not know who the villain is, but we can send you in the right direction."

"You are both so very considerate." Lane gave her a winsome smile. "I have many unanswered questions. I feel as if some of the townspeople have ... misled me."

Mr. Davis nodded, "I am sure some of them have. Club members, I expect."

"That is where you need to look, Mr. Parker." She paused, refilling his glass. "The murderer is targeting the club members. Perhaps it is a disgruntled husband or wife. There are some, shall we say, questionable and offensive activities among the members."

Mr. Davis winched his eyebrow. "This is not an acceptable subject to be discussed among the gentle-born."

"I concur," Lane nodded. "Let me ask, if you please, do you believe Mrs. Williams is involved?"

Mrs. Davis' mouth formed an O, as she fluttered her hands. "Oh, my gracious, no! The Widow is a generous and kind soul. She would never … never consider intentionally harming anyone."

"She is an asset to our town," Mr. Davis added.

Lane rubbed his jaw. "What about," pausing for emphasis, "the scandal in St. Augustine?"

Annoyance flashed in her eyes. "Unfounded and utterly ridiculous. We have benefited from Mrs. Williams' generosity and kindness."

"Your opinion of Mrs. Williams is commendable." Lane knew he had to change the subject. "It seems to be the overall consensus." He was losing their confidence. He should have waited. "Could you direct me to someone acquainted with Mr. Burke?"

"Mr. Brandt is … was his closest friend," Mr. Davis offered. "He may be able to help you."

Mrs. Davis blushed, "Mr. Burke also visited Mrs. Enlow, on several occasions."

"Mrs. Enlow?"

"Yes," Mr. Davis cleared his throat. "She has a boarding house on the south end of town."

Lane looked over at the clock. "If you would excuse me, I have another appointment. Would you mind if I came back at another time so we may continue?"

The couple stood. "Of course, Mr. Parker." They escorted him to the door. Mr. Davis stood behind his wife, raising his eyebrows. Lane nodded, verifying their appointment at the tavern.

* * *

It had been a month since the ball and Lane Parker had not made the slightest dent in locating the murderer. He had yet to receive a response telegram from his acquaintance in St. Augustine, and there were now more unanswered questions than when he had started. It was frustrating. To make matters worse, the desirous and illusive Mrs. Lydia Williams was avoiding him.

It was a brisk morning. Activity in the township had reached its peak before the luncheon hour. Lane had just left the sheriff's home for the fourth time in as many days. He clenched his jaw. A handful of residents had possible motives; many of them were involved with the murdered men. Richard Miller was on the list. According to the sheriff, he had only been involved with the members for just over two years; about the time, in fact, he had become betrothed to Catherine. Miller made frequent visits to the apothecary.

The sheriff was acquainted with almost everyone in the club. He foraged deep into their lives and could not find one member who did not have a legitimate alibi. They had meetings once a week but were sociable with each other daily. If someone from the club were the murderer, someone would have known and, most likely, would have informed him immediately.

The Widow had visited the sheriff the day before yesterday and his health was improving. She appeared to have a vast knowledge of medicine, considering she was a gentle-bred woman. She knew almost as much about medicine as the doctor. He, too, insisted that Mrs. Williams was a healer, not a murderer, and trusted her with his life. Was that not obvious? If the sheriff felt she was the murderer, he would never have allowed her to administer medication to him. The whole town trusted the woman. Mrs. Williams helped when people were ill or in unfortunate situations, cooking and cleaning, or watching and caring for the children. She prepared meals or had them delivered if she was too busy to bring them herself. She even helped pay some of their debts.

The sheriff had concluded that the victims were poisoned. After Lane's persistent questioning, the sheriff admitted that he had suspected The Widow in the beginning and had investigated her personal apothecary. He had searched the supply room, made a list, and had all the herbs identified. The room was organized and all of the medications labeled. The sheriff had not discovered any herbs or medicine that could possibly be mistaken as poison or used as poison.

As Lane approached the front entrance of Mrs. Williams' home, a horse and buggy carrying Catherine Miller raced away, her face mottled, tears streaking down her cheek. The stoic butler stood with the door open and waited.

Lane entered and greeted The Widow, who was putting on her gloves to leave. His heart pounded, struggling with his desire to hold her the way he had at the dance. Disappointment creased his face when Lane realized he would not be spending precious time with her. Common sense battled with his heart; she too was a suspect. Lusting after her, falling in love with her, would not be wise.

"I am sorry to do this, Mr. Parker. I know you wanted to speak to me, but Catherine's husband is very sick. I need to see him. Glenn is waiting for you." The carriage arrived as she spoke. The Widow tipped her head, grabbed the medicine bag, and whisked out the door, leaving the analeptic scent of lavender in her wake.

The butler stood waiting to escort him to his brother-in-law's room. As he walked toward the bedroom Lane wondered if he would be able to find the supply room where The Widow kept her herbs. He would like to investigate it himself, before she had the chance to hide anything.

* * *

Lydia was rapidly spitting orders to the housekeeper as she adjusted Richard's pillows. He opened his fever-laden eyes, pleading for relief from the pain.

"How long has he been like this?"

"I don't know," Catherine whined. "When he did not arrive at the breakfast table I sent the maid upstairs. He was fine at the meeting last night."

"Meeting?"

"We hosted the club members' meeting last night."

Lydia fumed, restraining her acerbic remarks. "What happened at the meeting last night?"

"They discussed setting up another fund, this one for Amanda Burke. For some reason they felt obligated to support her. They talked about the town, the Pinkerton man, and the sheriff. They were heatedly discussing the murders and what they would do about it. I do not remember who it was, but they had suggested ending the Gentlemen's Club."

"What did they say to that suggestion?"

"Oh, it didn't go over well at all. Something about Mrs. Enlow not taking proper care of their needs, that for a madam, she was chaste about performing particular sexual acts … not knowing how to have fun. Mr. Taylor mentioned having the meetings at his house for a while and then coming back to ours. Almost everyone was against that suggestion," Catherine laughed.

"They said the entertainment at our house was the best they had ever had since they started the Gentlemen's Club. I placed the last of the refreshments on the table and Mr. Brandt offered me a glass of sherry. I had two glasses of sherry and we all ate from the buffet I had set out." Catherine shrugged. "I wasn't in the room for too long after that. I was tiring and one of the gentlemen had spilled his drink on my bodice. The last thing I remember was him handing me a handkerchief to wipe it off. Nothing that would cause concern."

"What do you mean by the last thing you remember?" The Widow asked.

"It is odd. For some reason, whenever I hostess a meeting I get so tired and never remember going to bed or even walking up the stairs." She shrugged again. "I just wake up the next morning with a dry mouth and I'm very thirsty. It can't be the sherry; I never drink more than two glasses."

"Catherine, who prepared the refreshments and who gives you the sherry?"

"I prepare the buffet. Sometimes I get help with it, sometimes it is just me."

"And the sherry?"

"Richard or one of the club members gives me my glass of sherry."

The Widow sighed, biting her lip in concentration.

Caressing Richard's hair, The Widow quietly asked, "Where do you hurt?"

"Everywhere," he croaked.

"Open your mouth, Richard, let me have a look."

Like an errant child, Richard clamped his teeth together and refused to budge, his agitation apparent as he clenched the blankets under his chin.

"I cannot help you if you do not let me." The Widow coaxed him as she would a child, "Now come, let me see."

His throat did not appear red or swollen. The offensive stench of ammonia perforated the air. Lydia bit her lip. Carefully she pressed on the lower part of his swollen abdomen, working her way toward the heart. He flinched when she pressed on his liver.

She placed a cool cloth on his head and a damp towel across the torso.

Lydia sat down on the chair next to the vast bed. He appeared lethargic, agitated, and confused. Richard's normally pale skin was a golden brown, warning her of jaundice and possible liver failure. Her fingertips felt as if they were floating on water as she examined him. Either fluid was building up or there was internal bleeding.

She did not think it was internal bleeding, though, not with that coloring. What would make his liver fail so quickly? Reaching into her medicine bag, she pulled out several herbs and combined them on the table, giving the mixture to the housekeeper for a medicinal tonic.

Juan, Andrew, and Devry entered as she was explaining the preparations and portions to Catherine's housekeeper. Richard's reaction was startling. He became restless and fearful. When Devry walked toward the bed to help calm him, his agitation increased. He clutched the sheets to cover his face, croaking grunts of deep-seated apprehension.

Devry sprinted from the room in tears. What could she have done for him to react in such a horrid manner?

"Calm down, Richard." Mrs. Williams caressed his cheek. "She is gone."

"What is it, Richard? What could Devry have done to upset you?" Catherine pressed in confusion.

The housekeeper began to leave the room as the maid carried in cooler, damp towels, curiosity slowing their steps.

Richard croaked his fears. "She is trying to kill me. She is the one who is poisoning everyone. She is the one who helped you yesterday. I ate the pastries she brought. Now I am sick."

Devry? The group stood with mouths agape, staring at Richard. The housekeeper and maid scurried from the room. They knew the accusations would spread; the gossip mill would be in an uproar.

"But Richard, everyone ate some of the pastries. No one else is sick!" Catherine protested.

Andrew paled at the accusation about his daughter. He realized he would have to send Devry away to protect her from the unwarranted accusations. His decision to send her to Standing Rock with Karen Black Elk would stay firm. Patting the telegram from his wife Christine, he felt reassured of his decisions. He would inform Devry before the dance tonight.

Chapter Eight

Matthew groaned. An unfamiliar jingle of harnesses echoed in his dream. Always slow to awaken, his eyes barely registered the antique furnishings that surrounded him. Methodically, he rolled onto his back expecting to see the fan on the ceiling. A minute ticked by as he realized the fan was not there and the furnishings were not antique. They were freshly polished and new. He had arrived.

His mother's personal touch was evident as he sat up on the bed. The armoire doors were open, showing the clothing she had purchased for him. Two pairs of shoes lay on the floor in front of it. Saline solution for his contact lenses sat on the bureau next to his favorite cologne. The absence of a clock in the room left him wondering the time. Dressing, he approached the window and found the sun high in the sky.

In childish excitement, Matthew raced down the stairs, creating the sound of a thousand buffalo, alerting the household of his arrival. Entering the dining area, three expectant faces greeted him, each with their own unique reactions.

Karen jumped up and ran to him, encircling his broad shoulders. When she finally let him go, she bounced up and down in happiness, clapping her hands silently.

Andrew Little Red Hawk reached over and shook his hand. The young boy he remembered well, had now grown into an impressive young man, a man so very much the image of his father. If the eyes had not been green, he would have mistaken him for his father's ghost.

Andrew hugged him. "It is good to see you again, Gentle Raccoon, or do you prefer Matthew?"

"When I am not on the reservation, call me Matthew."

"Agreed, Matthew it is. How is your firefighting? Your mother had mentioned some rough wildfires when you had just started the job."

"I love being a firefighter. It's going well, thank you." Matthew grinned. "The wildfires were rough. Too much land was destroyed, but I must admit it was an excruciating way of initiating my first days in the field."

Andrew moved back, hand open and pointed to the dining table. "I would like you to meet my daughter Devry."

Devry held her breath. Standing in the dining room was the most wonderful, gorgeously handsome man she had ever had the pleasure of resting her eyes upon. He was tall and broad-shouldered. His eyes shined emerald green, feathered with eyelashes that would make any woman jealous. His long black hair waved down to the center of his back. Large, hard muscles bulged as he patted his mother on the back. The timber of Matthew Standing Deer's voice was deep and melodious. His lips were beckoning to her.

Devry's heart quickened, her body warming with unfamiliar sexual desire. She decided, without any doubts, that Matthew would be her husband.

* * *

Matthew turned, ready for his introduction to Devry, who was still sitting stiffly at the table. She was every man's dream. His mother had told him she was an exquisite beauty. She was exotic and the mirror image of her mother Christine, whom Matthew had met over 15 years ago.

Her hematite-colored hair was pinned elaborately in a large knot at the back of her head, yet it cascaded in curls down to below her waist. His head swam with enigmatic visions of a black-haired Lady Godiva.

When he bent to kiss her hand, he looked into her eyes and knew she was an innocent. A blaze of desire scintillated and surged through his blood. It grasped his heart and nested its embers deep within. She would be his and nothing would stop him.

Enjoying the cool evening air, Arabella, Elizabeth, and Devry stood huddled together drinking punch on the patio, relaxing as they waited for the last set of dances. The dance was festive and the grist of gossip passed among the ladies and men circling the room with each new topic.

"Oh my stars! You have to see him," Devry exclaimed excitedly. "Matthew is so perfect. He is the one I am going to marry."

"You've kissed him already?"

Devry's eyes grew wide and laughed. "No. I have not. Mark my words, I will. Nevertheless, The Widow was correct about needing hot coals to stoke the fire. All of those boys I tested with kisses, just did not bring the sparks she said it would. I know they are not for me."

"You may not have liked the way Taylor kissed, but I do." Arabella giggled, no longer upset because Devry had kissed him first.

"Oh!" Devry shivered in dramatic exaggeration. "At least I got away from 'that man' when he tried to kiss me."

"That man." Arabella smiled. "It is so funny when you call him that. Or, when you blink at him like a dumb bunny. You are so mean sometimes."

"Well, I don't need to kiss him to know *he* isn't the one for me." Devry wrinkled her nose.

"I do not believe Mrs. Williams meant for you to kiss every boy you dance with or has tried to court you." Elizabeth twitched with a dimpled grin.

"Most likely not." Mischief sparkled in Devry's eyes. "It was interesting, though, the different ways each one kissed. Some of them had wet kisses. I just wanted to wipe my mouth and …" she made a gagging noise, "some had real soft lips. Some of them were so rough my lips bruised. I do know that I don't like kissing men with whiskers or a mustache."

The three laughed together.

"Indeed, that is reassuring for those of us who do not have hair on our faces." A deep voice resonated from behind the girls.

Devry, Elizabeth, and Arabella whirled around in unison as if a choreographer had instructed them in a theatrical play. Each stood, stunned, as they stared at the young man before them.

"Oh! Matthew. We did not know you were there. These are my friends, Arabella Peck and Elizabeth Parson."

Matthew gallantly took Arabella's hand and kissed it gently. "I am enchanted to meet you."

He repeated the performance with Elizabeth, murmuring the same words.

"I've been looking for you, Devry. I believe I have the next dance." Matthew escorted her to the dance floor. Devry cast a joyful glance at her friends. Elizabeth smiled and winked back, knowing the mischievous grin would promise an interesting end to the dance. Arabella giggled behind her fan, making muffled kissing noises only Elizabeth could hear.

* * *

Matthew knew the strict rules of society and had absolutely no intention of following them. He retrieved her dance card and placed it in his jacket pocket. The first rule he intended to break was to keep her in his arms dancing for the rest of the night. His not-so-subtle announcement would deter anyone from trying to court her.

After the third set, Matthew took Devry for an evening stroll, satisfied in the unintentional disclosure that she preferred men without whiskers or facial hair. A kiss would seal the evening. He would have to restrain his desire for more than just a trifle kiss. Unlike the modern world, he understood that in the late 1800s a woman of twenty was an innocent. Having her run from him in terror would not suit his plans.

She was discussing suitable, lady-like, approved topics while Matthew listened with one ear, his eyes intent on finding the opportune moment for concealment from prying eyes. His heart pounded in nervous anticipation. Her scent, her being, enveloped him in a cocoon of warmth. Matthew's breath quickened and he forced himself to relax. He looked into her eyes, feeling lucky and blessed that he had this woman to cherish.

Low on the horizon, the moon smiled at them, and the stars winked as if conspiring with him. The songs of the night skillfully played their enchanting tunes. A slight breeze caressed a stray hair near her forehead, placing it strategically in front of her eye. He repressed his desire to move it, afraid to break the spell.

Matthew grabbed his moment. With a surprised squeak from Devry, he pulled her behind a bush.

"Devry," he whispered. One hand gently grazed her chin as he lifted her face toward his lips.

She opened her mouth, puzzled at his sudden movement. For a fleeting moment, surprise flashed in her eyes until she understood his intent and accepted his unspoken invitation with unabashed desire. She licked her lips in anticipation. His manhood jolted in response.

As faint as rustling leaves, he caressed her lips, sending a jolt through both their souls. Matthew pulled Devry closer, melting his body with hers as they merged and became one heart and soul. The roar of a flash flood pounded in the distance. The Earth slammed to a halt. His body ached to be deep inside, enclosed in her heat. In response, his lips took control and filled her. His senses reeled with emotions from unfamiliar territory.

An echo whispered quietly, *you can never go back*, as he plummeted into a chasm engulfed by something he did not fear. He reluctantly released her lips. The withdrawal made him feel as if he had vaulted into the freezing cold waters of the Arctic. His lips screamed in protest. He was drowning and she was his lifeline. Holding and hugging her body to his, Matthew kissed Devry again, sealing a vow he did not know he was making.

The band strings sang, beginning the last dance of the evening, as the two rushed toward the dance floor. With Devry in his arms, he swept her into a waltz. A contented smile etched pleasantly on his face, knowing he had more than surpassed the accepted amount of dances for an unbetrothed innocent. They both saw the tall, blond, and very red-faced gentleman approaching the couple as they made a turn in the waltz.

Matthew raised his eyebrows and grinned. "Sorry, sir, but the lady is dancing with me."

Gracefully maneuvering Devry in a swirl of glittering silk, Matthew chuckled, watching the man's face bottle with rage. The private ballroom dance lessons his mother had insisted on were giving him the expertise to skillfully keep them out of the enraged man's reach.

They were lost in their own private moment while the room buzzed; many had seen the evasive maneuvers. The elders gossiped, recounting the previous dance and The Widow's uncharacteristic behavior.

Karen heard the clucking and ripples of whispers, "wild and uncontrollable … undisciplined … we understand The Widow's faux pas … obvious what is happening … what a scandal …"

She silently watched her son, wondering what could possibly be on his mind to intentionally desire a social uproar. How was she going to explain his outrageous behavior to Christine and Andrew? Thank the heavens he was not traveling with them to the reservation. The scandal would be impossible to erase if Matthew was to travel with them now.

She scanned the room, seeking Andrew and his pending reaction to her son's odd behavior. She watched Mr. Brandt skirt the perimeter of the dance floor, following her son and Devry like a wolf circling his prey. His body reeked anger, his eyes declared murder.

Karen jerked her ankle at an angle, tilting it back and forth. Smiling, she watched Brandt trip across the room, stumbling with each step as he tried to follow the couple around the room. She was using one of her gifts and being petty. But, it was worth it to see the look of embarrassment on Brandt's face.

Chapter Nine

Lane Parker shook his head in sincere surprise. He should attend Sunday church services more often. It was the last place he had expected to find clues to the murders. The people of the town were bustling with the news of last night's scandalous dance. The enraged and apparent murderous wrath of Mr. Brandt fueled the gossip, loosening their tongues, opening torrents of information.

He had missed the dance. He had had no desire to waste his precious time when he knew The Widow was helping Catherine attend Richard Miller. Now he was kicking himself for not attending the soiree. Lane clenched his jaw in frustration; another murder seemed inevitable.

Mrs. Barnes had snagged him as he was leaving the church, insisting that he come to her home. She sat across from him, stiff and regal, like a queen blessing her minions with an audience.

"Mr. Parker, I have no hesitations. Many do not care for my lack of diplomacy and honestly. I do not care. If you do not want to hear my opinion, do not ask."

"Please, continue."

"Well then, I shall," she sniffed. "Mr. Burke has been, excuse me, had been a club member from the moment he realized that women could satisfy his base needs. He specifically chose Amanda for a wife because of her wanton desires. She was a hot-blooded pretty girl until the tonic and pregnancy started taking its toll."

"Tonic?"

"Yes. Do not interrupt me, young man." She pursed her lips. "The club members vote on a host. The wife entertains the men, in any fashion they choose. When the hostess becomes pregnant, they move on to another. I have tried to warn the women of the town, but they refuse to believe me!"

"How did you get this information?"

"My son is a member. Mr. Brandt brought him home one evening, intoxicated to the hilt. My son tends to babble when he has been drinking."

"What about the sheriff? Did you speak with him?"

Mrs. Barnes chuckled. "He is a member; however, while the sheriff may have abnormal desires, he would not abide murder."

"Tell me about Mr. Brandt."

"Ah, yes. Mr. Brandt likes it all. He has to feel in control. Mrs. Enlow and her boarders usually take care of that part of his needs. Mr. Brandt enjoys the feeling of superiority."

Lane stared at the elderly woman before him. "Is he a member?"

"I am unsure. Mrs. Enlow's dealings with the club members and her desires harmonize with Mr. Brandt's and the rest of the club members. They visit her boarding house approximately once a month.

"In my opinion, she has made the unfortunate mistake of falling in love with one of them. He spurned her love and the club members started ridiculing her. Mrs. Enlow was quite loud in her protests, announcing to the town how she would pay them back."

"Do you believe she is the murderer?"

Mrs. Barnes knew she had his ear. "She is in cohorts with The Widow. If, Mr. Parker, you were sincere in your desire to unearth the murderer, you would take yourself to the Black Widow's doorstep. She has created an illusion to fool the community." Refilling his cup, she nodded. "I suggest that you pose inquiries to The Widow and ask why she had to leave St. Augustine. If she is honest, she will tell you, Mr. Parker, that her voluntary departure from St. Augustine was on the heels of another murder investigation."

Lane interrupted. "What about his business?"

"Ah yes, Mr. Brandt's illicit business dealings … Mr. Brandt had become obsessed with obtaining riches. During the Indian wars, he manufactured munitions and sold them for exorbitant prices. As he became more affluent from the sales, other businessmen approached him and borrowed money to expand their businesses, or keep them productive while the low economy depleted their incomes."

"Mr. Brandt considered the use of his money a personal loan?"

"Yes, he would create a contract to protect both parties with the clause defining a purchase option, upon default of repayment. Since he rarely loaned money to someone who did not have a bank loan on the property, he would often give them the option to purchase back their property, at the market price."

"Mr. Brandt manipulated the situation?"

"Quite well, too. The borrower, unable to maintain payment for both loans, would find themselves in arrears and feel relieved that Brandt was willing to help them. Many of those who had died in the last year owed Brandt money; their deaths increased his wealth and position immensely." She sighed heavily. "I do not believe Mr. Brandt is the one you need to pursue. I suggest you keep yourself close to Mr.

Miller, considering … his present situation. He has made frequent visits to the apothecary."

A knock on Mrs. Barnes back door ended the conversation as quickly as it had started. "If you would excuse me, Mr. Parker. I have business that needs my attention." She stood and swept her open palm toward the front door. "Thank you for coming to visit."

Heading toward The Widow's home, Lane puzzled through the conundrum. Brandt's business dealings were not illegal, just unethical. Mrs. Barnes suspected that Mr. Brandt was a member of the gentleman's club, but no one, except the members themselves, knew. He was not on the list the sheriff had given Lane. How many names were missing?

Since Mr. Brandt had reason to have many enemies, Lane had too many suspects. Although many had not quite understood his unethical behavior, most did not consider him an enemy but a friend. However, the remainder made up a separate handful of possible suspects. Yet, it was his enemies who were murdered, one property owner at a time.

Mrs. Enlow had declared her revenge in front of the town. Lane shook his head. She did not have the ability nor the education to know which medications would cause death. If she were to consider murder, it would most likely be something less complicated. Her alibis were concrete and unwavering. She did not know how to cook, so how would she poison someone without suspicion?

His information from St. Augustine indicated that Lydia Williams, accused of killing sixteen men by poisoning them, surreptitiously escaped a conviction for murder. Upon her arrest, they had confiscated her complete supply of medicines.

The sheriff in St. Augustine had been thorough with his investigations, including the autopsies. He had questioned every pharmacist and apothecary within a fifty-mile radius.

No evidence showed that she had purchased or possessed any of the medicinal drugs found in those sixteen victims. Without proof of the poisons, the sheriff had released her. It had been a major scandal, separating the town into those defending Lydia's innocence with full-force passion, and those demanding her incarceration and death.

Lane spoke to the apothecary several times. He had answered multiple questions without hesitation. Richard Miller had purchased an abundance of dangerous drugs and medicines from the apothecary in the past year. Besides purchasing cocaine, morphine, and laudanum, he had been procuring an anesthetic called flunitrazepam.

When he further questioned the apothecary, Lane learned that this anesthetic caused adverse effects if used improperly. It could decrease blood pressure, impair the memory, and cause drowsiness, dizziness, and confusion. The pharmacist claimed that it could also impair vision and cause intestinal disturbances and urinary retention. Lane's internal beacon flared brightly.

Could that be the drug Richard used on Catherine? As a depressant, the anesthetic could cause excitability or aggressive behavior. It was also addictive. They would need to wean Catherine from the drug to avoid withdrawal symptoms.

He mentally listed the symptoms as he watched a crowd of people entering The Widow's back gate … headache, muscle pain, anxiety, tension, restlessness, confusion, and irritability. There could also be numbness, hallucinations, delirium, convulsions, shock, and heart failure.

Richard had accused Devry of trying to poison him. Could she have found it in the house and used this anesthetic on Richard? Dismissing accusations like that would be neglectful on his part, even though she was still a child. Where would she have obtained the knowledge? She had also been the only suspect who had never set foot in the apothecary's drug store. In addition, acute kidney or liver failure was not on the list of side effects.

Lane stood at the entranceway to Lydia Williams' backyard. This was obviously something else he should have done sooner. Before his eyes, burbled a kaleidoscope of people and animals. Laughter and squeals of happy children filled the air. Above the ruckus, a very distinctive and loud goose bellowed, quite agitated at someone or something.

He had never set eyes on a more eccentric or elaborate piece of property. The people he had spoken to had nonchalantly referred to it as her backyard, but what Lane saw before him was an elaborate park. Making his way toward the covered patio, he skirted some running children squealing in delight. The goose continued to resoundingly honk his objections.

It was an uncharacteristically hot day and half the town was there. Matthew and Devry sat on the covered porch, dining and obviously enjoying each other's company. Mr. Brandt stood leaning against a tree with his arms crossed, glaring at the young couple. Feral anger radiated from his eyes.

Animated in cheerful conversation, the elders of the community enjoyed the cool shade of the massive oak trees, observing the festive lawn party with practiced ease, delighting in the enjoyment of the children's play.

None of the other suspects appeared to be present. He had a feeling they would arrive soon.

In the distance, he saw a boathouse near the water. People were swimming and splashing about. Several boats drifted beyond the reach of the swimmers, the passengers relaxed, enjoying the warm sun. Swans, ducks, and geese meandered, oblivious to the human infiltration of their habitat, as if it were a common occurrence.

A few young boys fished from the shore and boat decks with their canes. Against the fence, toddlers petted the lambs, feeding them scraps while their mothers watched with prudent eyes. The sound of a violin tweaked his ears and he turned to see a group of men under a large gazebo.

Next to the gazebo, a maze of flowers flourished, with benches strategically placed for the enjoyment of those who wished to rest. A young couple with a child sat on a blanket next to the garden. The mother reading a book to her child made animated faces and movements, acting out the story. The child laughed and bounced in delight.

He heard voices filtering through the kitchen window, some of the town's women chattering and giggling among themselves. Through the whole gathering and above the din of laughter, the irritated goose would not stop wailing.

Lane's eyes rounded when he saw three very large tables full of every mouthwatering dish imaginable. He was surprised that the laden tables had not collapsed from the weight.

Uncomfortable in such a large crowd, he scanned the area for a familiar face. One of the ladies greeted him and handed him an ice-cold glass of fresh lemonade, indicating pleasantly where he could refill his glass. He stood silently watching a group of young teens gathering to play a competition unfamiliar to him.

Two teams of young teenage boys stood in a line of battle, their anticipation vibrating through the enthusiastic crowd. Tension increased as all silently waited for the signal to start.

The whistle blew, and Lane watched intrigued as the boys attacked each other, trying to wrestle their opponent to the ground. Cheers and shouts of instruction came from the spectators.

The goose honked louder.

"It's called Che-hoo-hoo," the doctor, sitting comfortably in a wheelchair, explained as Karen pushed him past Lane.

She wheeled him to the plank brunch table, walked over to the food, and started filling three plates. Lane pulled out a chair for Karen before sitting next to his brother-in-law.

"Who-who-what?" Lane laughed.

Glenn smiled and thanked Karen as she placed the plates in front of them. "Che-hoo-hoo is a northwestern Indian wrestling game. Little Red Hawk taught it to the youngsters. You see, he aspired to help them find something to keep their minds occupied and out of trouble. The wrestling match can have as many wrestlers as they want, as long as both sides have an equal amount. Every time they play, they choose a different leader to call sides and then set themselves up in the line of battle. They cannot attack their opponent until the signal to attack is given, or they are disqualified."

Lane nodded. He was going to strangle that blasted goose if it did not cease making so much noise. "Any rules, or is it a go-for-the-throat competition?"

"Rules are quite strict. If someone does not keep good form and follow the rules, he is ridiculed and shamed into embarrassment." Glenn chuckled. "Not too many teenage boys are going to allow themselves to be subjected to that type of ridicule, so they all play fair. It is against the rules to strike with their hands. Nor can they take their opponent by the neck. Of course, no cat fighting; they are not allowed to kick or pull hair."

The group watching the wrestling match swelled as the competition continued.

"This is intense! Look at those two boys. No quarter given there," Lane exclaimed.

He watched as two teenagers wrestled with great intensity. The shorter one broke free and ran a few yards away. At first, Lane thought he would give up and run away, possibly to another wrestler; but the boy spiraled suddenly and pushed himself into his opponent. The tactic did not work. His opponent pinned him to the ground. One of the men officiating declared him down and counted out.

Cheers of approval roared through the crowd. The blasted goose honked louder. The boy's opponent helped him up and they shook hands. Applause from the group of onlookers ensured the boys that they had had a good match. Arm in arm, the two slowly strolled over to a group of girls who were watching the encounter.

"A lot of people here," Lane commented. Cooked goose for dinner tomorrow sounded very enticing.

"Yeeeeup, not unusual for Lydia. It started a few months after she came to live here. People seem drawn to her. It has always been that way. Every Sunday, unless she is visiting family out of town, the people of the town come and have a nice friendly gathering. Everyone brings food and drinks." The doctor pointed to the table overflowing with food and the overflowing plates in front of them. "If they don't have food or drinks to bring, no one worries about it."

"You would think, with all that caterwauling, he would have lost his voice by now."

Glenn blinked at Lane, baffled. "Who?"

"The goose." Lane pointed to the locked door.

"Sir Elmer? Fat chance." The doctor laughed. "He'll calm down when Lydia feeds him. She'll be back soon."

"No, you misunderstand me, I mean the goose. Who's Sir Elmer?"

"The goose," replied Karen between bites of potato salad.

Lane stared at Glenn and Karen with a vague look of confusion. "She named the goose Sir Elmer?"

"No," they both answered.

Lane closed his eyes and inhaled deeply. "What is the goose's name?"

"Sir Elmer. Get on the same page, boy."

Karen covered her mouth, stifling the urge to burst out laughing.

"But, you just said …"

"We said *Lydia* didn't name him Sir Elmer. She named him Elmer. The neighbors added the Sir because of his being a royal pain in the …"

"The goose that is making all that blasted noise is named Sir Elmer? Wait, did you say The Widow's not even here?" Surprise and disappointment colored Lane's face.

"Yes, the goose is Sir Elmer. Lydia went over to the Miller's to check on Richard."

"I didn't see her at church. Was she there all morning?" Lane started rubbing his temples. He would cook Sir Elmer, the goose, if he did not stop harping so loudly.

"Only time you'll see Lydia at church is for a funeral or a wedding," the doctor dryly professed. "She'll be here soon, so you can wipe that disappointment off your face."

"I am not disappointed."

Karen laughed at the obvious denial.

Glenn snorted. "Sure, Lane. Any luck on the investigation?"

"Better today than yesterday. I have five suspects. Guess the scandal last night started wagging tongues. I was surrounded by gossip after the service ended."

"What scandal?" The doctor brightened with enthusiasm.

Lane laughed. It was about time the doctor had a good day. It was hard watching him deteriorate day after day. He was such an adventurous and energetic person.

"My son, I assume?" Karen asked.

Lane nodded and grimaced. "Well, it seems Matthew Black Elk breached an unforgivable etiquette rule by dancing with Devry for more than two dances in a row. He has made a powerful enemy."

"Standing Deer."

"What?" The doctor never failed to confuse Lane. "Standing Deer?"

"Matthew Standing Deer. Karen's second husband, John Black Elk, is his stepfather. Matthew's father was killed at the Little Big Horn massacre."

"When was that battle? I don't recall hearing about it."

"Custer's Last Stand," Glenn rephrased.

"On that note, if you gentlemen will excuse me?"

Lane nodded. Everyone knew about Custer. He stood silently, remembering the tales about the infamous soldier, as he watched Karen descend the stairs.

"Well? Are you going to tell me or am I going to have to use my own imagination?" The doctor growled at Lane.

Lane's mind quickly returned to the present conundrum. "I did not mean to upset her."

The doctor shook his head. "You didn't. It is just like any other battle memory. You prefer to keep it safely tucked away."

The men were silent for a few moments.

"Lane, you going to stand there staring at the crowd or are you going to tell me?"

"Yes, sorry. Last night seemed to have caused a cauldron of speculation. I do not think there was one person that attended the dance last night who did not warn me that Brandt was furious. Actually, their words were more specific, along the lines of his wanting to murder Matthew."

Glenn grunted. Lane knew information was coming. His brother-in-law was not much for words but when he spoke, Lane had learned to listen. Obviously, the doctor was figuring out how to word it, or what to say. Patience had not been one of Lane's virtues. It was a hard lesson, one he learned well as a Pinkerton man.

"Put the cards on the table for me." Glenn glanced toward the pond. "Tell me what you have been dealt."

Lane sighed, "There is only one person who has made comments about a scandal in St. Augustine."

"You have been talking with the town gossip. Good place to start but Lydia is innocent."

"Your opinion is in accordance with the rest of Tokata. She was the only person to have something negative to say about Mrs. Williams." Lane cleared his throat. "I was left with the impression that she may have a personal vendetta against men."

Sir Elmer was getting louder right along with the pounding pain that had gradually infiltrated his head. Maybe he would stuff it and mount the thing, too, forever to live in silence. Lane smiled to himself, picturing the goose stuffed and getting dusty in his attic.

"Mrs. Barnes fuels gossip. She is a bitter woman and envious of The Widow." Glenn took a bite of chicken. "However, out of all the information she gave you, there is something there, some clue that could put you on the right path."

"She had her own personal list of suspects." Lane grimaced. "Her son is a member."

"Appears the list is growing."

"Which list?"

Glenn grunted, "Both. The club members, which in turn increases the list of suspects, and increases the list of potential victims."

"Mrs. Williams and Mrs. Enlow appeared to be on the top, along with Mr. Brandt." Lane pushed his empty plate to the side. "Mr. Brandt and Mrs. Enlow visited the homes of the murdered on several occasions before their deaths. She told me to watch Richard Miller, implying I wouldn't have to search too far for the murderer."

"Brandt and Mrs. Enlow together?"

"Mrs. Barnes elaborated the sordid details of many of the club members' desires, starting with Mr. Burke. When I questioned her about Mrs. Enlow's alleged involvement with Brandt, she proceeded to inform me," Lane blushed, "of his unique and unusual sexual desires."

The doctor nodded, picked up another piece of fried chicken and pointed it at Lane. "Yes, he does have different needs. However, Brandt is not a murderer. He would pay someone to do it."

Just as Lane was going to pummel Glenn with questions, the goose stopped screaming and Andrew approached with greetings. He had escorted Lydia to Richard and Catherine's and they had made a quick stop to check on the sheriff. Andrew explained that Richard was now comatose and probably only had a few days before he would pass to the next world. He was happy to announce, after giving the bad news first, that the sheriff was recuperating very quickly with the medications and herbs that Lydia had given him.

Lane kept silent during the exchange, absorbing as much information as his aching head would allow. Andrew had commented that he should get Lydia to give him a tonic for his headache. It took a considerable amount of tongue-biting to avoid making a flippant remark. A woman doctor? God help him. With the doctor sitting there as well, he most likely would have gotten an earful.

He was attracted to The Widow. She made him tongue-tied like a greenhorn getting his first woman. His palms began to sweat whenever someone mentioned her name. The thought of her kicked his heart (and other various unmentionable parts of his body) into blood-rushing desire. Knowing she was a few feet away had his heart thundering so loud he would not have been surprised if Andrew and Glenn could hear it.

He wanted to take her to his bed and never let her leave the room. He would like to change the reference of her being a widow to being Lane Parker's wife. Lane was stunned. From where did that notion come? A wife, Lane Parker's wife; *Mrs. Lydia Parker* had a nice sound to it.

His gut instinct told him he should arrest her and then find proof, which of course, he could not do. South Dakota was a state now, protected by laws; even suspected murderers had rights. Unfortunately, regardless of what direction his queries took him, they always came back to The Widow.

The problem with his caution was that he had completely searched her storage closet of herbs. Taking a pinch from each jar, he had meticulously marked them and sent them to one of his old Pinkerton friends to have the herbs verified.

His instincts told him The Widow was guilty. His heart denied the accusations. Circumstantial evidence did not convict a criminal. Lane had to find undeniable proof, one way or another. Otherwise, he would never be able to honestly love her without seeds of doubt.

Chapter Ten

A small group of friends sipping iced lemonade sat under the breezy shade of the majestic oak trees at The Widow's home. Catherine sat stiff and immobile. A thankful numbness from the tragedy of the past week carried her through the hot afternoon. Oblivious to the conversations cantering about, she stared at the swans swimming and frolicking on the shore, amusing herself in her own private bubble.

Richard's funeral and the speed of his illness had left the town dazed.

They had watched the ex-Pinkerton man investigate and question half the residents, frantically searching for leads. During the funeral services, Lane Parker had kept looking at Catherine, guilt radiating from his handsome features. They knew he was searching relentlessly for the identity of the murderer, understanding the frustration engraved in his expression and stance. The only times they had seen him relax were at the dance with The Widow and at her home a few days before.

Their thoughts brought them to the chimerical memories of that Sunday afternoon. The cat and mouse game between The Widow and Parker had kept them entertained. Most Sunday afternoons, The Widow would join the elders under the tree and leave only to bring food to the women who had trouble walking.

Last Sunday afternoon was quite different. She had not stayed in one place for very long. The elders noticed how her eyes had followed Mr. Parker when she thought no one was looking. The Pinkerton man was more aggressive in the chase. They had watched him repeatedly approach her. The Widow would skitter away from his advances.

Today, with talk of murder, her eyes had kept darting toward the entranceway and the rear doorway, anticipating his arrival. A few innocent queries had Lydia blushing and changing the subject.

Secretly the small group of friends had started placing bets on how long it would take the tall handsome man to win her heart.

Love seemed to be the focus, as life must continue, even on such a mournful day. Devry and Matthew were the newest and most refreshing aspect of the marriage season. In the town's eyes, Mr. Brandt was an unlikely candidate for marriage to young Devry. Most had expected Mr. Brandt to continue his bachelorhood. He had not revealed any desire to join the marriage mart until this year.

They started discussing Brant's reaction to Karen Black Elk's son. Matthew's increased interest in Devry created concern among the elders; not that Matthew was unworthy, but rather, their concern was about his impending encounter with the contentious Brandt.

An eruption between the two men was imminent. Devry, as the young so often were, was oblivious to the burning hatred developing between the two adversaries.

Lydia excused herself and walked by a group of men sitting near the porch. She could hear their whispers of frustration, and sense their feelings of incompetence. They seemed like lost fledglings searching for home. They heard rumors that the club members had called an emergency meeting after Richard's funeral. What would the club members do? Who would be next? Would the Pinkerton man find the perpetrator before another murder took place?

As he walked through The Widow's house, Lane noticed that the residence, which usually glittered with effervescence, now breathed a quiet sadness. The poignant melody of a flute floated through the open window.

He casually leaned against the doorframe of the doctor's room as he watched The Widow bending over Glenn, helping him drink one of her decoctions. Her body blocked his view of the doctor, but he was more than willing to watch Lydia's gentle movements, unabashed and uninterrupted. Lane clenched his fist fecklessly trying to curb his desire to caress her backside.

Clearing his throat loudly, he entered the room. Glenn and The Widow turned slowly to greet him. Discreetly, the doctor closed a book that was open on his lap. From behind the door a loud, vitriolic screech caught him by surprise. The cantankerous goose gouged Lane, backing him against the closet doors. The invidious little savage was going after his manhood!

"Sir Elmer!" Lydia shouted and clapped her hands together. "Sit down."

With a hauteur known only to royalty, the goose sat immediately, in regal posture, and proceeded to yell at Lane. Glenn chuckled as Lane stood motionless, staring warily at the beast. He watched wide-eyed as she picked up the goose and placed him in a padded basket on the table behind the door. His hands remained cupped, protecting his private parts, when she grabbed his wrists to inspect them.

"You're bleeding," Lydia stated without compunction and pulled him toward the door. "Come into the kitchen; I'll bandage them for you."

Dazed, Lane glared at Glenn, who was trying to restrain his laughter, and then at the back of his hands, as he watched blood trickle from his wounds. *Holy Jesus! The blasted thing went after my manhood. I'm going to neuter the beast! How does one go about neutering a goose?* Addressing the different ways he was going to break Sir Elmer's neck interrupted his thoughts, bringing visions of a stuffed and mouthwatering roasted goose.

Clenching his jaw, Lane watched her grab a jar and bandages from the cupboard. Gently, she cleaned his wounds, her languorous movements inflaming his desires. Her breast came within inches of his hands as she bent to retrieve more water, and his manhood twitched. He moaned, fearing Lydia would see what she was doing to him.

Thinking that she had hurt him, Lydia apologized. Lane shifted uncomfortably in his seat. Looking around at the various pots and pans was not helping. He could smell the sweet lavender scent she used. It was alluring, intriguing, and invigorating.

She explained how Sir Elmer's possessive behavior had started from the moment he had been able to walk. She had found the egg, still warm, but somehow moved from the nest. Nurturing the egg until the bird had hatched, she had fed him as she would a baby.

She placed a salve on Lane's wounds and bandaged his hand. He winced expecting it to hurt. Surprised, he looked in her eyes and she smiled.

"I do not use iodine or alcohol."

Her gentle smile mesmerized him. She did not pull away as he placed his bandaged hand on her head. Slow and sweet, like warm golden honey, he leaned toward her lips, waiting for her to reject his advance. Lane had seen the desire in her eyes but until now she had been skittish and evasive whenever he had approached.

When she did not pull away, he leaned closer, within a breath's touch. She closed her eyes and leaned toward him. He could feel the heat between them, but at that moment the door swung open and they both sprang back.

Andrew saw what he was interrupting and immediately apologized. Explaining that he was there to visit Glenn, he quickly left the red-faced and embarrassed couple. Without another word, Lydia finished bandaging his other hand.

As they entered the bedroom, Glenn and Andrew smiled at them. Glenn had a satisfied smirk painted on his face with a twinkle in his eyes that spoke loudly of their whispered conversation. Andrew concentrated on the books on the shelf as if the answers to the world's questions were there on the book covers.

An uncomfortable silence ensued until the goose hailed his presence to all in the room. Sir Elmer had had enough of the childish behavior and proceeded to tell the group his objections. He glared at Lane as he loudly informed the group of his personal discomfort.

Glenn chuckled. "It appears Sir Elmer is jealous of our Pinkerton man."

Andrew smiled. "I wonder how one competes against a goose for a lady's attention."

"Perhaps the competition for her hand will entertain us on those rainy days?"

"Can the incumbent candidate succeed against one whose position has never wavered?"

"Ah, but you missed the most precious attack," Glenn laughed. "I've never seen Lane move so fast before. It seems Sir Elmer knew where his weakness was and went for it."

"Really? Tell me about it, my friend." Andrew smiled and leaned back in his chair.

Lane glared at the two men. Had it been anyone else they were discussing, he most likely would have joined in the battle of wits. Unfortunately, he was competing against a goose for the lovely widow's attention … a goose whose feathers would be a welcome addition to his pillow.

Lane smiled as he scrutinized the goose, picturing it stuffed and dressed. His mouth dropped open. Did it just humph and stick his nose up at him?

"Enough. The two of you could try a saint. Let's discuss something a little more harmonious, shall we?" Lydia suggested. "Were Karen and Devry on time for the coach this afternoon?"

"Yes, they are on the way. Devry is quite excited. I will be leaving tomorrow morning after I send a telegram to Christine. She will not arrive there in time for the ceremony but will be meeting me at Sitting Bull's camp. We will be gone for a few weeks and return home together. Matthew will be taking over the ranch while I'm gone."

Lydia tilted her head, listening, and frowned. "Did you hear someone yelling?"

All three of the men shook their heads.

"I could swear I heard someone call for help."

Eduard Colon rushed through the house searching for Andrew and Lydia. Andrew jumped up and rushed toward the butler. Lane and Lydia followed his retreat.

"What is it? What has happened?"

"It is Master Standing Deer." Eduard paused, breathless. "They found him in the path leading to the Lunch House on the ranch. He has been shot. They are bringing him here now."

"Shot? Where? How bad is it?"

"I don't know. Anthony found him. Some of the men are bringing him on a makeshift travois. They should be here soon."

They escorted Eduard to the kitchen to let him rest and have a refreshing cup of hot tea. Lydia scrambled into the back room used specifically for patients. Andrew put a pot of water on the fire while she prepared the room for Matthew. She set out various scalpels and medical tools, bandages and medicine on a tray. The housekeeper brought towels into the room as Lydia tugged back the bed cover and sheet.

Chapter Eleven

The noise and chaos in the yard alerted the group that the men had arrived with Matthew. The townspeople at The Widow's were frantic. One of the men grabbed a horse from Lydia's stables and rode off to alert the sheriff. Fear raged through the crowd. What was happening to their peaceful town?

When Lydia had seen all the blood on him, she raced to the bed and placed more towels over the sheets. The men laid Matthew down and solemnly left the room. Andrew and Lane cut the bloody clothes off the young man while Lydia and her housekeeper carried in a pot of steaming water.

"I will need more washcloths," Lydia ordered and the housekeeper scurried away. "Someone needs to sit with Glenn, please!" She called out to whomever was within hearing range.

The three continued to clean the blood and locate the wounds. It was amazing—all that blood and no puncture wound. Lydia used a cold compress on the swelling lump on the back of his head, a lump he most likely received when he fell.

She proceeded to clean the gash caused by the bullet. The wound began on his hand, and then slashed a long puckered trail up his arm to his shoulder. It was bleeding profusely, though it was not a deep cut. Biting her lip, she wrapped some gauze around Matthew's arm and proceeded to make a fresh poultice.

Andrew and Lane changed the bandages on his head as she unwrapped his arm. Carefully, she applied the poultice and then rebound Matthew's arm.

All three sighed in relief.

"He might not even have a scar," Andrew surmised.

"No, probably not. I hope he does not stay out for too long. That could be his biggest problem." Lydia added. "Head wounds are so touchy."

Lane scowled. "I'll be back. I am going to ask those men who found him some questions."

About fifty feet from the Lunch House, a group of men surrounded the sheriff. Lane tied his horse and the group separated. He stood back and listened as the sheriff rapidly fired questions. No one had seen anything.

When they heard the reports from the gunshots, they had immediately hit the floor for cover. After a few minutes of silence, the men gradually opened the door and scanned the area to see if it was safe to leave the premises. That was when they spotted Matthew lying face down on the path.

The sheriff had one of the men lay down in the same position, on the same spot. As the man stood up, he thanked everyone and sent the men on their way. Lane turned to look where the shots could have come from when the sheriff walked in the opposite direction. The sheriff tapped Lane on the shoulder.

Holding his hand out, he showed Lane the remnants of a bullet. "Looks like a .22 to me."

Lane nodded his head. "How many people you know own a .22 rifle?"

"Off the top of my head? Three. The Widow — her grounds man uses it for hunting, Mr. Barnes, and Curry up at the old mission."

Lane blew air through his teeth and the sheriff shook his head. "Lydia was with me. Mr. Barnes was in the backyard the whole time. He was sitting with the gentlemen outside on the back porch."

"Where was her grounds man?"

Lane sighed and kicked some dirt. "Don't know." Irritated, he snapped at the sheriff. "She doesn't have a motive."

"Don't go getting all upset with me. I don't think she is guilty either, but it don't look so good. You ask your lady friend some questions and I'll check with Curry. Seems if you go up there, he will probably shoot you, not knowing who you are. He's real quick with his trigger finger and mighty itchy to stay alone on his hill."

"He won't shoot you?"

"Nah, I go up there every once in a while and threaten to destroy his still. He can tell it's me just by the sound of my horse. I visit for want of some of his whiskey. Good stuff, best I've ever had." The sheriff grinned, shook Lane's hand, and walked toward his horse.

Before the sheriff rode away, he turned to Lane and waved. "I'll meet you at The Widow's."

On the ride back to Lydia's, Lane tried to reword every question in his mind to avoid sounding as if he were interrogating her. Nevertheless, no matter how many times he changed the wording, he was still questioning her on another murder case.

He shook his head, disgusted and discouraged with himself. He was in love with a possible murderer. She had her hands dirty with everything. St. Augustine, the suspicious poisoning of the club members, and now Matthew possibly shot with one of her rifles. It did not make sense. At least the murders in St. Augustine and the murders here paralleled. Matthew's situation did not quite fit with the killer's pattern. They had to be dealing with two separate cases.

Lydia entered the parlor and saw, immediately, the seriousness of the situation. Lane looked angry, upset, and troubled. Walking over to the cabinet, she poured them both a glass of bourbon. She carefully placed the bottle on the coffee table. Handing the glass to him, she delicately touched his face.

"Matthew woke up for a few moments but fell back to sleep."

"I want to question him."

"Not yet, Mr. Parker. Give him time to rest and recuperate."

"Lane. My name is Lane. My father is Mr. Parker."

"As you wish, Lane. What have you found?"

Taking her hands with both of his, he clenched his jaw. "Sit down, Lydia. I have to ask you some questions."

Sitting on the chair across from The Widow, Lane looked to the fireplace, as if searching for answers in the mortar and bricks.

"I don't want you to feel as if I am accusing you of any kind of culpability. There are so many unanswered questions involving your past and, as it stands, the present."

Lydia nodded. She had sidestepped this confrontation as long as possible, but had known it would come down to this. He was astute and thorough. It was one of his several attributes she found attractive. Sadly, none of her answers would declare her innocence. Puzzled, she tried to understand. "Why am I being questioned for the attempt on Matthew's life?"

"How many firearms do you own?"

"Firearms?"

"Yes, firearms. As in shotguns, rifles, and hand guns?"

"I have several." She added with an ostentatious sniff, "We do have to eat."

"How many do you have, Lydia?"

"I just told you, several," she snapped.

Lane took a deep breath. This was not going well. "What brand are they?"

"Well, let's see. I have three Remington rifles, a split breech carbine, a rolling block, and a cavalry carbine. I have several revolvers, a Colt Walker, pocket revolver, and three Remington Peacemakers."

It was amazing. She was answering his questions, but not giving complete responses. She was good. He wished he had seen her work her magic in the courtroom in St. Augustine.

"Which one is the .22?"

Lydia blinked. *Where are his questions leading?* "The Remington rolling block rifle."

"Does anyone have access to your guns?"

"Yes."

"Are you intentionally being obtuse? I will get the answers one question at a time, if that is what you want. You are not in a courtroom where every word will be scrutinized."

Lydia raised her eyebrows. "The only difference is there is no jury, but it appears to me as if there is a judge."

Lane sighed. "Who has access to your guns?"

"James."

"Your grounds man?"

"Yes."

"Did he have access to your rifle today?"

"No."

"How do you know?"

Lydia was getting quite irritated with his patronizing attitude. "I have a key." Indignation burned in her eyes.

Pulling out the key ring, she jingled it in his face. "I keep all firearms locked in the closet."

"Are you sure he did not have access to the rifle today?"

"Yes, I am sure." Lydia growled her response through clenched teeth.

Lane was quiet for a moment, staring at the ceiling. He appeared calm and unaffected. Lydia wanted to hit him with the bourbon bottle.

"Can I see it?"

"Of course." Lydia left the room with an irritated swish of her skirt.

When she returned she handed the rifle to Lane. He dismantled it, finding no evidence of recent use. The rifle was clean. James obviously took great care of the rifle.

"Do you know anyone else who owns a .22 rifle?" Lane asked as he handed her the rifle and watched her place it on the table near the door.

"Yes." She countered curtly as she seated herself across from him, tapping her foot in irritation.

"Who?"

"It is a common rifle. Most likely, half the people in town own one."

"Who?"

"Was Matthew shot with a .22?"

"I wouldn't be asking these questions if I thought he was shot with anything else."

"Where?"

"Close to the Lunch House."

Lydia bit her lip. "There are only a few places near there where someone could fire. It would have to be someone who was very accurate."

"That is true. The person would have to be a sharpshooter. Lydia … who?"

"I do not want to accuse anyone. I know what it is like to be accused of a crime when one is innocent."

Silence permeated the room. Lane would have sat there glaring at her all day if she did not speak up. He was like a wolf stalking its prey, waiting patiently for its victim to make that one spurious move.

Lane shrugged, "I'll wait all day for an answer … who?"

"I don't know anyone who would be that accurate. Except …" Lydia took a deep breath, "except Curry. Rumor has it that he was a sniper in the war. But, it doesn't really make sense."

"What doesn't?"

"That Curry would miss." Lydia tilted her head toward Lane. "If Curry shot at Matthew, he would be dead. Curry would not have missed."

"There were two shots according to the men at the Lunch House. He is that accurate?"

"Yes, he is that accurate. Two shots? Curry wouldn't need two shots."

Lydia could not fathom Curry missing. When they had shooting competitions, no one wanted to compete against him. Had someone paid him to scare Matthew? Curry could have intentionally grazed him with the bullet, as a warning. What was the first shot for? How in blazes did he cut a line right up Matthew's arm?

"The sheriff has gone up there to talk to him."

"If anyone can get answers from Curry, it'll be the sheriff." Lydia started to rise from her seat. "Well, that's settled. I have to check on my patients, if you will excuse me."

"I'm not done." Lane grabbed her arm.

Lydia gritted her teeth and sat next to Lane, emitting a deep sigh. She had worked so very hard to forget the past and continue as a respectable citizen after the raking she had received in St. Augustine. She had become a paragon of virtue and still the past came back to haunt her.

However, she was attracted to this man sitting next to her. She did not want to be virtuous or chaste. This was the first man who had resurrected her womanly desires. Lydia wanted to wallow in his seduction. She craved carnal sexuality—every blissful, sinful manner in which she could have him.

Yet, circumstances had caused a rift where none should have been. Lydia felt as if she did not have a choice. The nightmare of her past would follow regardless of her innocence. And, regardless of how she answered his questions, a seed of doubt remained. Could they overcome this hurdle? If she had been accused of anything else, Lane most likely would have been able to live with it. Suspected murder, though, was a seed no normal self-preserving adult would ignore.

"I'll be direct, Lydia, and make this easy on the both of us. I already have all the information available to me from the sheriff and an acquaintance of mine from St. Augustine. I'm not going to waste your time or mine on questions that I feel have already been answered."

Lydia nodded. Holding the glass, she prayed that her hands would stop shaking.

"Do you have access to anesthetics other than the apothecary?"

She glanced away from him, not able to bear the hostile accusation is his eyes. "Yes."

Lane was dumbfounded. He expected Lydia to deny any access to anesthetics. He had searched her personal medical supply area thoroughly; went through the pantry where she prepared and stored the medicinal herbs.

"How? Where do you get them?"

"From the doctor. His medicine cabinet is in the closet in his bedroom. Glenn gives me the key whenever he wants me to get anything out of it."

"His bedroom at his house, the one I'm staying at?"

"No, here at this house."

"You have access to anesthetics at this house?"

"Yes." Her voice sounded rough as she breathed quickly, as if she were pleading with him to understand.

"Oh Lydia, my love. This does not look good at all."

"I know how bad it looks. I am innocent. You have to believe me." Her eyes welled with unshed tears. "Please, believe me. I am a healer. I don't hurt people."

He could see the bridling fear. Leaning over, Lane held her close. He wanted to believe her. He could feel Lydia trembling underneath his arms as he cradled her and kissed her forehead.

"Hush now, listen to me. Have you used any of the anesthetics?"

"No." She shook her head. "No, I don't know how to use modern medicine. Anytime I went into Glenn's medicine cabinet, he would just tell me what to bring to him. He prepared everything. I just delivered his preparations."

Lane kissed the tears on her flushed cheeks. "It's all right. If what you say is true, the doctor can vouch for you."

Lydia sniffed. "See? Even you said, '*If* what you say is true.' You must believe me!"

He held her tight, feeling her body relaxing a moment at a time. Caressing her arm with one hand, he raised Lydia's face to his. As he leaned in to kiss her complacent and willing lips, a knock sounded at the door. They both looked at the ceiling and groaned, interrupted again.

"Enter," Lydia called to the unknown intruder.

The sheriff entered and Lydia handed him a drink. Not one to waste time, he immediately went into the reason for his arrival.

"Well, I spoke to Curry. He was up at his still just like I thought he would be. He said if he had wanted the boy dead, we'd be burying him in the next few days."

"Did he admit to shooting him?" Both Lane and Lydia asked simultaneously.

"Nope, said he was up at his new still since early morning. He wouldn't admit to it, anyways."

"New still?" Lydia pointed out. "Where would Curry get the money to build a new still?"

"Good question." The sheriff lifted his glass in salute. "Same question I asked him. He said he did a friend a favor. The friend paid him by buying him parts to make a new still."

"Like shooting Matthew?"

The sheriff chuckled at Lane's sarcastic remark. "Told him Matthew had his signature, straight up his leg."

"But it wasn't his leg, it was his arm." Lydia was confused.

"That's where I got him. Curry said the boy was hit in the arm and then drew a line right where the bullet grazed him. That's when I arrested him. He's at the jail as we speak."

"How did you know? That's exactly where Matthew was hit."

"I didn't. Shucks, Mrs. Williams, I called a bluff." The sheriff glimpsed out the window as his face blushed a bright crimson.

"Who hired him?" Lane asked.

"Can't get it out of him. Even when I told him he would rot in jail for attempted murder. He just threw his hat on the cot and said I knew da … excuse me, Mrs. Williams. Curry said I knew that if he wanted the boy dead, he would have done it. The boy's alive cuz that's how it was supposed to be. Just a scare."

"Well, if you gentlemen will excuse me, I'm going to check on the boy who has had *just a scare.*"

Chapter Twelve

Two weeks had crawled by as Matthew recuperated from his concussion. His arm was healing fast. The salve The Widow had applied smelled similar to what Sitting Bull had used when he was a child years ago. It might not leave a mark, which, though he may have foolishly wished it did (picturing the ladies fluttering around him in awe), he realized it would be difficult to explain once he returned home.

Mrs. Williams had been overbearing and overprotective, not allowing him to exert himself or leave the grounds. When he had mentioned her overly zealous patronage, her reply … *accept it.* She was not about to let anything happen to him while he was under her care.

Whispers had managed to come to him in the past week carrying suspicions of who had paid Curry to shoot him. Matthew was counting his blessings, for he was informed almost immediately that if Curry had wanted him dead, he would not be complaining about Mrs. Williams' obsessive nurturing.

No one had bothered to ask him whom he had suspected. If they had, he probably would not have told them anyway. But he would resolve the situation himself. Murder was not on his mind. Matthew laughed as he opened the door to

The Widow's porch. He might be wearing white man's clothing, but he was still a Sioux warrior. He would take care of his quarry the Lakota way.

He was looking down at Sir Elmer piously honking at him as the goose ran under his legs and out the door. The swoosh of skirts alerted him that he had interrupted Lane and The Widow for the second time this week. Sir Elmer's raucous screech was piercing and Matthew closed his eyes in pain. The back of his head throbbed as he opened them and watched the intrepid lawman scoot backwards, away from the attacking goose.

Caustic anger radiated from the helpless man's eyes. Matthew knew the only reason why the goose was still on this Earth was because the man was in love with The Widow.

Sir Elmer's fealty was complimentary, but Matthew was not sure he could tolerate the attacks the way Lane had. In just the last two weeks, the goose had managed to break skin on Lane's nose, knee, both hands, and now his elbow.

The Widow picked up the ranting, jealous goose and purred sweetly in his ear as he continued to berate Lane while she returned Sir Elmer to his room. Matthew promptly apologized as Lane grabbed a handkerchief to place on his elbow.

Lane shrugged and sighed. "One of these days I'll be able to taste her lips."

"You mean you haven't kissed Lydia, yet?"

"No. Every time we get this close," holding up two fingers, "someone or that soon-to-be-roasted goose comes in. Do you have any idea how frustrating that is?"

"Why don't you take her out alone on a picnic or something?"

"I've tried. She's afraid to leave Glenn."

"When Mom gets back maybe she can watch Glenn while you two spend some time together."

"I've been waiting patiently for your mother's return. I know she is the only one Lydia trusts with administering medication."

"That makes two of us, but I don't think I'm being patient about the wait."

Lane raised his eyebrow and laughed. "I don't think it's your mother you are waiting impatiently for."

Matthew had the grace to blush. "They'll be here soon."

The carriage ride had been long, arduous, and unusually void of conversation. The wind whistled violently, warning of an impending storm. *Ominous,* Karen kept thinking. It unsettled her when she had those feelings. She looked up into the dark, foreboding sky and prayed the rain would not begin until they had made it safely home.

She did not enjoy carriage rides and this mode of travel was definitely a deviation from her customary unconventional means. Having Devry there restricted the use of the gifts given to her years ago.

Karen had been able to reminisce on her visit with Sitting Bull and her Lakota friends. She knew in her heart she was a strong person with the utmost faith in herself and humanity, but wished she possessed Sitting Bull's unwavering spirit. It almost reached the point of envy. The strength in his soul created a celestial aura. His heart was immortal. With everything the Lakota had lived through, despite all the disasters and tragedies, he still reached for the heavens with an intensity no one could diminish.

Sitting Bull led the ceremony with exceptional refinement and skill. Devry's induction into womanhood was magnificent, as the Lakota cherished the spiritual and sacred ceremony. Glancing at her young companion, Karen noted an astounding transformation in the young woman.

"My warrior awaits me," Devry professed after a lengthy silence. "I've been searching for him ever since I realized that some day I wanted to marry. As we travel across the plains, I know he stands proud waiting to make me his wife. My warrior is my light and my soul. I can feel him and see him in the eternal space of time. I can sense his power inside me, waiting for my return. Nothing and no one can hinder what He has given us."

The intensity of Devry's words did not surprise Karen. It startled her that she had found someone she desired so soon. She wondered which warrior Devry had decided would be her life-mate. She did not recall a moment when the young woman had been out of her, Christine's, or Sunshine in the Morning's sight. *When had she fallen in love?*

Karen's heart palpitated. *Was that the ominous disaster she had felt in the air? Could the warrior Devry had committed herself to be one who would want her to live at the reservation, or would he come to live in the white man's world? Would he turn away from Devry when she refused to live on a reservation? Would he be one of the survivors?*

She inhaled a deep breath. "Who has stolen your heart, Devry?"

Devry face was enfolded in smiles, her sweet soul reflecting in her eyes. "Matthew."

Karen gazed out the window, scandalized. Her face paled; her stomach roiled, her heart twisted in fear, anger, disgust, and sadness. She was appalled that this … fourteen-year-old … had declared her love for her son. *Matthew is much too old for Devry. He will be declared a pedophile in our world. He will never be able to return home.*

"No," Karen growled. *How did I miss the warning signs? I should have spoken to him immediately about his actions at the dance. Doesn't he understand?* She shook her head, disappointed in his selfish maneuvers. He was not the sort of person to play games with people's feelings. *What is Matthew doing?* The more she contemplated his churlish behavior, his inconsideration for someone else's feelings, the more outraged she became. *Matthew is in for a thrashing like he has never experienced. Encouraging a young girl's impressionable heart like that!* She tapped her fingers on her leg in irritation.

Devry's eyes widened, hurt at the response from a woman she respected as much as her mother. Her heart sank as tears trickled; a lump strangled the breath in her throat. She could not understand Karen's horrified reaction. *What is wrong with her? Why is she turning away appalled at the thought of us joining as man and wife?*

Karen regained her composure, "Devry, please don't believe it is you. You are a wonderful, enchanting woman. If you were older, wiser, a little more experienced with life, you would understand my objections. If he falls in love with you, his life, everything that Matthew has worked so hard to accomplish ... taken from him. In our world he would be condemned to misery and ridicule."

"I don't believe you. Just because you don't live here in South Dakota doesn't make your world any different from mine."

"There is too much you do not understand. You are not at an age to marry in our society's eyes ..."

"How can you say that? You just witnessed my ceremony. Women marry at my age all the time. I started my season. My father is considering as we speak who would be a good match for me." Devry cried. "I know he would approve of Matthew."

"That is not the problem. Of course, your father would approve of Matthew, just as I would if you were not fourteen years old. I would not ..." She exhaled loudly, "I would not ... if you were at least eighteen ... I would not have objections. Even then, that is too young."

"I thought you liked me," Devry whimpered. Tears streamed down her flushed cheeks.

Karen hugged the heartbroken girl. "I'm so very sorry. In my heart, I cannot give my approval … if that is what you were seeking. I apologize for taking that hope from you. You will find your place on the unwinding path and the right man to be your husband. You will have your rainbows and make a wonderful wife. Matthew is not that man. I'm sorry."

Devry pulled away, livid and inconsolable, and stared out the window. The rest of the ride home would be miserable. She had painted a picture of them discussing the wedding plans; she had dreamed of having Matthew's children, sharing more love than one could imagine. Instead, her hopes and dreams … shattered by Karen's disapproval.

He *was* the man of her dreams. Stolen kisses and stolen moments when they had found themselves unescorted left her in a haze of desire. When their bodies had touched, when their lips had joined, she felt liberated. She ached for his touch, craved the pulse of energy as she melted against him. Matthew was in her thoughts, always there, drifting with her through the day, infiltrating her dreams at night.

He was the chosen one; her life-mate … she had seen it and felt it at the ceremony. The winds had whispered their consent, tendered the path she was to follow. Her vow was steadfast.

Chapter Thirteen

His mother and Devry arrived home that afternoon. Matthew had just missed them by minutes. He had tried to get home at a reasonable hour after he had received a note that they had arrived safely, but ended up working at the ranch late into the night. One disaster after another seemed to consume his day. He wondered how Andrew managed to gain any free time.

Matthew walked into the sitting room exhausted, poured a drink, and sat down next to the fireplace. His mother had already been asleep for hours. Matthew rubbed his neck and shoulders. They ached as if he had never worked a hard day in his life. The guys at the fire station would be laughing at every groan.

He was startled as gentle hands pushed his away and began massaging the area.

"I do this for my father when he has had a long day," Devry whispered sensually in his ear.

She pushed and kneaded his aching muscles, relaxing his entire body. He was melting under her clement touch, yawning from exhaustion and wistfully wondering if he could perform as tired as he was. Her fingers sent shivers of longing pulsing through his blood, and his member throbbed with each stroke.

She did not end the onslaught until his upper body felt ethereal, a total contrast to the rigidity in his aroused lower region.

Devry walked around the couch and sat next to him. She had an evening robe covering her nightgown. He could see the frilled lace peeking out of the collar. His heart pounded with the thought of what waited for him underneath the flimsy fabric.

Matthew read the carnal desire in her eyes, the innocent need for his lips on hers. He watched, as a feather of red blushed her features when she became aware of the bulge in his pants. She had an intriguing magnetism, inflaming his senses in torment. She radiated virginal innocence.

However, he was not a virgin, and needed to keep that prominent in his mind. His virility and constant burning desire to feed his sexual appetites had provided him with experience, exploring willing flesh over the years.

"I missed you," Matthew whispered as he caressed her eager lips.

Their kiss was deep and profound, resonating with fire. He endeared her lips, fondling and caressing them until she opened her mouth. She tasted as sweet as the darkest honey. He kissed her eyes, neck, and chin, willing her to surrender.

Devry pulled on his shirt, opening the buttons as quickly as her fingers would allow. Her lips caressed and kissed everything within reach. Her fingers danced across his tight chest.

His body sizzled with need. No one had ever affected him this way. Matthew wanted to throw her on her back and satiate their burning desires. *That would not do.* He must keep control.

His lips tingled in anticipation as he fell into the chasm of her love. He became aware of every movement, every touch, caressing and kissing his neck and chest. Flames of passion marked his heart.

Matthew kept reminding himself that she was a virgin, to take this slowly. He kept forcing his mind to stop before it was too late. If he did not keep his desires under control, he would dishonor himself, his family, and friends. Languorously, he made love to her lips. Intensifying each caress, he greedily devoured the alms she gave him. Lost … he was lost in desire and fulfillment … and the satisfaction of completion. He opened the evening robe and pulled her nightgown down.

His lips burned as he kissed her neck, easing his way to her luscious peaks. He suckled them until they were red and hard. Looking into her eyes, seeing the burning plea of possession, Matthew reached for the nightdress and pulled it up, exposing her legs. He may not be able to penetrate her, but he could have just a taste. A sweet taste of everything she was willing to offer lay within his reach.

His hands gently tickled her soft thighs as he traced his way to her hidden desire. She grabbed his neck, her nails scratching him as she uncontrollably bucked with every finger-stroke. Matthew groaned in engorged pain as his member throbbed and begged for release.

Devry's body jumped like flames seeking oxygen. She jerked with each graze of his tongue, her chest heaving with excitement. She whimpered as the throbbing pressure grew, curling her heart around his essence. Her body screamed as she restrained a cry of release, fighting the unknown.

"Don't fight it, my love," he whispered, coaxing to allow her frenzied release. "Let it go." His body shook as she stiffened, holding her breath, as fire peppered her from the inside. Tears filled his eyes and somewhere deep inside Matthew grabbed the strength to withhold his intense desire to penetrate Devry and fill her with his seed.

Her breaths came quickly as he felt her body melt against his. Matthew leaned his head against her shoulder, wincing as his own release spilled onto his leg. Their hearts raced, pounding in rhythm … he was still in painful need to enter her but kept his promise to himself, unsure of how that made him feel. He had always made a point to please the women he was with; made sure they had received their pleasure before he sought his own release. This was a different experience, a completely selfless act of compassion.

As he released their entwined bodies, he wondered when they had lain on the floor. Devry's hands were shaking as she sat up and clumsily attempted to cover herself. Matthew assisted her, and when they looked in each other's eyes, they both started laughing.

The day after Devry and Karen had arrived home, Lane had taken Karen aside and had asked for her help playing matchmaker with Lydia. Her reaction had been caution, but once she understood his plans, she had readily agreed to sit with Glenn. Lane and Lydia were together now, alone on a picnic somewhere in the hills. She hoped The Widow would lay down her guard.

Glenn was comatose and there was not much Karen could do except maintain his comfort. His skin had the golden-tan pallor of the sickly. She would randomly hold his hand and talk to him, unsure of how far into the coma he had slipped. She bathed him, brushed his curly red hair, trimmed his nails, and gave him a good close shave. His fingers had trembled while she was shaving him, and she could almost hear his Scottish accent warning her to be careful.

She sat across from Sir Elmer, who was being unusually quiet. She attempted to focus and read the same page repeatedly, until she finally yielded to her wandering thoughts.

Juan had come to visit earlier and to ask if she or Lydia would visit Catherine. He was understandably worried about her health and behavior. Lydia had prodded Richard for answers and received the information about the drugs he gave to Catherine. Karen was shocked when The Widow told her that he gave Catherine morphine, laudanum, and flunitrazepam.

Flunitrazepam was an anesthetic. In modern times, it was known as *roofies*, the date-rape drug. It was a dangerous addictive medication. They would have to preen her off the addiction gradually. With the combination of the drugs Richard gave Catherine, Karen was surprised that the woman was still alive.

The withdrawal was not going easily. She complained of headaches and muscle pain, her behavior swinging between extreme anxiety, restlessness, and confusion. Juan understood her depression and irritability, and helpless loss. She was too young to be a widow, with no children of her own. He wanted to deny Richard would do such a thing to his daughter, but knew in his heart that she needed their help.

Karen sighed. Andrew and Christine would be arriving soon. They should be able to help Devry understand why Matthew could not marry her. It was a sensitive and delicate situation. She did not take pleasure in dissuading the union. Karen had not spoken to Matthew about it yet. She did not know where he stood or what his opinion would be concerning Devry.

Instinct told her it was unwise to forbid the courting. If Matthew were interested in Devry, he would perceive it as a control issue. Would he overlook the fact that she was only fourteen? Karen shook her head. Matthew had enough common sense to make the correct decision.

Devry, however, looked at it as a rejection. That was not what Karen had wanted to portray to the young woman. Unfortunately, that was how it sounded to a young and impressionable heart. Should she have kept her opinion to herself and approached Matthew, warning him of Devry's plans to marry him?

She and Devry had been back for over a week. Although they stayed in the same house, neither had spoken to the other. Devry avoided breakfast until Karen left to help Lydia. Matthew was busy running the ranch for Andrew, leaving the house before dawn and not returning until late at night.

"Good afternoon. How is he doing?" Lydia inquired.

Karen jumped at the sound of Lydia's voice. "What are you doing here?"

Lydia laughed. "You mean besides the fact that I live here?"

Karen smiled until she saw Lane. He did not look happy. As a matter of issue, he looked furious.

Sir Elmer jumped down off his bed and started yapping a greeting to his beloved Lydia. When he realized that Lane was in the room, he turned to honk at him and attempted to nip his leg, fluttering his wings violently and darting his beak with fierce bellicosity.

Karen covered her mouth to hide her laughter when Lane growled at Sir Elmer, "Don't even think about it."

Wide-eyed, the goose cautiously and wisely walked backwards a few steps, frowned, and sat down, pouting. With a loud honk toward Lane, Sir Elmer stuck his nose in the air and proceeded to ignore the man.

Karen made a poor attempt to hide the amusement in her eyes. "So, what happened?"

She watched Lydia lift the cloth napkin off the basket and hand some chicken to Lane.

"Mrs. Hayes had her baby. Her son flagged us down as we were leaving town. It appears she …" Lydia turned to look at Lane and blushed.

"I think I'll go check on, um … the horses."

Lydia smiled as Lane rushed out of the room, hitting his knee on the doorframe in the rush. They could hear the uneven click of his boots on the wood floor and his unmistakable cursing throughout the house. Sir Elmer bounded onto his bed, laughing. If a goose could smirk …

"Her water broke. She was not due for another two months. The baby came fast. When I walked in the bedroom, one foot was already waving at me."

"Oh!" Karen shivered and winced. "That hurts just thinking about it. Are they doing well?"

"Yes, both mother and son are doing excellent." Lydia started laughing, wiping a tear from the corner of her eye. "Oh … oh! You should have seen Lane's face when he saw that foot! Neither one of us was expecting the labor to be so advanced. I've never seen a man's face turn red that fast."

"You would think that as many times men have seen animals deliver, it would not faze them to watch a human born. But instead they get all gushy."

"It was priceless." Lydia smiled. "He was staying outside and kept sending her son in to see if I needed anything."

"Poor Lane. I guess he never thought he would be in these situations when he decided to stay with Glenn. So much for some time alone. Did he ask for a raincheck?"

"Pardon? A what?"

"Baseball, hot dogs, apple pie, and …" Karen bounced, grinning, "Sorry, my humor," clearing her throat, "it is a voucher used for spectators, when a baseball game has been rained out. Did Lane ask to see you again?"

"No." She shook her head sadly. "I would imagine he is very frustrated at this point. Too many obstacles seem to get in our way. It's not wise for me to become involved with anyone anyway, especially a former Pinkerton man."

"Goodness! Why? You are still young. You have your whole life ahead of you. What difference does it make what his last occupation was? It's not because of your family, is it?"

"My family would love him. I have never really been very conventional and they accept that. They would welcome him into the family without compunction."

"This isn't characteristic of me to pry. Forgive me for being so forward, or tell me it is none of my business, but what is deterring you? What are you afraid of?"

Lydia bit her lip. "I am afraid. No, afraid is too simple a word. I am terrified. There is so much of me that I have kept locked away. I am not sure I am able to take the chance to allow someone that close to me again. We all have skeletons. I know that. Mine are just more severe than most."

Karen took her hand. "Lydia, please consider opening yourself to another relationship. Whether it is Lane or someone else, don't let the chance for happiness pass you by because of fear."

"I just have so many doubts." She clasped her hands together and sighed as she sat next to Karen.

"Doubts about Lane?"

"Yes, no." Lydia laughed nervously. "He's an ex-Pinkerton man. Being accused of murder in the past, and now there are murders here in Tokata." She shook her head. "Who wouldn't wonder about my innocence? You can't honestly tell me he doesn't suspect me."

"That is a real concern. Serial murderers are very smart, and they do tend to move around to evade being caught," Karen explained solemnly. "Also, it seems that it would be someone close that a person would never suspect."

"Serial murderers, is that what they're called?"

"Yes, when you have murders by the same person over a period of time." Karen grimaced. "However, it is unusual to have a female serial killer. They are usually men."

Lydia pursed her lips. "Mostly men? Odd. Still, the seed of doubt would be worse for him. How could Lane commit himself to me if he had the slightest suspicion that I would be what you call a serial murderer?"

"You definitely have a conundrum on your hands. Until he uncovers the murderer, there will be doubt."

Chapter Fourteen

Preparing to leave to visit Andrew and Christine, Juan and Catherine led their horses from the stable. Catching movement out of the corner of their eyes, they stopped abruptly. Mr. Brandt was sneaking out Catherine's back door! They stood hidden in the shadows, suspicious of his intentions. She had refused to open the door to the man along with other members of the club.

It had been weeks, and Catherine was still weaning herself from the drugs that Richard had given her.

"Be careful," she whispered as Juan approached the skulking Mr. Brandt.

Catherine watched her father approach the man. The agitated and animated movements of his hands did not lessen her apprehension. Often she had teased him that he would not be able to converse if someone tied his hands, but the quick motions alerted her to a problem.

Warily, she watched Brandt hurry away from the house and rode toward Juan, leading his horse. "What did he say?"

"He claims he was trying to assure himself that you were well."

"Through my back door?"

"That's what I asked. He said he had knocked on the front door and when he didn't receive a response, went around to the back to see if you were outside."

"And, Mr. Brandt let himself in my house because?"

"He claims he heard something and went in to investigate. When he did not see anyone in the house, he left through the same door he entered. It sounds innocent enough."

She snorted. "He lies. There was no one in my house."

"Catherine, we cannot assume the worst. Mr. Brandt has attempted to visit you and see to your welfare."

"Father, you're too trusting."

"And you, daughter, are too cynical."

Juan and Catherine entered the living room amid cheerful laughter. Greetings and kisses, in addition to sincere condolences, greeted the new arrivals. Juan had brought his wife Domina over earlier and then left to escort Catherine.

Their arrival had interrupted a controversial discussion on women's suffrage. Christine was passionate in her beliefs. Although the men wanted to protect their women from the sadistic political system, no one in the room disagreed with her. Christine had the gumption to travel to Washington and fight for those rights and everyone in the room respected her for it. The men were wise enough to keep their mouths closed and their humble opinions to themselves.

"It's not just women's rights that are involved here," Christine added passionately. "Indian rights are being fought for also. There are also some heated debates in D.C. right now about Mississippi."

"What's going on in Mississippi?" Matthew took the bait, smiling.

Curious eyes turned to Christine. "They are trying to add a clause to their state constitution withholding votes from those who do not comprehend the U.S. Constitution."

"Isn't that taking a step backwards?" Karen asked.

Domina piped. "Sounds like it to me. Why would they want to do that?"

"I honestly believe, if I may give my one-sided opinion, it is to prohibit the illiterate Negroes from voting."

"Don't leave many people voting, does it?" Matthew quipped.

"Matthew!" His mother reprimanded.

"Well, it's true. Obviously, they do not want to have a true democracy. They'll have a handful of white, educated voters running a predominately black state."

"It's just the beginning," Andrew joined in the debate. "The southern states are searching for ways to get around the 14th Amendment."

"The only way it's going to change is with a woman's vote and that won't happen. Men do not want to relinquish their control." Christine's vehemence startled the group.

"That is unfair," Andrew shot back.

"You, of all people, should understand."

"You are not the only one fighting oppression."

Christine blinked, stunned that she was yelling at Andrew. "I'm sorry, Honey. I guess I've gotten used to exerting my opinion so fervently just to be heard."

"How about a change of subject?" Catherine asked. "How was the visit with Sitting Bull?"

"It was wonderful!" Christine exclaimed.

"Yes, it was good to see our old friends. We also learned the truth behind the Ghost Dance."

All eyes turned to Andrew.

"Sitting Bull is much more colorful with his words. However, I shall attempt to describe the Ghost Dance for you.

"It is said that Wovoka, a Paiute from Nevada, recovered from scarlet fever right after a total eclipse of the sun. He had seen a vision, a prophecy, that if the Indian believed in the faith of his heart, sang ceremonial songs, and danced, his deceased relatives would return. The Buffalo would return and the wasicu would be destroyed. If we respect and abide by the prophecy, Mother Earth will be reborn with the coming of the green grass, in the spring of 1891. A fresh layer of fertile soil shall be set upon the Earth; sweet grass will cover the land; clear, fresh running water will flow from the rivers; trees and plants will thrive and grow tall to feed and house the creatures of the land. The Buffalo will thrive and the wild horses shall return."

Andrew cleared his throat. "When Kicking Bear and Short Bull returned from Nevada, they taught the Ghost Dance to the Sioux. They described how Wovoka had flown over them on horseback teaching them Ghost Dance songs. All Indians, no matter what tribe, who join in the Ghost Dance, will rise into the heavens, while the soil and land replenishes itself. They will then return with their ancestors and live upon the revived Earth. The wasicu will not walk upon the land."

Andrew scanned the room. "They call Wovoka, Christ," he added carefully.

A hiss of repressed anger blazed through the room. All listening to the story of the Ghost Dance were Christians, excluding Andrew himself. He understood their reaction and had compassion for their shock. Waiting a few moments for the impact to settle in their minds, Andrew watched as a kaleidoscope of emotions danced across his friends' faces.

"Because of the unacceptable circumstances on the Dakota reservations, the Lakota have embraced the passionate aspirations of the Ghost Dance. It is spreading to all the Sioux reservations. They gather at the Strong Hold on the northern part of the Pine Ridge reservation where they convene the Ghost Dance ceremony.

"Black Elk has designed the Ghost Shirt. Kicking Bear has convinced the Sioux that if the dancers wear their Ghost

Dance shirts, decorated with the magic symbols given to them by Wovoka, the soldiers' bullets will not harm them."

Silence hung heavily in the room. Andrew waited patiently; he understood the myriad questions parleyed among the friends.

"Have you joined in the Ghost Dance?" Domina asked, breaking the silence.

Andrew shook his head in denial. "I cannot. In my heart, I believe it is wrong. My wife, my soul mate, does not have Indian blood. The belief is that all non-Indians, all wasicu, will be destroyed. The Ghost Dance does not single out non-Indians who will die and others who will endure. I have many friends who would die for me that are not Lakota. I will not turn my back on them."

"Will it cause an Indian uprising?" Catherine bit her lip.

"I honestly don't know. I did not see any dissension. There are rumors of a letter written to the Secretary of the Interior giving information and warnings of Lakota plans of resistance."

Juan frowned at the lack of reassurance. "What does Sitting Bull have to say about all of this?"

Andrew looked over to Karen. Slowly she glanced around the room, understanding the concern of the people around her. No one wanted the Indians destroyed or hurt. Everyone present had attempted to improve the life of the reservation Indians. Each, in their own way, had fought for the Lakota, for their freedom and for the rights they deserved as American citizens.

"Sitting Bull has his doubts," Karen explained. "He does not believe that the dead will return. If allowing the Ghost Dance on his reservation encourages the hope of the Lakota, then he will not object. He is aware that the white people living around the reservations and the Indian agents are getting nervous about the Ghost Dance. It worries him that they are transporting soldiers to some of the reservations. He fears what the soldiers' return will mean the death of more of his people."

"If he is so afraid that it will hurt his people, why is he allowing it?"

"The people need their hope," Karen explained. "Sitting Bull does not want to destroy any chances of his people keeping their faith or squash their optimism for a better life. Kicking Bull requested permission from Sitting Bull to teach the Ghost Dance at Standing Rock. He granted that request."

"Good for him," Christine interjected. "The Indians have every right to perform any sacred religious ceremony they choose. Our constitution protects that right. Pick any other religious sect encouraging prayers and ceremonies for a day of ascension, and the government wouldn't hinder them."

"It is disheartening that they have to perform their religious ceremonies in secret. When will people learn not to persecute others for their religious beliefs?" Domina turned to Devry. "Was your ceremony hidden also?"

Devry radiated with pleasure. "Yes, it was. It did not stop it from being the most beautiful ceremony I could ever have imagined. I ... my choice for my husband was included in my prayer songs."

Andrew and Christine looked at each other, puzzled. It was the first they had heard of their daughter's intentions. Karen turned bright red with repressed anger as her heart thundered, awaiting the announcement.

"Well Devry, please do not leave us in suspense," Domina encouraged.

Devry beamed at Matthew and he smiled in return. Both were recalling the last few evenings they had shared together.

Andrew and Christine's eyes opened wide in surprise. Seeing Matthew's response, Karen turned a deeper crimson. Juan, Domina, and Catherine were the only ones in the room who did not foresee a problem.

Biting her lip, Devry sighed happily, "Matthew."

"Matthew," Andrew said quietly, tilting his head toward Karen. "Are you sure?"

Andrew and Christine had mixed feelings. They both felt honored. The friendship they shared with Karen lay forever in their hearts. They were happy that Devry would choose such a worthy man. Nevertheless, would Matthew want to take their daughter back to his strange magical world? How often would they see their precious daughter if he did?

"Yes Papa, I am sure."

"Matthew, how do you feel about this pronouncement?"

"I am honored. At a more opportune time, I believe we should discuss our future nuptials and decide on how you would like me to proceed. I was planning on the Lakota way in making my proposal. I will concur to any way you choose to fulfill my obligations."

Karen sat forward, determined. "No." A whiplash of fury descended upon the room. "I will not allow it."

The room exploded. Matthew was stunned.

"What?"

"Why not?"

"What's wrong?"

"You insult us! I thought we were friends." Christine cried as tears filled her eyes.

"I hate you," Devry yelled.

"Stop! She must have a good reason for such a vociferous objection." Andrew spoke over the clamoring voices, his face pale. "Why Karen? What is it?"

Karen looked at her good friend and then to her son's furious face. "It is not Devry. She is a wonderful, beautiful young woman."

Matthew clenched his jaw, repressing the urge to scream profanity at his mother.

"Your marriage will not be accepted in our world without causing you problems, Matthew. My Lord, what are you thinking? Do you want to escort the whole family to our world so they can sign the papers consenting the marriage? How can you condone marrying someone so young? Jesus, Matthew, use your brain and not your …"

"I am using my brain!" he interrupted. "She is not that young."

"Not that young?" His mother snorted. "Oh! That is disgusting! Just the thought nauseates me. What are you thinking?"

"Oh! I hate you!" Devry screamed at Karen and stomped out of the room.

Matthew stood, watching Devry run through the door. "I can't believe you! How can you be so insulting to people that you profess as friends? I have never seen you act this way toward anyone. Yes, she is young and inexperienced, but come on, Mom, so am I. It's not like I'm announcing that I'm gay or marrying a twelve-year-old."

"Close enough!" She yelled sarcastically at him.

"She's twenty!"

"Twenty? Twenty! Is that what she told you? She's fourteen, Matthew!"

Matthew sat down, stunned. His heart was in agonizing pain, his stomach churning. Everything … all his dreams had just collapsed around him.

His voice croaked as he looked around the room. "Four … Fourteen?"

Andrew and Christine nodded their heads.

Matthew paled and covered his face with his hands. "Oh my God, I think I'm going to be sick."

Chapter Fifteen

Lydia paused, gathering her thoughts in front of the crowded congregation. People crammed themselves into every available space, the doors of the church open for those who stood outside. She looked at the open casket and prayed she would get through this moment in time.

Taking a small knife out of her reticule, Lydia reached up and cut a piece of hair from the nape of her neck. Her lips moved in prayer as she leaned over the casket and ceremoniously placed it in Glenn's hand. Returning to the pulpit, she scanned the townspeople before her.

"Doctor Glenn Carson was my friend, my mentor, and the brother of my heart. His spirit blessed and touched us, branded with the goodness of his character. I believe, to the utter reaches of my soul, that he is in a better place. He is now with his beautiful daughter and wife.

"He had an abundance of love inside him for everyone. He taught me that life was not cold, that I could do anything as long as I had faith. That is how Glenn lived his life. Through all the tragedies we have all experienced, his faith was there to help carry us through the hard times.

"He taught me there were few things in life we could actually control. We have the gift of choice. It was up to me to choose the path of my life. He taught me that life was a kaleidoscope of changes. It was my decision as to how I wanted mine painted.

"Many years ago, when my heart was at its weakest, he explained to me that everything comes, everything passes, and everything is replaced. A change is in the wind now, and we cannot hold him back. Our memories we will cherish.

"I will miss his smile, the twinge of his Scottish accent, and his sense of humor. Most of all, I will miss his uncensored love."

Lydia's voice broke as unbidden tears streamed down her face. Juan stood and approached the podium, putting his arm around Lydia for comfort and encouragement. He reached over and handed her a handkerchief. Taking a few deep breaths, she continued.

"Glenn will always be with us, in our hearts and in our memories. Our time with those we love is never long enough, but we have them with us in our hearts. He will be there, always strong, smiling, and encouraging. I shall look to the stars and see His spirit watching over us, knowing that Glenn is in His loving care."

Silence permeated the town; a mournful essence veiled the skies. Not a soul walked the streets. Dark ominous clouds blanketed the funeral procession as they walked sullenly toward the burial grounds. The Earth wept with the people. Across the river, the cemetery waited patiently for its newest tenant. It was a secluded place, where one was laid to rest among trees and flowering gardens.

The doctor was well known, highly respected, and cherished among the townspeople. He had always been an honest and generous man, a dedicated and meticulous doctor, never deceiving anyone and never expecting more than one could give. His death was a great loss to the community and many felt cheated by his passing.

They watched the undertaker's carriage struggle along the narrow road. Many of the townspeople were gathering memories, wanting to remember the good doctor's face, his dimpled smile, and his merry eyes, always gleaming with a happiness that reached out to his friends and patients.

They pictured him with the gold chain and watch hanging from his pocket, the one his wife had given him as a wedding gift. Many could hear his voice, a deep, resonant sound that brought cheer to those around him, even in times of despair. They had looked to him for comfort from his positive outlook, and his effervescent desire for life.

He was now with his daughter and wife in the next life. His watch rested on the mantle next to his picture, in the home that now belonged to his brother-in-law.

All those who loved and respected him surrounded the grave of Doctor Glenn Carson. His closest friends, after moments of silence, honored his memory by recalling the drinks of cheer, the smell of his cigars, his precious art, the battles, and his complete passion for life.

All took the drizzling rain as tears from heaven. The brown earth sagged in sadness under their feet; shovels of dirt struck against the wood of the casket. The congregation stood in paralyzed unity while the minister mumbled a few more words in Latin, then closed his Bible with a resounding thump.

Lane Parker stood in the corner of Glenn's office watching the whole town walk in and out of the house. The women scuttled about, covering the formal dining room table, the counter tops in the kitchen, and every other available space with food.

He had never seen so much food in his life. Did the whole town have to be here? He wanted to mourn alone, not have people surrounding him, cooing words of wisdom and condolences.

Glenn's will and testament sat on the desk unopened. Juan had brought it to him hours ago, telling him not to allow anyone to rush him into any decisions. Mr. Brandt had already approached him with an extremely generous offer to buy the house. Lane had not considered selling the house, but the generous offer played chimerically in his thoughts.

He warily eyed Brandt, sitting across the room. The man did not look well. A sheen of moisture dotted his pale face; he was sweating profusely. He appeared about ready to fall off the chair. Lydia was handing him a plate of food, encouraging the man to eat.

Mrs. Barnes was sitting next to Catherine, insidiously babbling about The Widow. Lane overheard her cutting words of warning.

"Look at The Widow, Catherine." She tapped the young woman's arm to get her attention. "Mr. Brandt will be dead next. You wait and see. The Widow is single-handedly murdering all the club members, just like she did in St. Augustine."

"You are implying The Widow killed my husband, Mrs. Barnes," Catherine replied caustically. "She tried to save him."

"Oh, you poor child. She is good at hiding the evil within her. Of course, she made it look like she was trying to save him. She does claim to be a healer. With the good doctor gone, who will control her now?"

Catherine stared blankly at the older woman.

"Why is that young man shunning Devry? Every time she goes near him, he walks away."

She turned to see Matthew shaking his head at Devry. Her heart went out to her cousin. Everyone close to Andrew and Christine knew that their friend Karen and her son came from a different type of society. Once Karen explained her objections, it was understandable given the problems it would cause. She recalled Matthew's destitution as he sat on the couch that fateful day, humbled and aggrieved.

"Maybe they had a bit of a spat. You know how young people can be."

Lydia approached Lane with a plate of food. He quickly escorted her onto the veranda, away from the insipid conversation.

Lydia protested, "You must eat."

"I will, if you promise to stay here with me for a while."

"Are you trying to protect me from Mrs. Barnes' vicious tongue?"

"You know?"

Lydia laughed. "She has never been anything but honest in her dislike of me. Mrs. Barnes truly believes what she says. I respect her honesty, though I do not care for her inaccurate description of my beliefs. She feels quite adamant about her opinions."

"She has a point about Brandt. He doesn't look as if he is well at all."

"True, but I don't think he has eaten all day. He gets that way when he doesn't eat."

Lane nodded his head. "With him being one of my suspects, it'll definitely put a twist on the investigation."

"Brandt is one of your suspects? I was under the impression that you were watching him because of Matthew."

Lane wanted to kick himself for letting that bit of information slip. He needed to be more cautious around The Widow until this murder case was over. He sighed. He could not retract it, so he might as well observe her reaction.

"Yes, I didn't really see him as a solid suspect until Catherine told me they saw him sneaking out of her house."

"Catherine enlightened me about that, too. It really upset her." Lydia looked through the doors at Mr. Brandt. "Do you want some lemonade with your meal? I'm going to get a glass for myself."

She accepted his suspicion without a blink of her eye, as if they were discussing the weather. Lane watched as The Widow walked away. Most men would not consider Lydia a beauty, but in his eyes she was stunning. Her mourning dress billowed around her ankles, her hips swayed gracefully. The dress went up to her neck, sequestering generous breasts. Breasts his fingers ached to caress.

Lane groaned. He had not even kissed her yet.

When he saw Lydia standing at the podium during the service, she seemed so vulnerable and forlorn. He had wanted to kiss her tears away. He had felt the pain of her loss when she had spoken at the funeral. Such radiating love could not hide a murderer. The aberrant behavior would have shown its ugly head by now.

He watched her enter the office with a servant carrying trays of lemonade. Juan and Andrew approached him and quietly told him it was time.

Lane entered the room solemnly. Slowly, methodically, he opened the envelope and leaned against the desk.

"I, Doctor Glenn Carson, being of sound mind and body … bequeath to the following:

Lydia Wetmore Williams — all of my medical supplies, including medicines and tools for her future use;

Juan and Domina Rivera — the collection of handguns, and my grandmother's china closet and the china collection;

Andrew and Christine Little Red Hawk — the collection of bows and arrows along with the new Winchester carbine rifle, and my wife's emerald necklace and matching ring;

To my brother-in-law, Lane Parker — all of my worldly possessions, not mentioned herewith, with one stipulation; that he not sell the house. He may dispose of any other personal property as he sees fit.

Night had fallen quickly and the sound of crickets filled the air. The house was quiet. Lydia was in the kitchen cleaning. Everyone else had gone their way.

Lane sat next to the fireplace and stared at the will in disbelief. Glenn had told him that he was inheriting the house, but not everything else. It was ironic how an offer was made and the will stipulated that he keep the house. How had Glenn known? He never did finish the conversation they had started a few Sundays back. Was Glenn trying to convey a message?

The doctor willed his medicines to The Widow. Glenn would never have done that if there were any suspicion in his mind that Lydia would abuse them. Was that his way of declaring the woman's innocence?

He offered to retrieve the gifts from Glenn; all said to wait. There was plenty of time. It was pointless for him to worry about those things now. He had an estate to care for.

Glenn had been very comfortable financially. It was overwhelming to learn that he had that kind of money within his reach. Lane had always lived frugally; his lifestyle as a Pinkerton man did not offer him many options for luxuries.

Lydia entered the room and offered to pour him a glass of bourbon. She handed him his glass and sat daintily next to him.

"How are you holding up?"

"I'm fine. He was sick for a while. I appreciate you taking care of him the way you have."

"I would have done anything for him."

"Can I ask you a question?" He gently stroked her hand as he spoke, sending chills of pleasure up her arm.

"A lawman question or a Lane question?"

He laughed. "You are a cautious one, aren't you? I didn't know there was a difference."

"A huge difference. When you wear the lawman face, you are serious and unbending. I prefer the Lane. Go ahead, ask."

"It was something you did during the service. I am curious. Why did you cut a piece of your hair and give it to Glenn?"

Lydia smiled. "It's a custom from my first husband's tribe. A part of my spirit, a gift from me to carry with him to the afterlife, as a symbol of my love for him."

"Why have you never remarried?"

Surprised by the quick change in subject, she fluttered breathlessly. Blushing, she felt clumsy, as she became ensnared in the rhythmic caress of his hand. "I've been to dinner and dances with gentlemen a few times. There has never been anyone who appealed to my interest more than a simple need for companionship."

Lane was caressing her arm. Lydia could feel the heat from his gentle fingers through the lace of her dress. She yearned for his lips on hers, wanted to taste him. She needed him; it had been so very long since she had desired a man.

"No one?"

Silently, she shook her head and returned his heated gaze.

Lydia was startled when Lane stood up, slicing the poignant moment as he crossed to the door and locked it.

He shrugged. "Just in case someone decides to interrupt us. It seems to be a habit of the folks in this town."

With an impish smile, Lydia lifted her glass in salutation. A burble of jittery excitement raced through her veins. "What do you have in mind for a need to have the door locked?"

Sitting down, Lane took her face in his hands and kissed her, tasted her, seduced away the resistance she might have given him.

Lydia's scent of sweet lavender enveloped him. He met no resistance as he greedily kissed her lips. They were hot, soft, and pliant. Her unfettered response consumed him in heated flames. He indulged his desires as his hand strayed to her neck, feeling her pulse quicken as he deepened the kiss.

His member strained, violently objecting to its confined quarters, pleading release. He heard a beseeching whimper.

Standing on unsteady feet, she took his hand and guided him to the door. Lane puckered his brow as he watched her twist the key, unlocking the door to their precious privacy. She smiled, leading him toward the back of the house. When they reached the top of the stairs she hesitated, unsure of which direction to pursue.

Amazed at the boldness of her gesture, thrilled that he had found someone to love so thoroughly, he escorted her to his room. Locking the door behind them, he heard Lydia's giggle as she sat on the bed, unbuttoning her dress with shaking hands.

Shrugging, Lane turned from the door, walking toward her with determination beaming from his eyes. "Just in case."

Chapter Sixteen

Another dreary day. The rain danced on the windows and lightning flared as the thunder rolled over the land. Lane leaned against the doorframe of the doctor's medical supply room, watching Lydia pack boxes, one for the apothecary and the other for medicines and tools she wanted for herself.

She was such an extraordinary woman. Their lovemaking the night before had shown him a passion he had never expected. His fantasies and dreams had not come close to the intensity they had shared.

Lane recalled the night before with vivid clarity. His fingers and hands tingled at the memory of caressing her smooth silky skin, of how Lydia's bold responses encouraged the rhythm of their lovemaking. He could hear her whispered sighs of passion. His body reacted from the recollection and he surreptitiously adjusted his growing member.

"What are we going to do with two houses?" he asked while she placed medical books on a chair.

"Two houses?"

Seeing her puzzled expression, he glided over and circled his arms around her, kissing her on the forehead. "I don't want you to leave. Will you be my life-mate? My wife, my love, the mother of my children?"

Lydia blushed. "You don't have to marry me …" she stuttered. "I … I … it is not as if you seduced me and stole my virtue. I … was … oh!"

She turned quickly, embarrassed, and started putting more jars in the box, her movements jerky and animated.

Lane laughed as he turned Lydia slowly toward him. "Do you love me?"

Nodding her head, "Yes, I do."

"Will you do me the honor of becoming my wife?"

Tears filled her eyes. "What about the murders? I know you have suspected me."

"Just minor doubts, but the doctor put them to rest."

"What could Glenn have possibly said that was different from anyone else you have asked about me?"

Smiling, he caressed her face. "It wasn't only what he said. It was what the doctor did."

Lydia stared at him, puzzled. He could see her mind working.

"If he had any seed of doubt about you, any unspoken suspicion, Glenn would never have given you his medical supplies in his will."

Hugging him, she mumbled, "That is true."

"Will you marry me, Lydia?"

"Yes, I will. I love you."

Hugging him, she smiled and felt a piece of her heart grow.

He played with a lock of hair that had fallen out of her bun. "How about this Sunday? I do not want to wait any longer than I have to. Is there anyone I need to speak with, for permission?"

"This Sunday! Oh my, but there are so many preparations!"

"You want a big wedding?"

"No. I would prefer the time to have a dress made and to discuss what our future plans are." She kissed his nose.

"As you wish. We'll marry on the following Sunday."

"You are exasperating! How about a few months from now? October?" She caroled with a smile, belying the harshness of her words.

"But that's too far away. I don't think I can wait that long."

"Wait that long for what?" Arching her eyebrow, she smiled seductively.

"Is there someone I need to speak with?" Lane asked, feeling himself harden at the languorous lilt of her voice.

"No. I will send an announcement to my uncle and brother."

Lane blinked. "I didn't realize you had a brother."

She looked at him, surprised. "I talk about him all the time. Charles works with shipping and the railroad. He and his wife live in Newport near my uncle's home."

"Of course," Lane chuckled. "I didn't realize he was your brother. I thought he was another cousin."

"If you think I have extravagant picnics, wait until you experience one of George's at the Chateau-Sur-Mer. Oh, you will love it there! It is such a beautiful place. Each year I visit my relatives in Newport. Normally, I take my holiday near the end of summer, but the last two years I have taken it at the beginning of the year. Last year, I went earlier for my cousin Edith's debutante ball."

"Your uncle's a senator for Rhode Island, correct?"

"No. He was governor of Rhode Island and ran for the Senate last year but was unsuccessful. I'm sure he'll try again."

"Won't he object to you marrying a commoner?"

Lydia smiled. "You are far from being a commoner. There will be no objections. George is not pretentious in any way. He will accept you for who you are." She paused, tapping her finger on her lip, animated in deep contemplation. "You will have a problem with one minor detail though."

"Oh?" Lane frowned as he closed the box she had filled with medicine and carried it to the door.

"Sir Elmer." Lydia laughed. "He hasn't taken a liking to you at all," she drawled, batting her eyes like the most innocent southern belle.

"I gathered as much, by the slow torture he has inflicted upon me. Do you really want to wait until October?"

"Autumn is my favorite time of year." Seeing the look of discouragement and the uncharacteristic pout on his lips, she winked. "Oh, you poor dear. How about the end of August?"

Lane brightened. "That's my girl. August it is."

A quiet knock sounded behind the couple. "What's in August?" Devry asked, as she and her father entered the room.

One week before the wedding, Mr. Brandt, frustrated with his failure to lure the elusive Devry into his arms, walked into Mrs. Enlow's sitting room. He needed a woman and he was tired of abstinence, tired of trying to win over someone so beautiful. How could a woman, so stunning, have absolutely no innate desire for passion?

"Here, let me take your coat."

Grateful, he turned and handed her his evening jacket. She was wearing his favorite gown, one he had commissioned especially for her. His heart pounded with desire as he licked his lips. She wore nothing underneath the lace bodice, her voluptuous breasts straining and yearning for his touch. The bulge in his pants tightened in anticipation. He could always depend on her to satisfy his needs.

"You're angry." Brandt stroked her ear.

"You haven't come to visit for a while."

He raised an eyebrow. "It wasn't very harmonious the last time I was here."

"No one cares for rejection, my dear."

"That is true. I apologize for hurting you. I … I was shocked. I had not expected your continued declaration of love, especially after you vented your anger in front of the whole town."

"A most unfortunate temper tantrum. I apologize. You are here now, that's all that matters." Mrs. Enlow pointed to the table. "Make yourself a drink. I'll return shortly," she cooed.

Excusing herself, she rushed to the rear entrance of the house. Scribbling a note, she handed it to one of the boys to deliver. The young man ran as quickly as he could, the promise of a coin fueling his effort. He delivered the note, waited, and then ran away, another unexpected coin clasped in his hand as he tightly grasped the bag he was to give to Mrs. Enlow.

Sir Elmer sat on Lydia's bed watching Catherine and Devry, buzzing around his mistress. It was another day, with people that he had to deal with. What were these women doing today? He looked around the room, smelling the change in the air.

Something was happening and no one had informed him as to what it was. This was not picnic day, the usual day for everyone to infringe on his privacy and his home. This was garden day and they had not gone outside yet. Yesterday was laundry day and they worked in the garden. He was not happy. This week was all in a shambles.

People were not supposed to be here today. This was their exclusive day together. Saturday was *his* day, not for the rest of these interfering humans. People! They think they can just do whatever they want. He fervently wished they would leave.

Sir Elmer mumbled petulantly as he watched the women help The Widow with a gown.

Lydia admired herself in the mirror as Catherine's experienced hands clasped the small pearl buttons. The wedding gown was ivory silk satin with elegantly embroidered gold and lavender lace. Pearls and embroidered silk sparkled beneath the translucent layer of ethereal silk chiffon that flowed over the gown, creating an angelic appearance. The detachable, twelve-foot train was finished with the same intricate lace trimmings and ethereal silk chiffon.

Her golden-brown hair, decorated intricately with ringlets, entwined through the tiara. The gold and lavender chiffon headpiece cascaded down the center of her back.

It was Saturday, September 6, in the year of our Lord, 1890, and her life would change for better or worse in less than twenty minutes. They delayed the original wedding day to allow her uncle, cousins, and brother to attend. Lane had waited graciously and patiently for this day to arrive.

Sitting in the closed carriage in front of the church, her Uncle George patted her hand, reassuring her thrumming nerves. Her stomach rumbled its objections.

"Ready, my sweet?"

She nodded and smiled. "I am so pleased you are here."

"We would not have missed this for the world, my dear."

As he disembarked from the carriage, someone shut the doors of the church and waited for Lydia to arrive at the steps. Taking a deep breath, she nodded to her Uncle George, and he asked the deacon to open the doors.

Sir Elmer was incensed. He had watched the group enter the carriages and ride away. As he stood at the front doors waiting expectantly for an explanation, his Lydia had not said one word to him, just kissed him on the nose and left. Something important was happening today and he was going to discover what it was.

Sizzling in vexation with each step, he stomped toward the end of the road, watching the final carriage meander out of sight. Oh bother, he was going to have to fly. Spreading his wings, he took flight, keeping the group within easy reach.

Landing behind Lydia's carriage, Sir Elmer skulked near the rear wheel to watch Lydia and her Uncle George enter the church. Hopping up the stairs, he stood at the entranceway and watched warily.

Frowning, he heard the preacher.

"We are gathered here today to join this man and this woman in holy matrimony ..."

Matrimony? *Matrimony?* They were getting married? With silent and vitriolic steps, he marched down the aisle. There was no way he would allow this farce to continue. He would not allow this arrogant buffoon to marry his Lydia. How dare this man think he could just strut in and take over. Take his woman away from him? Who did he think he was?

Sir Elmer was a man of purpose. His goal: to block the wedding in any manner he could.

The congregation watched, mouths open in astonishment, as Sir Elmer bit Lydia Wetmore Williams' future husband on the backside. Lane howled in excruciating pain as he swatted the feisty, invidious goose, tears pooling in his eyes.

Tears of laughter filled the church.

The preacher made a feckless attempt to calm Lane and the rest of the congregation. Chaos and unfettered laugher filled the church. Throwing his hands in the air, the preacher sat down and joined the congregation, watching the chimerical show before him.

Lydia mumbled apologies as she scooped the goose into her arms. After calming the bird, she handed him to Juan. Sir Elmer squawked his disapproval, his voice echoing off the church walls. Lydia turned a disgruntled eye toward the goose and he sat back.

Deep anguish filled his eyes as he pouted, crushed that she would choose someone else to love. He stared at Lydia, beseeching her to still love him. Lane stood gawking, open-mouthed at the destitute reaction of the beast. Lydia lifted her hands, pleading to him to wait just one more moment.

Walking over to Sir Elmer, she held him close, hugging him, reassuring him that she still loved him. Carrying him back to the altar, she placed him between Lane and herself. Sir Elmer looked at Lane, tilted his head, and smirked. Wide-eyed, Lane watched the goose snub him, turn his face toward the minister, and wait for the man to proceed with the ceremony.

The congregation finally settled down, a few snickers tickling the air. Lane nodded to continue and Lydia looked to the heavens for comfort. Standing proudly, the audacious Sir Elmer listened intently to the minister.

"... May he speak now or forever hold his peace." The preacher paused and scanned the members of the church.

As if waiting for the question, Sir Elmer sprang forward, wings outstretched, and stood in front of the congregation bellowing his protests. A few giggles circulated through the church; some attendees held their Bibles in front of their faces in an attempt to shield their laughter. Lane turned a deep shade of purple, repressing the urge to sacrifice the goose on the sacred altar. Lydia hid her face in the bouquet but could not hide her giggles.

Looking at the goose, the preacher solemnly nodded, acknowledging Sir Elmer's ranting objections. "Is there anyone *else* who would like to express their objections?"

The ceremony continued without another eruption or mishap from the heretical goose. He stood between the couple as if he too were joining them in holy matrimony.

Grumbling, the goose kicked Lane, his piercing eyes riveting resentment at his nemesis. The preacher patiently waited for Lane's response. Beaming at the goose with a self-satisfied grin of triumph, he answered, "I do."

As they faced the congregation for the first time as man and wife (and goose), Lane glanced at Sir Elmer. The goose stuck his tongue out at him.

Chapter Seventeen

Karen tapped her foot as the band played a lively waltz. Bright sunshine blazed its happiness upon the guests as they danced and mingled, enjoying the festive atmosphere and delicious buffet. The reception held at Andrew and Christine's home was simple with a twist of elegance. It was a celebration and gift to their friends to share the happiness of Lane and Lydia's union.

"This is a wedding reception, Matthew. We are supposed to be celebrating. Do you think you could possibly find a generous smile in that frown for one day?" Karen pleaded with her son.

"I'm sorry, Mom. I'm frustrated."

"Besides the fact you can't marry Devry, what is bothering you?"

"How could you tell?"

Karen laughed. "I'm your mother."

Matthew sighed. "I still want to discuss Devry with you. However, you are right. That is not what is on my mind at the moment."

"What is bothering you, Son?"

"The murderer is after Brandt. I am pissed. I wanted to deal with him myself."

His mother's eyes widened, in fear. "You want to kill Brandt? Have you lost your mind?"

"No. I do not want to kill him, just muck around with him a little. He is not dead yet. I might still be able to inflict some pain."

"Whoever the guilty party is knows exactly what they are doing. It is wrong, Matthew. No one has the right to judge anyone. There is a self-righteous, pompous man out there, playing God. It is not our place to create our personal Judgment Day. I expected better from you."

Karen watched Matthew bite the inside of his cheek, a habit he displayed when deep in thought. His eyes scanned the dance floor, until he found Devry dancing with her father. Confusion strummed his features.

Saddened by the loss her son felt, she wished she could mend his heart but knew she could not. This feeling of helplessness caused her heart to ache. Karen knew she had to allow her children to fly with their own wings, fledglings soaring to their own beginnings. Unfortunately, this time she had to interfere.

"If Devry was willing to wait until she was older, would you accept the marriage?" Matthew asked quietly.

Karen grimaced. "That depends. How much older?"

Hope flared in his eyes. "Eighteen?"

"Would she be willing to wait that long?"

Matthew smiled, showering her with hugs. "I know she will."

With a quick kiss on his mother's cheek, he departed and tapped Andrew on the shoulder. Andrew turned and waited for Karen's consent before he relinquished his daughter to Matthew. Joining Karen, the two friends watched as the young couple glided on the dance floor.

"So much for interfering," Karen said, as she tasted her wine.

"We did raise them to be independent. What did you tell him?"

"They have to wait until she's eighteen."

Andrew laughed. "Do you think they'll listen?"

"No, although I believe her age is a hurdle for him as well."

"Oh, there is no doubt there. His face went whiter than yours; didn't think that was possible."

"Brat."

"They do look like they are in love. They shine when they are together."

Karen sighed.

"You look beautiful," Matthew grinned. *Why does she have to look so much older than her true age?*

"I missed you. Why did you stop wanting me?"

"I apologize, Devry. I would never intentionally hurt you. You have to understand that my mother is true in her belief. She was protecting me. Taking you as my wife at your age would make me an outcast in my world."

"Why?"

"It's the way it is. The thought of you being so young leaves me cold. I have so many mixed feelings right now. I look at you and know you are my love and then …" Matthew inhaled a deep breath, "… then I see you as the child you are and it makes me nauseous."

"I make you nauseous?" Her voice croaked.

"No! Yes! Oh God." *Why is this happening?* "If we are meant to be, it'll happen. When you are older and closer to adulthood and we still feel this love for each other, we can become man and wife."

"I am not a child," Devry whispered.

"Yes, you are! You just turned fourteen a few months ago." Matthew shivered, aghast at the reality of her age, at what he had done. Thank God, he had restrained himself. He groaned as the memories haunted him. They had done everything else a couple could possibly do, yet he had restrained himself from penetrating her.

Matthew squeezed his eyes shut, inwardly cursing the memories. "You haven't even finished school yet. I graduated from college. I have a career as a firefighter. I cannot lose that. It's a part of who I am."

"Why are you stopping?"

"The music stopped."

"So, we'll dance the next set."

"No, we've already danced two dances. I am not going there again. Not now, anyway."

"Fine. Then we'll sit and finish this conversation."

"There isn't anything else to say." Matthew remained standing, shuffling his feet uncomfortably while she sat down at an open table.

"I'm not finished," Devry protested.

"You're not going to change my mind. No matter what you say. You are still fourteen. It won't work."

"Fine." Devry stood, and with a swoosh of her skirt stomped away.

"Well, that didn't go well," Matthew spoke to the deserted space where she had stood.

Domina asked as she approached. "What did not turn out well?"

Matthew shook his head and sighed.

"She will yield, Matthew. Give it time for the winds of change to administer their own plans. Come, let's have a dance and you can tell me of your plans to visit Sitting Bull."

Devry joined Catherine and Lydia's brother.

After a few moments of strained silence, Devry looked at the two of them. "Did I interrupt something? I can leave and join Juan at his table."

Charles Wetmore responded quickly. "No. We were discussing the rumors that were circulating the room about one of the residents here."

Devry lifted her eyebrow in question.

"Mrs. Enlow was brought in for questioning," Catherine whispered as she looked around the room.

"For what?"

"For the attempted murder of Mr. Brandt and the murder of the club members. I was just informing Charles, I mean Mr. Wetmore, about the club members." Catherine blushed prettily from the slip.

Ignoring her cousin's usual calculated antics when it came to men, Devry scanned the room searching for the sheriff. "Mrs. Enlow? That doesn't make sense."

"The sheriff overheard Mrs. Davis talking to someone about Mr. Brandt being at Mrs. Enlow's home a few days ago. He rushed over to Lane and they whispered something, and then the sheriff left."

"Lane left?" Devry was stunned. "His own reception?"

"I was sitting next to Lydia when Lane informed her of the sheriff's sudden departure," Charles added.

"No." Devry shook her head in denial. "Mrs. Enlow doesn't have the intelligence to continuously hide something like this."

"Maybe it was contrived to appear as if she was guilty?" Catherine whispered.

Charles speculated. "There is a possibility she expected people to underestimate her."

"They're wrong," Devry stated with purpose. "They need to find someone who has a medical background. Someone who has knowledge of drugs."

"Well, Devry, that points to yourself, me, the doctor who is no longer with us, and Mrs. Williams." Catherine laughed. "I mean the newlywed Mrs. Parker."

"Don't forget Mrs. Black Elk," Charles added.

"Karen Black Elk?" Devry was stunned. "No, oh my stars, no. For one thing, she is rarely in town, and she doesn't practice doctoring here." She scrunched her forehead. "Something about not being allowed to practice medicine here, and not interfering with the doctor's patients."

"Besides, the last time she came for an extended visit was two years ago. Except for a few short visits here and there, she hasn't been in Tokata," Catherine added.

Charles was puzzled. It was obvious that Devry and Catherine were not capable of being conniving and dangerous. He knew his sister was not guilty. She was not capable of pre-meditated murder. It had to be Mrs. Enlow or Mrs. Black Elk.

The sheriff was on his way to The Widow's estate. He thoroughly questioned Mrs. Enlow and her servants. They searched her home for any possible evidence. He was discouraged until his deputy told him one of the boys had delivered a note to Lydia Williams on the same evening Brandt visited Mrs. Enlow.

The Widow and Mrs. Enlow, conspiring with each other? Now *that* would be an interesting trial—if he found evidence. However, it just did not taste right. There was something in the back of his head, something he could not quite grasp, that told him he was following the wrong leads.

While he waited for the apothecary to arrive with the deputy, he entered her medical supply room. The sheriff was amazed at the organization. Everything ... every bottle, jar, bag, and box … was clearly marked and dated. Some of the jars recorded usage of the herb and warnings to not mix them with certain medicines.

"She is more organized than I am," the apothecary exclaimed as he entered. "Those decoctions cannot be opened."

Pointing to a group of bottles, he lifted one and looked at the date. "It'll ruin the medicinal properties."

Smelling the bottles, he identified them and gently put them back to their designated spots. He walked over to the shelves, opening jars and meticulously inhaling and evaluating the scent of each one. An hour later, he was finished.

"Nothing, sheriff. Everything here is marked as it should be." He stood silently waiting for a reply while the sheriff looked about the room. "If that is all, I would like to return to my business."

"Yes, of course. Thank you."

The sheriff watched the apothecary leave. Chewing his unlit cigar, he quietly shut the medical supply room and followed his deputy outside. Nothing . . . they had found nothing.

He could not deny that he was relieved. It was not illegal for a neighbor to send a note to another neighbor. Blushing prettily, Mrs. Enlow said she had requested some herbs, female herbs.

He was at a loss.

Chapter Eighteen

Devry, Catherine, and Lydia were clearing out the kitchen cabinets, making room for Lane's contributions to the household. The utility room and pantry had already been prepared for the influx of crates and assorted boxes.

"What do you want me to do with these herbs?" Catherine held a jar up and pointed to the cabinet with medical supplies. "They are out of date."

"Just empty them into the grass bin outside the door and I'll mix it with the garden mulch."

"What about the salves?"

"Put them aside and I'll put them in the medical pantry later."

Catherine went outside and dumped the herbs in the bin. Grabbing the trowel, she mixed the grass and herbs, sprinkling them with water from the watering canister.

"I turned the mulch for you. One less thing for you to do. While I was outside I think I heard a carriage coming up the drive."

Devry raced to the window, hoping to get a glimpse of Matthew. He was helping Lane pack his boxes and move his belongings to Lydia's. For the last three weeks she reprimanded herself for acting the petulant child, the child

Matthew accused her of being. She *had* been unreasonable and selfish, his point proven by her childish antics and farcical behavior. An apology was forthcoming and she would humbly give it to him.

She did not want him to leave for the reservation thinking that she was not willing to wait. Matthew had to know that he was the morning sun, the evening moon, and the stars in her dreams. She would rather live in his world than without his love in hers. He would take her love with him, and she would stand tall and wait for her warrior.

The men entered through the rear door, arms full of boxes and crates overflowing with kitchen supplies. Lane kissed Lydia on the forehead as Catherine and Devry directed where to place the crates. He waited patiently as Catherine moved an assortment of empty herb containers from the counter.

"You can't be throwing herbs away to make room for my things," Lane protested.

"No dear, they were past their dates and needed to be disposed."

Lane frowned. As meticulous as his wife was about her herbal medications, he found it difficult to believe she would have so many that had expired. Smiling, he realized that circumstances, with other pressing matters, had kept her occupied in the last few months. Some things may have been neglected.

Catherine nudged Devry when she noticed Lane and Matthew's flushed faces. Pouring two glasses of iced lemon water, she handed one to Lane and the other to Matthew.

"Juan and Domina are coming with the cart. Where do you want to put the furniture?"

"Andrew, Karen, and Christine have cleared out the front sitting room."

Matthew laughed.

"What is so funny?"

"Picturing my mother moving furniture in a gown."

Karen walked through the doors, Andrew and Christine behind her. "Well, I don't think it's so funny. I like my pants, much more comfortable than wearing long dresses."

"She did mumble once about 'stupid dresses' getting in the way. You have to admit men do have it a bit easier when it comes to clothing," Christine chuckled. "Some day I am going to try men's pants. That will get the elders clucking."

"We should all do it on the same day!" Catherine suggested.

"That will give them something else to talk about besides …" Devry stopped mid-sentence and blushed, "I'm sorry, Lydia. I did not mean to bring it up."

Lydia and Lane shook their heads. Lydia hugged Devry.

"Do not worry about it," Lydia comforted her. "The sheriff did not find any evidence, and I gave him a sample of the herbs I had sent to Mrs. Enlow. He had confiscated the herbs she possessed and they compared the two packages. The apothecary verified what they were used for."

"I just wish they would catch the murderer," Catherine said.

"I don't plan to give up my search. The killer will make a mistake and I will be there to catch it," Lane declared.

"We wouldn't expect anything less," Lydia commented. "Besides, until the culprit is found I will never be completely clear. Will I?"

"I know I am missing a major clue. I just cannot seem to point my finger in the right quarter. I have an odd feeling that someone knows something and refuses to come forward."

"Who would feel they needed to protect a murderer?" Devry asked.

"I don't know. However, I do know I'm not letting go."

Lane patted Matthew on the shoulder and they headed out of the room. Andrew and Devry remained in the kitchen while the rest went to the front to greet the new arrivals coming up the drive.

"They will never find her," Andrew said under his breath.

Devry whipped her head around, astonished at the whispered words. Did she hear him right? Did he say 'her'? She stared at her father, shocked, as she watched him leave the room.

It was a long and challenging day. Evening stars twinkled through the open windows. The cool breeze caressed the weary friends who had gathered to share a table at dinner.

Devry was listening to the men discuss Matthew's impending trip to the reservation. She could not believe he was leaving and traveling in the winter months. Didn't he realize the dangers of traveling through the hills in the winter? It would be a hazardous journey for him. He was leaving in the morning, and they had not had any time alone.

He spoke, with animated excitement, about seeing Sitting Bull, Gall, and Black Elk. His plans were to arrive at Standing Rock and then proceed to Pine Ridge to visit with Black Elk. The flames in the fireplace flickered light on his features, creating a halo around his black hair as he spoke wistfully of the Lakota.

When she looked at him, she saw her dreams of tomorrow. Some things she would never understand, but she knew her heart was wherever he was. Hope filled her because she knew one day they would be one. She would be in his heart again. When Matthew returned from the reservation, she would be there waiting, with unconditional, unwavering love. Together, they would share the happiness and the sorrow. She would be there for him.

Later that evening, Devry was in her room preparing for bed. Her nightdress and robe lay on the bed, ready for her to don after her bath. She had tried unsuccessfully to get

Matthew's attention earlier. He had dodged her quite easily. Her decision was final: tonight she would give herself to him, place the gift of her heart and soul into his hands. She would let him fill her with his seed and they would share a brief joy and laughter until they were together again. She would give him her unselfish love.

Matthew stared out the window. He felt frustrated with Devry's attempt for his attention. However, he had to give her credit for her persistence. At least he knew she was not ready to give up on their love. At this moment in time, he could not be alone with her. It was daunting. He would think of her, feel himself harden, and then he would remember her age. Her age was an excellent prophylactic; Matthew was flaccid the second it came to mind.

He loved her but could not allow what she was planning. Bad form, that is what it was. The timing to fall in love with someone so young was cruel. Nevertheless, time was what he had to face—four long, drawn-out years during which she would be tempting him, enticing him with her seductive eyes, her perky, begging-to-be-caressed breasts, and the swing of her hips.

He went to the bedroom door, locked it, and crawled onto the bed, groaning. *Fourteen, fourteen, fourteen!* He could not forget it! It was going to drive him over a deep abyss. Devry had the voluptuous body of a grown woman and the mind of a child. Beautiful hair that he would love to spread on a bed of flowers while he took her, possessed her, and made her his love for eternity.

Matthew pounded his pillow, venting his frustration. *I want Devry now. But she's only fourteen ... fourteen ... fourteen!* Flopping onto his back, he stared at the ceiling, listening to the sounds of the night. He cocked his ear, unsure if he had heard the whisper of feet in the hallway. He sucked in his breath, his heart pounded, and he closed his eyes hoping it was only someone passing by his room.

Devry scratched at the door and attempted to turn the knob. Matthew put the pillow over his ears as he rolled over groaning.

Damn! His eyes were leaking.

Chapter Nineteen

As the first sign of freezing rain tapped on the trees, Matthew covered his bundled body with another layer of protection. Securing the boots on the horses, he listened to the eerie call of the winds. Pulling the hood of his rain gear over his face, he concentrated on the path ahead. Matthew traveled on foot toward the reservation, keeping the horses' safety and welfare in mind. Holding the reins of the lead horse, he looked up to the sky and prayed that he would make it to Standing Rock before the storm blew.

The temperature had dropped below freezing. He scanned the crushed snow left from the last storm, watching for a dangerous coating of ice forming beneath their feet. Just a small amount was enough of a hazard for him and the two horses.

His fingers were stiff with the cold, his face numb from the rain splattering off his hood. Flurries started dancing in the air and he once again scanned the area for a place to shelter. Matthew recalled a small cave, an old dugout from a long-ago miner, about a mile up the way. If necessary, he would make his own shelter, but he preferred the cave. It would be a better haven for the horses.

Slowing his steps, he realized that he was starting to perspire. He needed to be careful. Hypothermia was not on his list of priorities. Everything he was wearing was lightweight and loose, the layers of clothing trapping air to insulate his body. If it were crucial, he would remove his flannel shirt underneath his coat.

Matthew yawned and his teeth started chattering. *Not good.* He needed the shelter of the cave. The wind was whipping about; gushes of cold snow swirled around them, temporarily blinding him.

"Mushroom, we have to get to the cave." The horse whinnied in agreement.

He was shivering. The danger signs of hypothermia rang in his mind. Disorientation, uncontrollable shivering, slurred speech, drowsiness, and exhaustion. He clenched his jaw; there were more symptoms, but he could not recall what they were.

Snow was falling fast, and a roiling whoosh pushed them forward. Matthew lost his balance on the coating of ice and dropped to his knees. Blinding snow cut slashes in his face, his raised collar and hood useless against the thrashing gusts of wind.

He could see the path to the cave opening. He stared at his goal, repeating to himself. *Just a little bit more.* Limping, Matthew brought the horses into the cave. Relief settled the tension he had not realized had been building throughout his muscles. Stretching, he rubbed his face with his wet mittens. Groaning, he realized his mistake immediately. He took his mittens off and put on another dry pair. Pulling out a towel, he dried his face, carefully, as he felt the bite of the snow on his skin.

After the second attempt, the fire flamed bright from the aged wood he had found in a corner, heating the small cave as he wiped down the horses. Part of the dugout had collapsed but it was still large enough to house the horses and him. Two mice watched his movements from a corner, unsure of the uninvited guests who had laid claim to their home.

He would not be arriving at Standing Rock today. The temperature had dropped quickly, issuing him a warning of the coming blizzard. The blinding wind-driven snow, severe drifting, and dangerous windchill were life-threatening. Always prepared for the worst, he had four more days of food and water. Would it be enough? He remembered a larger wood supply, but that was almost ten years ago. Would it still be there?

Tying a rope around his waist and attaching it to the chair near the makeshift door, Matthew headed toward the side of the dugout. About ten feet from the opening he miraculously found a woodpile. Carrying as much as he could, he added more wood to the small stack that someone had generously left behind.

The storm was turning fierce. Thrashing winds were coming from the southwest, howling like coyotes at the moon. With the combined winds and the extreme drop in temperature, the windchill would most likely drop below –5 degrees. He shivered again, wishing for the warmth of the Florida sun. His stomach muscles ached from constantly clenching them against the cold.

Quickly, he stripped off his clothing and put on some long johns, drew up a pair of skins, and added layers of shirts until he was comfortable. Putting water on the fire, he prepared a sparse meal.

"My favorite," he mumbled. "Lukewarm soup."

He needed to raise his body temperature slowly as he wiggled his numb fingers, wishing for the companionship of Captain Morgan. Matthew grabbed the blanket he had placed near the fire and wrapped its warmth over his head and around his shoulders. The heat from the blanket and the warm soup was comforting, relaxing. He yawned again and forced pleasant memories to occupy his mind.

Sharp pains exploded through his bones, crippling the movements of his fingers and arms. His legs felt heavy, weighed down as if steel bolts held them to the dirt floor.

He edged his way, like a decrepit man, to retrieve his medicine bag. As he prepared a decoction, he thought of his friends at the reservation.

He looked forward to seeing Gall again. Gall had fought against the invasion of their land with the fierceness of any true Lakota warrior. He had originally been a part of Red Cloud's band until he had joined forces with Sitting Bull. Over time, he had become Sitting Bull's war chief and fought against the United States. Gall had led the Hunkpapa warriors against Major Reno at the Little Big Horn campsite, and then joined Crazy Horse in the battle against Custer and the Seventh Cavalry.

Gall had fled to Canada with Sitting Bull but had returned to the Lakota Territory after a disagreement between the two men. Matthew's mother had discussed the rift with Sitting Bull. When he attempted to talk about his speculations with his mother, she would shake her head and say her conversations with Sitting Bull were in confidence, and their private discussions would not pass her lips. She would not break a code she had lived by all her life.

Matthew wondered if Gall had not been willing to stay in Canada. It was not their land. He perceived that Sitting Bull was tired of fighting and Gall was not yet willing to surrender, nor was he willing to stay in a land that was not their own.

Matthew understood Gall's innate desire for survival. Once he had surrendered to the government, he accepted the defeat and attempted to encourage the Lakotas to accept and embrace their new way of life. Gall had become a prominent member on the reservation. He actively campaigned for the farming programs and education of the children. The previous year, his influence among the Lakota's and the federal government had increased tremendously when he had become a judge on the reservation's Court of Indian Offenses.

The rift between Gall and Sitting Bull increased when he had conceded to the reduction of the reservation, allotting the federal government more land. Gall had become good friends with Indian Agent James McLaughlin, seemingly siding up with the enemy, and then had consented to sign away more land. Sitting Bull had been furious.

Sitting Bull had agreed with Gall on many issues. Neither of the men participated in the Ghost Dance; nevertheless, both had allowed it to continue. Though the Lakotas had never been an agricultural tribe, he approved their farming programs, understanding their necessity. Sitting Bull also sent his children to the schools and encouraged the Lakota to learn the white man's ways, knowing that education was a gift for their future welfare, for the generations to come. They could take everything else from the Indian, but no one could take their education from them.

Sitting Bull had also consented to allow his children to learn the Christian faith. Through Matthew's mother, Sitting Bull had learned the Christian beliefs but stayed strong with the old ways. He listened to the priest's words of wisdom and understood the spiritualism; for he believed much of the Christian ways coincided with his own spiritual beliefs. Sitting Bull respected their choice of religion but did not embrace the Christian faith as his own.

He found many of their ways confusing. He could not comprehend how they only worshiped their god once a week. Every breath he took, every bite of food he received, and every aspect of life he experienced was accompanied with prayer. The Lakota did not designate just one day a week to honor the Creator, but every day, every moment.

Catholic priests were the only Christians that Sitting Bull observed worshiping and praying every day. Like him, they had laid their souls in the palms of God. Wakan Tanka was the same Supreme Being, the Creator, with a different name.

When Matthew was younger, Sitting Bull had taught him many spiritual beliefs. During his absence from the Lakota people, his parents had taught him the Lakota ways, in addition to teaching him about the Christian faith. The combination was empowering and utterly humbling.

Together they taught him to live life with a passion, to never let go of hope or faith. He had watched with the insight of a child as his mother had been emotionally knocked to the ground. He was impressed with her strength, as she picked herself up, never giving in, never giving up. How liberating it was not to hang on to sadness or bitterness; to know that tomorrow was another day, another choice, and another chance.

He recalled a time when he had struck out in a baseball game. Every time he went up to bat that day, he struck out. He was frustrated and angry, mad at the world. He was ready to quit, to never play ball again. She had told him, it was not a bad day, just a bad moment. Her words rang in his ears.

Life is an adventure. Know that there will be days when you strike out, but remember to live life with every intention of sliding into home base, knowing that you will have added one more score to the game.

It had taken him years to understand what she had been saying.

There were times when Matthew felt as if he was a useless speck of dust. After the last set of wildfires he had fought, he felt weary. Tears of frustration had filled his eyes at the loss of the burned acreage, the death of the helpless animals. Darkness and pain had smothered him. Like the flames that had destroyed the earth, he had succumbed to the sorrow, his strength drained.

Through the darkness, he knew that God was at his side, to bear the load of defeat and to comfort him. Matthew had swallowed his pride; the sun would shine again. He had placed the weight of tragedy in the palms of God. There was *always* tomorrow.

Jumbled random thoughts skittered through his memories. The freezing cold made it difficult to concentrate. His father's image waded through the throng, halting the passage of confusion.

When Matthew had lost his father, he had hated the white man, the government. His heart had knotted into a ball of bitterness and hatred. Ironically, it had been Crazy Horse who eased his heart, telling him that there were white people and then there were wasicu. *Learn the difference, know the difference, and live the difference.*

He stared at the bouncing shadows. His thoughts converged on a new notion, a sudden intuitive realization from the gathered wisdom of those closest to him. Matthew spoke to the flames snapping before his eyes. "We the People build a nation, a nation does not build the people."

The cave was warm as Matthew stood to check on the horses. Air escaped through holes in the dugout and he braced an extra blanket to block the flow.

"Is that better, Shadow?" She whinnied and nodded her head in thanks when he swapped her blanket for the warm one that had been around his shoulders. Matthew quickly replaced Mushroom's blanket with the one he had laid near the fire.

Matthew squatted near the flames and made broth with dried venison, then drank some of the decoction he had made earlier. The pain was finally gone from his limbs.

The storm howled vigorously. The cave walls managed to block the wind as it moaned a threatening song of warning.

Satisfied with his meal, Matthew crossed his legs and relished the moment of solitude.

After his visit with Gall and Sitting Bull at the Standing Rock reservation, he would ride over to Pine Ridge and visit Black Elk and his Lakota friends. Two Feathers would be there, and Sings to the Wind, his mother's friend Bonnie, who had chosen to stay with the Lakota Indians. Most of all, he looked forward to seeing Black Elk.

Black Elk, who had only been thirteen when he had fought at Little Big Horn, was only a few years older than Matthew was. He smiled. Black Elk had joined the Buffalo Bill Wild West Show, and he was looking forward to those particular tales of adventure. Mostly, though, he was excited that he would be visiting a childhood friend that he missed dearly.

Chapter Twenty

Matthew walked slowly and cautiously to the front entrance of Gall's home. Three days of freezing temperatures and minimal rations had left him weary and hungry. Now he was angry, spitting angry. Four Special Police had stopped him near the reservation entrance and had searched his supplies. They had confiscated his rifle and he wanted it back. He was fuming. He understood now why his mother had told him to hide his handgun.

When he had protested for his rights as an American citizen, the one who had taken his rifle hit him with it and told him to shut up. If he hadn't had three guns pointing at him ...

The door opened before he had a chance to knock. Gall stood looking at him, his hard features stoic. His eyes scanned the four men standing one hundred feet behind the bundled man at his door.

Pulling back his hood, Matthew rapidly spoke to him in Lakota. "Gall, you knew me as Big Eyes. I am Gentle Raccoon now. My mother is Spirit of the Mountain."

A smile washed across his face, brightening the welcome as he opened the door wider for Matthew to enter. The room was warm and cozy, blocking out the drudgery of the reservation, creating an atmosphere of serenity.

Someone took his coat and Gall hugged him. "Welcome to my home. Your mother told us to expect you. Come, sit by the fire, and warm yourself, fill your belly with good hot food."

Matthew gratefully sat down, a bowl of steaming hot stew placed in his hand. The woman was gone before he had a chance to thank her, so he extended his thanks to Gall.

While he was eating, the woman returned and tended to the cuts on his face. The wounds stung, and she apologized each time he flinched. A young boy, who took his horses to the shelter, brought in his supplies. Gall lit his pipe and they smoked together. True to Lakota form, Gall waited patiently before he spoke again.

"How are you, *kola*?"

"Except for my encounter with the Special Police, much better now, thank you. I was caught in the storm and stayed in a cave about ten miles from here."

Gall laughed and shook his head. "You have not been on the reservation for more than ten minutes and you have already had a confrontation with the Special Police?"

"They commandeered my rifle, no reason for searching my supplies, no cause for suspicion. When they asked, I told them where I was heading. I answered all their questions, gave them no reason to treat me like a criminal." Matthew paused, "I want my rifle back."

"You did not provoke them? Give them cause to discipline you?"

"I did not swing at him, if that is what you mean. When he took my rifle, I tried to grab it away from him. Told him he had no right taking my rifle. There were laws protecting an American citizen. It is not like I could have done anything. I had three guns pointing at me."

"The reservation is in a volatile situation right now. They do not know who you are. I'll see what I can do to get the rifle back."

"What's happening to have them so anxious?"

"It is getting very precarious. Agent McLaughlin has sent a telegraph to Washington, D.C. requesting more troops. Sitting Bull's acceptance of the Ghost Dance has caused great concern and disruption. White settlers are panicking, sending letters about Indians crazed and wild, dancing in the snow. Kicking Bear was escorted from Standing Rock this morning."

"What harm could the Ghost Dance do? It is part of a religious ceremony, is it not? It gives the people hope."

Gall shook his head. "It is more of a cult than a religious ceremony. Hope must take its faith from reality."

"Do you not endorse the Ghost Dance?" Matthew frowned.

"I agree with some of it, not all of it. It sounds like a washed, one-sided version of the Second Coming of Christ."

"Religious freedom gives them the right to practice the faith of their choosing, whether we agree with it or not."

"I will not dispute that, Gentle Raccoon. However, we must keep peace on the reservation. The Ghost Dance is causing dissension and hysteria."

Matthew bit the inside of his cheek. "It's not supposed to be causing dissension and hysteria. Something does not sound right. Gall, we need to telegraph my mom. Something is seriously wrong. It's not supposed to be this way."

The next morning Gall and Matthew stood in front of the clerk at the telegraph office.

"What do you want to say?"

"The change of history is upon us," Matthew informed him. "Sign it, *Wica*."

"Odd choice of words; interesting timing, too." The clerk eyed him speculatively. "I was told earlier that Agent Royer sent a telegram from the Pine Ridge Agency this morning requesting seven hundred troops to restore order." He looked at Gall. "The Ghost Dance has caused problems over there, also."

Gall and Matthew walked silently toward McLaughlin's office. Soldiers rushed to their specific destinations, the cold hurrying their footsteps. Matthew watched the activities, wary of the obtrusive show of force.

Entering McLaughlin's office, Gall introduced Matthew to the man who, unknown to all, would soon change history. He denied knowledge of the confiscation of Matthew's rifle. A golden-colored calico jumped to his lap, purring in pleasure as McLaughlin absently rubbed and scratched behind her ears.

"Did you see who they were?" he asked Gall, when Matthew had informed him he did not know the names of the officers that had followed him to Gall's home.

"Only one I saw clearly was Bull Head."

McLaughlin nodded and left the room. A private brought in three cups of steaming coffee, put more logs on the fire creating a large blaze, then silently left. The agent returned with a grimace of pain as he seated himself at the desk.

He shrugged at Gall. "Hot coals just don't warm me enough. I need the white man's fire. This cold weather chills me to the bones." Looking at Matthew, he spoke quietly. "Please understand the caution that must be followed. We must be ready for any possible outbreak of trouble."

Matthew acknowledged the words, but was not sure if he wanted to accept the man's concerns or apology.

"We heard that Agent Royer sent a telegram this morning for troops to be sent to Pine Ridge," Gall reported.

"So I was told." McLaughlin sighed. "It worsens each day. This Indian messiah's promise of invincibility and the return of the ancestors are hurting the Indians more than helping them. I understand the desire for the return of their old way of life."

McLaughlin took a drink of coffee, unsure of how to explain his guarded opinion to Gall's guest. How could he express his fears without sounding obsessed about how dangerous and destructive it would be?

"It was a shrewd plan that backfired. Wovoka's timing was incredible. He seized the opportunity, using superstition, promising the return of the old ways and the annihilation of all whites. The Indians who have lost hope are grabbing onto the concept as a last breath for redemption. For those Indians who have accepted the Christian doctrines, they can relate and accept the ascension because it is similar to what they are being taught in the Holy Bible."

When a knock sounded at the door, the agent stopped speaking. The private entered and placed the rifle and bullets on the desk in front of McLaughlin. Dismissing the private, he waited until the door shut.

"My main concern is to supervise the domestication of the Indian, to civilize them."

Matthew flinched at the use of the words, his temper burning in his veins. He clenched his jaw, attempting to suppress the verbal thrashing streaming through his mind.

"They are already a conquered people. The government treats them like prisoners without rights. They are American citizens and should not be treated like criminals."

McLaughlin blinked. "American citizens? No, they are not. What made you believe the Indian was considered an American citizen?"

"They're supposed to be," Matthew growled. "When the Lakota surrendered, they should have become citizens of the state."

"We didn't become a state until last year." McLaughlin looked at Matthew oddly. "When they surrender they become a ward, not a citizen."

"Then they should have become citizens when South Dakota became a state. So, what you are saying is that when Gall, Black Elk, and Sitting Bull surrendered, they did not become citizens of this country? That no Indian living on this reservation has rights as an American citizen?"

"That is correct. They are not American citizens. They do not have a citizen's rights. They do not vote. They do not have the freedom to go where they choose and are required to stay on the reservation."

"That doesn't make sense to me. I understand that when there is a war situation, then there are prisoners of war. However, prisoners of war are soldiers and warriors, not women, children, and the elderly. Why are they considered prisoners of war? The way they are being treated, I wouldn't want to be a citizen of this country either."

Indignant with Matthew's attitude, McLaughlin asked sarcastically, "Are you a citizen?"

"Yes, I am." Matthew stared at McLaughlin, daring him to refute his statement.

"Can you prove it?"

"Yes, I can. Can you?" Matthew spit back at the man.

Gall cleared his throat and grinned. "Technically, Sitting Bull did not surrender."

"He didn't?"

"No." Gall suppressed a smile. "His son surrendered his rifle at Fort Buford in Montana, as a symbol that the next generation must become friends with the Americans."

"But he did say he wanted to be remembered as the last man of his tribe to surrender his rifle," McLaughlin added. "Along with the request to travel to Canada freely and a reservation of his own on the Little Missouri River."

Matthew chuckled. "I cannot blame the man for trying."

"Contrary to what you may hear about me, I do have great respect for the Lakota leaders and people. I am in a precarious situation. I must control a people who have had centuries of freedom. There is no other option but to increase the troops to control the rebellious."

"Would you have just laid down and surrendered without a fight?" Matthew asked McLaughlin.

"No, I would not have. However, that is not where I am, is it? I am required to keep the peace on this reservation. I will do what must be done."

"Why can't you see that it will cause a fury?"

"The soldiers are not here for the peaceful, law-abiding Indians. Sitting Bull's acceptance of the Ghost Dance has caused problems. Many continue to follow him as a spiritual leader. If he decides to participate in the Ghost Dance, peace on the reservation will be lost."

"Isn't he staying away from everyone in his cabin at the Grand River?"

"Do you honestly believe that?" When Matthew shrugged, McLaughlin continued. "Sitting Bull has his subtle ways of influencing those around him. The more we request that he stop the Ghost Dancers, the more he digs in his heels and allows it. This impasse will cause tragedy."

"I'm sorry, but more troops will alert the Indians and goad them into preparing to defend themselves. By sending for more soldiers, you are asking for a conflict. How would you feel if the cavalry started surrounding your home?" Matthew was amazed how calmly he spoke.

"The same way I feel now. Protected."

Matthew snorted. "Yeah, right, until bullets start ricocheting off the walls of your office."

"No one is safe when bullets start to fly," Gall added sadly.

"Unfortunately, the Ghost Dancers believe they have become invincible. I don't see any other options to control them."

"Do you really believe that you are doing what is best for the Indian?" Matthew asked.

"I'm doing what has to be done."

"I didn't ask that. Do you believe this is what is best for the Indian people?"

"It is necessary."

"Answer the question," Matthew growled.

"Yes!" McLaughlin slammed his fist on his desk. "Yes. I do. I do not like it, because no one should have their land taken from them. However, it has happened. That is life, people are conquered, wars happen. I am giving them the best chance they have to change their way of life."

There it was. All the cards placed on the table. Silence hung deadly and thick in the room. McLaughlin fingered Matthew's rifle. Gall stared out the window, Matthew at the floor. The three men sat numb, caught in a black widow's web, unable to control the forces around them.

Chapter Twenty-One

Matthew arrived at Sitting Bull's camp on the Grand River and was amazed at the sight before him. There were many more Indians here than he had expected. People sat around small fires while the children ran and played.

"*Hau.*" Matthew greeted a lone flute player whose tune danced a peaceful melody among the laughter.

A month had passed and Matthew had not heard from his mother. He rubbed his eyes in frustration. She returned to their world and would return to this one randomly to assess his progress. His words would not be reassuring to her. He knew she would rush to the reservation to help the Lakota.

Matthew had received a letter from Devry, giving him a rundown on the happenings in Tokata. The sheriff had finally released Curry. The man refused to name the person who had hired him. Catherine had drastically changed; she was withdrawn and unsure of herself. Devry was sure that in time, she would return to her former self. Lane and Lydia were doing well, though Sir Elmer was still pecking holes in Lane. The murders had stopped. No one in the town had so much as a cold, never mind murder. Devry and her parents would soon arrive at the reservation with Karen and she looked forward to spending more time with him.

He hoped his mother would be arriving soon. He felt helpless as he watched the Lakota trap themselves in a perilous web of their own design. By participating in the Ghost Dance, they were stoking the anger and greed of the government. It bound their hands and cornered them like branded cattle.

Somehow, history was changing. History as he knew it accepted the Ghost Dance, allowing the Indians to perform the ceremonies. None of this was supposed to be happening. Had Sings to the Wind manipulated the past again? Like she had before the Battle of the Little Big Horn? He recalled his mother's anger. Bonnie had been his mother's closest friend, and had traveled to the past. She had chosen to stay and live with the Lakota, with the promise not to try to alter the future. Providence had painted a picture that was shifting as history unfolded an untold story, emerging … a new history on a fresh canvas brushed with the strokes from the Breath of Heaven.

Sitting Bull had stopped coming to the agency for rations. His family would arrive for their bi-weekly portions while a bodyguard remained with him in anticipation of an impending arrest. Rumors dashed through the reservation that all Indian leaders involved or encouraging the Ghost Dance would be detained or arrested.

Gall had returned a few days ago and had informed Matthew that President Harrison had instructed the Secretary of War to commence military action on the Sioux reservations to thwart any imminent conflicts. The soldiers were to stay until the threat of the Ghost Dance ended. Gall had divulged that Major McLaughlin had received the telegram from the Indian Office informing him of the military movement.

Gall and McLaughlin had ridden to Sitting Bull's cabin in an attempt to persuade him to end the Ghost Dance.

"This is a precarious situation. It is creating rebellion among the peaceful Indians on the reservation," McLaughlin explained.

Sitting Bull had listened attentively. "I understand your fears and apprehensions. I do not participate in the Ghost Dance."

"They will listen to you." McLaughlin pleaded, "Can you ask them to end this foolishness?"

"No. I will not use my influence to stop others from performing the ceremony. I refuse to take hope away from my people. This country was born on the principles of freedom. Was it not? The Indian should be able to pray and perform religious ceremonies, without condemnation from outside forces. They should have the freedom to practice their sacred ceremonies without persecution. The citizens of the United States have the right of religious freedom. Why does the Indian not have this same right?"

"But, this is not a true religious ceremony," McLaughlin exclaimed.

"That is your opinion. We do not tell you how to pray to your god. Did this country not declare its independence many years ago against a repressive government? The Lakota should have the same independence."

"You have got to stop them."

"No." Sitting Bull nodded at Gall, who had kept quiet during the exchange, then walked to his cabin without another word.

While McLaughlin and Gall were gone, Matthew had written countless letters attempting to assuage the ignorance of what was happening in Sioux territory. His fingertips ached; he cursed his lack of a keyboard and printer, realizing how spoiled his world was with its modern amenities.

He wrote letters to every newspaper, senator, congressman, or organization he could reach, explaining the seriousness as well as the volatility of the situation. The Cheyenne and the

Sioux seemed to have received the least compensation of all the tribes once the military obtained control.

Gall entered the cabin, noticing all the papers on the table. "You have been busy."

"Well," lifting some of the letters and dropping them back on the table, "someone has to listen."

"McLaughlin is not the enemy."

"He could be doing a lot more than he is."

"Gentle Raccoon, he can only do what they allow him to do."

"What? What has he done?"

"He, too, has written letters and spoken with government officials. He has requested compensation from the sales of the arms and mounts, from those that had been disarmed and surrendered. Every month, I sit with him when he sends requests for more stock, farming supplies, food, and clothing."

Matthew countered, "In my letter I state that the lack of supplies has caused the Lakota to hunt cattle belonging to white settlers. The government has failed to support the Indian reservations in the manner that they had promised."

"Gentle Raccoon, the white settlers struggled here as well, until they admitted defeat. The soil is not good for raising crops. Many have tried. Humbled with unsuccessful attempts, the failure of their crops has spurred thousands of white settlers to leave their homesteads and travel west or return east to start again."

"The government needs to send more food for families to survive through the winter months."

"You are not telling me anything I do not already know. At least, the white settlers had the freedom to leave. That option is not available to the Indian."

"Has anyone considered opening a trade store?"

"Who would do business with an Indian? Besides, Gentle Raccoon, there is not enough food for the families to keep themselves fed through the winter months. How would they be able to trade or sell their crops?"

"What about work? A man could make it, with the white man's money."

"Not too many businessmen will hire an Indian, on or off the reservation, even for those who have learned the white man's ways."

"It all goes back to money, doesn't it? In the letter, I did mention the monies owed to Standing Rock for the right-of-way privileges the Sioux have given the railroads. They have waited for that money for almost ten years. It could buy cattle, stock, and clothing. They could have their own self-sustaining ranch."

"McLaughlin has been fighting for that money, too. He has seen official records showing that the government received the compensation from the railroad. He requested an increase in rations; instead they cut them in half."

"Someone is lining their pockets."

"It is not McLaughlin, Gentle Raccoon. The man sometimes uses his own funds to help the reservation."

The government had failed, disillusioning the Indians who had agreed to live peacefully on the reservations. Matthew had ended his letters with a plea to render assistance to those Indians who were peaceful and law-abiding citizens of this great country.

McLaughlin, Gall, and Afraid of Soldiers had a meeting to discuss starting a ranch with the cattle that white settlers had abandoned. Matthew had enough knowledge to assist in running a ranch, but to organize a new ranch was beyond his abilities.

The Indian agent had pounced on their idea with enthusiasm, inquiring if Matthew had the knowledge to train the Indians in the cattle business. He had informed the agent that he had enough to keep them going, but someone else would have to get it started. However, he did have a rancher in mind with the expertise to handle such an endeavor. He would request Little Red Hawk's assistance.

Matthew sat atop Mushroom staring at the cabin before him. A lone man approached, his face partially hidden from the hood of his buffalo coat. Slowly, the man pushed his hood back and Matthew looked into the face of his mentor, the man he called *Leksi*, his uncle. It was good to see him. Sitting Bull smiled and hugged him. With his arm around Matthew's shoulder, they entered his cabin.

He introduced him to his son, Crow Foot, who was sitting at the table. The three sat together sharing the afternoon meal.

"How are you, Gentle Raccoon?" Sitting Bull asked after the meal concluded.

"Doing well, considering the turmoil surrounding us."

"And your sister, *Kimimala*?"

Matthew smiled. "Changing with the wind every chance she can. She is still attending college, a university, and has changed her major again."

"Your sister will find her path. Spirit of the Mountain told me you fight fires for your world."

"Yes, I followed grandfather's footsteps before he became a doctor. I considered joining the military, becoming a warrior for our country, but at the time I believed I could do more by becoming a firefighter."

"From what your mother has told us, it is a worthy cause, a warrior's way of life."

"To some people, I guess it is. However, I have a different path that I am following. Tell me, *Leksi*. What is happening to our people?"

"They are finding hope again. The heavy weight of despair is being lifted from their hearts."

"It has to stop," Matthew intoned.

"You take the white man's side?" Crow Foot spit out the feral words. "*Wasicuncinea*! Leave my father's home if you want our people to die away in dishonor and despair."

Sitting Bull raised his hand. "There is a reason for *Wica's*, Gentle Raccoon's, words. Let us listen."

Matthew calmly spoke to Crow Foot. "Call me half-breed all you want. You do not insult me. I am proud of my parents and my ancestors."

Matthew gathered his words and thoughts, completely aware of his precarious situation. He had to be cautious as he explained his objections. It was not the Ghost Dance he objected to, but the repercussions of what might happen if it continued. He also wanted to observe the ceremony for himself, to grasp a better understanding.

"I don't know what may occur if the ceremonies continue. They do not inform me of what is happening until after the fact. What I can tell you is what I am seeing and what I speculate will happen.

"Though I have not been told these words are true, there are rumors that you will be arrested on the twentieth of this month, Sitting Bull. It will happen when the people come for their bi-weekly rations.

"Both Indian agents from Standing Rock and Pine Ridge have requested more soldiers. They arrive every day; hundreds are arriving at Standing Rock as we speak. I have heard that the same is happening at Pine Ridge. This military movement is preparation for war. Their wagons are over-laden with firearms and ammunition. Cannons are being prepared, brought out of storage. They are preparing to permanently suppress the Lakota by every means available to them."

A silence ensued.

"Then," Crow Foot exclaimed, "we will fight."

"With what? Your handful of resistance against their guns would be futile."

"*Wasicuncinea*, you stand for the white man and declare your side," Crow Foot impugned.

"You are young and hot-headed. Do not insult me again. I take no sides, for I am a combination of two great nations. Each has given me the best it has to offer and has made me a better person. I do not want to see Sitting Bull killed, or anyone else die needlessly."

"At least we will die in honor. I deny all that is white."

"Then I pity you, Crow Foot. You have blinded yourself to the good that is there." Looking toward Sitting Bull and mentally dismissing Crow Foot, Gentle Raccoon continued to express his concern. "They prepare for battle. You would be able to do more for your people if you walked upon Mother Earth and continued to lobby for Indian rights."

"I am not afraid to die, nor will I bow down and not fight for my people," Sitting Bull explained quietly.

"You are flagrantly rebelling against the government, defying the authority of the Indian Agent McLaughlin. He believes you are encouraging the rebellious behavior by encouraging the Ghost Dance, instilling the beliefs that the Dancers will be invincible and that Judgment Day will see the eternal destruction of the white race."

Sitting Bull smiled. "I am honored that Indian Agent McLaughlin believes I have that much power and influence over the Lakota people. Nevertheless, I do not. If they so choose, they will perform the Ghost Dance with or without my consent. It is better for the Lakota to perform the ceremony here, in my little corner of Mother Earth, where they bother no one who does not wish to accept this new sacred ceremony."

"An excellent point, Sitting Bull. Do you believe in the Ghost Dance?"

"No, Gentle Raccoon. I do not. I do not believe they will become invincible against the white man's bullets, nor do I believe our dead ancestors will return to us. I encourage the hope it instills. I do believe, to the depths of my soul, that they have the right to perform the religious ceremony if they so choose. I would not block them anymore than I would stop a priest from saying Mass."

"The Lakota people need you. Can you avoid arrest? Prevent the people from getting hurt?"

Sitting Bull nodded.

Chapter Twenty-Two

The day was done and Major James McLaughlin looked forward to taking off his boots and having a stiff drink of bourbon in front of the fireplace. A deafening knock on his office door caused him to jump and spill ink on the letter he was signing.

"Sir, a missive has been sent from Lieutenant of Police Henry Bull Head. I thought you would want to see it immediately. The dispatch rider awaits your reply."

McLaughlin snatched the letter out of the soldier's hands and clenched his teeth as he read the missive.

> *... At this moment, preparations are being made to leave the reservation. Horses have been packed with the obvious intention for an extended journey. We request permission to arrest Sitting Bull immediately before he disappears in the hills where we may not be able to track or retrieve him.*

"Send the policeman in who brought the letter. I want to question him."

The dispatcher entered and stood with hands behind his back. Before McLaughlin had the chance to open his mouth and question the man, the post commander, Colonel Drum, walked into the office. "Oh good. I caught you before you left. Any news to relate from Grand River and the Ghost Dancers?"

McLaughlin took a slow, deep breath and handed him the missive. Colonel Drum read the letter quickly and looked up. "We can't avoid this arrest any longer. Sitting Bull must be detained, immediately."

"I would suggest that you have the Special Police arrest him in the morning, at daybreak. If they are the ones to detain him, I believe it could be done without bloodshed or conflict." McLaughlin scowled. "The second those Indians see any military forces, there will be a full-blown conflict on our hands."

"Agreed." Colonel Drum rubbed his jaw line. "We'll send two troops from the 8th Cavalry with orders to proceed at midnight to the upper Grand River. They will wait on the road to Sitting Bull's cabin until the Special Police arrive with Sitting Bull."

"It would be best for them to escort the Special Police with the prisoner and foil any attempted rescue by his people. I'll send the courier back with a letter explaining our plans and our desires to avoid conflict or bloodshed."

"Send a barrel of whiskey along with him, as a reward," added Drum.

Gray Eagle, Sitting Bull's brother-in-law, stood in front of Sitting Bull's cabin at daybreak, next to the three other volunteers. He hoped his presence would ease his friend's mind, reassuring him that someone was there to keep him safe during the confrontation with the Special Police. Thirty-nine Special Police stood in a separate group waiting for Lieutenant Bull Head to choose who would enter the house.

The door slammed inward. Matthew jumped out of his bedroll and reached for his gun. The sound of rifles slapping against palms reverberated through the air. Matthew looked up to see ten rifles pointed at him.

"Don't move, Gentle Raccoon," someone spoke quietly. "We are not here for you."

Bull Head came through the door, shutting it quietly. Crow Foot moved silently in the corner, until a lone police officer turned his gun on him. Lieutenant Bull Head stepped forward through the throng. "Sitting Bull, we are here to take you into custody."

Sitting Bull stared at Bull Head for a moment, then scanned the force in front of him. Looking at his son and then Gentle Raccoon, he accepted his fate.

"We shall dress, if you have no objections."

Crow Foot and Gentle Raccoon dressed within minutes, looking at each other, confused by the timing of the arrest. For a slight moment, Gentle Raccoon could see the doubts flickering through Crow Foot, wondering if Gentle Raccoon had sent the Special Police on his father. After a few moments of consideration, he realized that no one was that good an actor; besides, he had not let the man out of his sight.

Gentle Raccoon was furious. Someone must have been watching Sitting Bull's cabin, expecting his flight. Who would have spied on the Lakota Chief and spotted the clandestine movements of the evening before? Who had betrayed him? No one but himself, Crow Foot, and Sitting Bull had known they were preparing to leave. Sitting Bull had planned to inform the household immediately before their departure.

Sitting Bull was taking his time, walking languorously about the cabin, enjoying his morning as if he had not one care in the world. His two wives had jumped up to assist him and he had waved them away, murmuring for them to sit at the table. The longer he took to prepare himself, the more agitated Crow Foot became.

"Father, why are you accepting this?" Crow Foot asked. "You have done nothing wrong. Do you really believe no harm will come to you? Do you believe they are not here so they can silence your words forever?"

Crow Foot watched his father's slow movements as he packed a few more items into the bag.

"Gentle Raccoon, you know the laws of this country. Do something," Crow Foot pleaded.

"I'll ride in with him if Bull Head will allow it." Gentle Raccoon explained to deaf ears, "Resisting arrest is not wise."

"Father, listen to me. Do not let them take you. You cannot let the white man win. They will find a reason to use a bullet on you, just like they have anyone else who has resisted them."

Sitting Bull acknowledged his son's agitation and looked out the window. Pouring himself a cup of coffee, adding cream from a pitcher, he dropped a liberal quantity of sugar into the cup. Sitting on the chair next to the fire, he scanned the throng of people who had unceremoniously invaded his home.

Looking at Bull Head, he crossed his arms and announced stubbornly, "I will not go willingly."

Gentle Raccoon leaned against the wall, crossed his arms, and leaned his head back. *No, this is not happening.* He closed his eyes. *Please, Sitting Bull, do not resist. Do not resist.*

Lieutenant Bull Head grabbed Sitting Bull and pulled on his arm. Sitting Bull dragged his feet, swinging his arms to free them, temporarily dislodging Bull Head's hold. Forcefully, Bull Head dragged Sitting Bull through the door.

As they left the cabin, the men kept their guns and rifles pointed at Crow Foot and Gentle Raccoon. Three Special Police kept their rifles trained on his two wives and children, keeping them near the door of the cabin. Gentle Raccoon looked up to see the cabin surrounded by Lakota. He bit his lip. This was why Sitting Bull had taken so long to prepare for his arrest. He had been waiting for the camp to come to his defense.

The members of Sitting Bull's camp surrounded the Special Police. Many were fully armed, all were outraged. Matthew's stomach clenched. He could feel the raging fire radiating from the people as he walked beside Sergeant Shave Head. It did not bode well.

Gray Eagle, Red Tomahawk, and Shave Head attempted to reason with the crowd, explaining to them that it would be in Sitting Bull's best interest if he acquiesced, allowing them to escort him to the Indian Agency. Many moved to the side or retreated, increasing the opening for the escort to pass.

Gentle Raccoon cocked his ear, listening. Did he hear Sitting Bull tell someone to shoot Bull Head and Shave Head first? A whisper, like the sound of wings fluttering, filtered through the silent crowd. Gradually the sound increased until Gentle Raccoon looked up to see if a gathering of eagles had descended from the sky. A breeze pulsed in rhythm with the sound brushing across his upturned face.

"Now!" Sitting Bull yelled.

"No!!!!" Gentle Raccoon screamed.

He watched, terrified, as bullets flew around him. The scene before him unfolded as if he was watching a panoramic movie, the vision clicking in slow motion. Catch the Bear ran through the crowd and fired upon the Special Police. Strike the Kettle came from behind him, whipped his gun around, and shot Shave Head in the stomach. The pulsing beat of unseen wings pounded louder … unknown hands pushed Gentle Raccoon away from the conflict.

Catch the Bear pulled another shot and hit Bull Head. Reeling from the impact, Bull Head turned, shooting Sitting Bull in his left side. Each fell simultaneously. Lone Man, a private of the Special Police, gunned down Catch the Bear.

Grabbed from behind and knocked to the ground, Gentle Raccoon watched Crow Foot, Black Bird, and Spotted Horn Bull drop from bullets. Dazed, he saw Sitting Bull lying on the ground breathing heavily, his hand holding the wound in his side. As feet trampled around him, someone tried to grab Sitting Bull's legs to get him away from the fighting. Sitting Bull's head exploded from a bullet. Gentle Raccoon watched in disbelief as fragments of the great man's skull splattered the crowd.

Rolling over, he crawled away from the horror and vomited until bile splashed against his hands.

Hand-to-hand combat ensued. The nightmare surrounded him as he felt himself carried into the melee, swept into the ferocity of fulminating forces. Gentle Raccoon joined in the ruckus, connecting his fist with jawbones and noses. A chaotic insurgence of hatred fueled the warriors.

Over one-hundred-fifty warriors, most unarmed, battled forty Special Police. The women and children, realizing the odds were against them, joined their warriors in the conflict, using knives and sticks that the soldiers confiscated quickly and easily. After disarming the women and children, the police detained them in a nearby cabin.

Thirty minutes later, the burst of violence had subsided to one small group. The Special Police had managed to gather the warriors, corralling those who had used the buildings for cover, and pushed them back into the woods.

Gentle Raccoon watched the mourners walk the path to bring Sitting Bull to his final resting place—the final handshake. Unfettered tears poured from his eyes. The man had touched all who had been an intricate part of his life. He had been a loving and gentle father, a wise and gifted leader, and an inspiration to all around him. A patriot of the Lakota, with a spiritual essence of deep religious faith embedded in his soul—Sitting Bull would be a man never forgotten. Tatanka Iyotanka … his life, his blood, his being would continue through eternity.

Aho.

Chapter Twenty-Three

Matthew sat on his horse, overlooking the Pine Ridge reservation. He observed the movement in the Home Guard campsites that Governor Mellette had created to guard the homesteaders living near the reservation. They were armed cowboy militia ready for war, skirting the Pine Ridge reservation with anxious trigger fingers.

He had left Standing Rock bitter and disillusioned. Like the vision Sitting Bull had foreseen … he had been killed by his own people. Those who survived had fled to Chief Spotted Elk, Sitting Bull's half-brother, to seek protection.

Controversy and conflicting accounts concerning Sitting Bull's demise instigated heated debates. Matthew was appalled when he had read one newspaper account that claimed Sitting Bull "should have been hung higher than Haman," referring to biblical stories in Esther. How quickly they had forgotten that he was a man of peace and had developed a deep friendship with the white settlers. Instead, the papers encouraged racism and hatred toward the Indians.

Had Sitting Bull's death been planned? Did they manipulate the situation so the government and military would not be blamed for his death? The Indian Agent McLaughlin had to have known Sitting Bull would have rebelled against detainment. How far would the government go to steal the land from the Indians, to hide their greed … to silence those who might uncover the agents who filled their pockets for their own personal gain? Had there been an unspoken agreement to assassinate Sitting Bull?

Such dishonor and shameful behavior from his own people and government! Sitting Bull fought for the rights of the Indian against an unjust system. He had that right. This was America! This was not a fascist or communist country. He had that right to stand for his beliefs.

Matthew had known Sitting Bull all his life. He had never seen him waver in his beliefs. He had heard stories of his younger years when he had been a member and leader of the Strong Heart Warrior Society. At fourteen, he had experienced his first battle against the Crow.

As time passed, he had become concerned with tribal welfare and had become a member of the Silent Eaters. Sitting Bull was in his thirties when he had met Matthew's mother. A few years earlier, he had fought against American soldiers for the first time. Matthew was two years old when Sitting Bull became a chief.

Sitting around the campfire listening to legendary stories was one of Matthew's favorite pastimes when he visited with the Lakota. Smiling, he recalled his father's words telling a courageous tale of one of Sitting Bull's exploits.

The Lakota had been skirmishing with American soldiers on the Yellowstone River. The railroad was coming through, and the Indians had been pestering the soldiers. They knew it would be difficult for the white man if they caused havoc on the railroad line. They cut down telegraph lines, even before the repairmen were out of sight.

Groups of Lakota warriors would attack and then retreat, creating confusion. I was sitting with a group of Lakota when Sitting Bull had approached us. Sitting Bull was up to something. It was evident by the subtle glint of mischief in his eyes. He did not say a word to us.

Curious, the four of us followed Sitting Bull. We walked through the center of the battle lines to the edge and sat down on the ground as if we were ready to watch a show.

Without a word spoken, he pulled out his pipe. Unconcerned with his surroundings, Sitting Bull lit the pipe and passed it to me. We shared and enjoyed the smoke, watching the bullets whipping by us. After we smoked, he cleaned the pipe ... thoroughly. He smiled at each of us, and together we stood and casually walked to the Lakota side of the skirmish where we continued the battle with the soldiers who were guarding the railroad workers.

Matthew laughed. He wished he possessed that kind of audacity.

The trouble had not stopped there for Sitting Bull and the Lakota. The railroad and the discovery of gold had created more problems for his people. He had fought against the infiltration of prospectors and settlers who came to the Black Hills, the Paha Sapa. No one should ever have been searching for gold there. It was sacred land to the Lakota. The Fort Laramie Treaty had guaranteed that the Black Hills belonged to the Sioux tribes. Of course, that did not hinder the government. Once Custer had found gold, the announcement created a chaotic rush to the Paha Sapa.

The Lakota defended their land again.

Sitting Bull had been there, defending his people and defending their rights. By 1876, the Commissioner of Indian Affairs had ordered all Lakota onto reservations. The government considered Sitting Bull's refusal hostile and aggressive.

It was the government's greed, the hateful racism of the soldiers, and the putrid mind of one invidious man who had killed his father, Standing Deer. Matthew spit on the ground. George Armstrong Custer. At the Battle of Little Big Horn, American soldiers blindly followed their heretical leader into a massacre.

His mother had taken her own rifle and fought against her countrymen. The America that she loved and cherished was attacking her family and friends. The battle had changed them all. To this day, she was a voice, a very loud voice, defending the rights of the Native Americans in this time, and their own.

It still filled his heart with anger. Crazy Horse and Sitting Bull had tried to explain to the boy he had been, the lost soul he had become. His father had died a warrior's death defending his people, the women, children, and elders. At ten years old, Matthew had seen a reality no child should have had to see.

He closed his eyes against the vision of death before him and remembered the religious ceremony on the evening following the Little Big Horn battle. Sitting Bull had presided over the ceremony, praying for the souls of the lost warriors and the American soldiers who had fought and died in the battle.

The government had reacted fervently to the loss at the Little Big Horn. Thousands of soldiers and cavalry, dispatched to the Dakotas, relentlessly pursued the Lakota until, one by one, the Indians were forced to concede.

Sitting Bull had refused to surrender. He had taken his people to Canada and had remained there peacefully for over four years. He had returned, reluctant, arriving in Montana in the summer of 1881. His people could no longer survive in Canada. The buffalo were gone, the food scarce.

Matthew turned his horse to skirt Pine Ridge, wary of the Home Guard, wondering if he would be next on the list of casualties. He prayed all his letters were received with open minds. Hindsight made him glad he used his mother's maiden name, signing all the letters as Matthew Anderson. If he had signed them Gentle Raccoon, would he still be alive?

Trouble had already started with the Home Guard. He had heard they had sent snipers who had randomly shot into the Ghost Dancers at the Strong Hold.

Before Sitting Bull's death, the Home Guard had also cornered warriors from the Pine Ridge reservation, killing and scalping about seventy-five of the Ghost Dancers. There had been discriminate whispers of a massacre of Indians traveling in a wagon train to Buffalo Gap to visit non-Indian friends.

Gentle Raccoon was worried. Blood was boiling; the cauldron was filling with ingredients that would serve a dish of venomous tragedy. He had done everything he could to help bring awareness of the demise of the Lakota. He prayed for a quick response.

Congress was in session and had been for a few weeks. He had not been the only one sending pleas to the government on behalf of the Indians. Many had sent telegrams and letters beseeching them to honor the treaties and fulfill the promises the government had made. If the Lakota started receiving the promised compensation, it would reduce the hostilities and resentment and the Lakota could concentrate on issues that were more important.

A thriving reservation, full bellies, and healthy children would encourage a positive attitude among the people. The Lakota could then pursue their rights for freedom, to become citizens, to vote and become a part of the democracy.

Two Indians approached him as he edged his way closer to the reservation. Wary and ready for another encounter like the one he received at Standing Rock, Gentle Raccoon sat rigid on his horse. His right hand gripped the handle of his revolver. Their vigilant approach slowed to a canter.

"Do you have your papers?" the shorter one asked.

"I do not have a permission slip," he calmly said, distaste dripping from his words. "I do have a letter from Agent McLaughlin verifying who I am."

"You speak the Lakota tongue well, for a white man," the taller man commented, holding out his hand to take the letter.

"I shall hold on to it until we arrive inside the reservation."

The two sat silently and stared at Gentle Raccoon. After a few moments, they turned their horses about and told him to follow.

As they approached the entrance to the reservation, many eyes watched them in curiosity and unbidden hostility. Tension lay across the Home Guard campsite, a smothering blanket of festering resentment. The crowd stood a few feet from the horses as they passed.

One young boy who appeared to be in his mid-teen years lifted his gun, attempting to intimidate Matthew. Reining to a halt next to the boy, Matthew noted the reddish tone to the boy's cropped hair, the leprechaun green in his eyes. Without muttering a word, he pulled his hood back and leaned toward the boy, staring into his eyes.

The boy's eyes widened but he held his ground. Green eyes stared into green eyes, a ritual of stoic combat, until, after a few moments, the boy looked away. Confused, the young boy looked at Matthew's dark skin and dark hair, wondering if he was black Irish, curious about why he was at the reservation.

As the three rode away from the group, Matthew heard the boy comment to one of the Home Guard militia, "Did you see how green his eyes were? They were practically cousin to mine."

"Just means he's a half-breed, Squirt," someone replied.

"My mom says those are the ones who are dangerous. They are the ones who are going to ruin the country, thinking they have the right to walk about free … like they own the land."

"You mean, boy," another piped sarcastically "like the Irish immigrants coming into this country thinking they can take our jobs away from us? They think they have a right to be here, too."

Matthew turned around to find the boy jumping onto the man who had spoken, pummeling his face.

"I have every right to be here! My father is from Ireland. You take that back. This is a free country."

Another man dragged the boy off the older militiaman on the ground. The young boy looked at the three Indians and stared at Matthew. Looking around at the Home Guard militiamen, the boy shook his head in disgust.

"I should have kept going west with my folks. I quit."

Walking away from the group, he entered a tent and carried out his bags. Grabbing his horse, he mounted, kneed the horse, and rode away from the campsite.

The older militiaman shook his head. "Stupid Mick."

Matthew and his two escorts silently looked at each other. Turning away from the confrontation, they rode onto the reservation.

Chapter Twenty-Four

The freezing-cold winds rattled the windows of the cabin. Reunited, the group of friends sat around the fire warming their hands and sharing stories and memories of years gone by. Devry, Little Red Hawk, and his wife Christine, known on the reservation as Little Owl, had accompanied Karen to the Pine Ridge reservation. Devry was caressing the soft tuft of hair of Two Feathers' and Sings to the Wind's newborn baby. She had been listening intently to their colorful rendition of their courtship, until her mind wandered toward her desires for Matthew.

"Floating Flower … Devry." Spirit of the Mountain touched her arm, smiling. "Your thoughts must be pleasant, but Sings to the Wind asked you a question."

Sings to the Wind laughed a merry, knowing tickle. "I am not offended, Floating Flower, for I can see there are twinkling stars of love in your eyes. Who has caught your heart?"

Colors of melancholy dusted her features as she answered Sings to the Wind. "Matthew, Gentle Raccoon."

Sings to the Wind's eyes widened and her mouth shaped a surprised O. "Oh, that is a pickle! However," she paused as she hesitantly eyed Spirit of the Mountain, "it may not be all that much of a problem if you wait a few years."

"That was the decision, regardless of how I felt about it," Floating Flower sniffed.

"How does Gentle Raccoon feel about it?"

Sighing loudly, she responded. "He agreed with his mother, once she finished explaining her objections."

"I see." Sings to the Wind bit her lip, repressing her desire to sigh in relief. Her husband, Two Feathers, patted her hand.

Mixed feelings fluttered through her heart. Many years ago, she had traveled to the land of the Lakota with Spirit of the Mountain from another life, another time. She chose to leave that life and live with the man who owned her soul. It was a commitment that had been a hard, yet satisfying decision. However, she had also been much older than the fourteen-year-old young lady sitting before her.

Sings to the Wind believed Gentle Raccoon would not choose to live in this world. He might let the notion roll around for a while, but she doubted he would stay. That would mean Floating Flower would have to live in the modern world. That decision would bring a myriad of complications.

How would he get her a birth certificate and medical records proving her existence, a Social Security number or proof of school records? It had been hard enough to get Standing Deer's records created, but now it would be almost impossible. Since the war had started, security in the United States had become intense and thorough.

Sings to the Wind wondered when they would follow through with the plan, and how long Matthew was willing to wait.

As usual, Spirit of the Mountain read her mind. "When she is eighteen."

"Well, indeed. If both are willing to wait, a contract for arrangement could be written and signed. Just in case things don't quite work out," Sings to the Wind suggested.

Spirit of the Mountain stifled the urge to kick her friend and laughed at the childish antic in her thoughts. "Why don't we just wait until she turns eighteen and see if their desires and love still exist. This decision would lock them together forever." Her heart thundered and she licked her lips nervously. "Really, Sings to the Wind, divorce would never be an option. Think about it."

"Divorce?" the group echoed, appalled at the concept.

"I didn't even consider divorce. I never believed it was an option," Floating Flower's retort was scathing.

Spirit of the Mountain sighed. "The divorce rate in our world for couples who marry under the age of twenty is forty percent. For first marriages it's at fifty percent."

"Divorce is not an option," Floating Flower stated again.

"Our mode of transportation to this world is not to be used on a whim. It would be a rare occasion to visit your parents. Do you understand that? Do you understand that you can not visit your parents any time the desire comes to you?"

Floating Flower frowned while Spirit of the Mountain continued.

"I am not sure you would be able to return to your world without one of us. I do know that if you did, you would not be able to return to our world, unless one of us was with you." She sighed, tapping her fingers on her lip. "How to explain … everyone knows that I, Gentle Raccoon, and Sings to the Wind are not from *here*, that our world is different. Sings to the Wind was known as Bonnie, in our world. She chose to stay with the Lakota. If Sings to the Wind wanted to return, she would have to come with either me, or Gentle Raccoon. It took years before I was able to understand and control some aspects of our mode of travel. Floating Flower, I cannot guarantee that you would be able to return to your world, to this time. Or if you attempted to travel without us, if you would actually arrive where you wanted to."

"I'm confused."

Spirit of the Mountain laughed. "Yes, well, we get that way, too. From what we have figured out, a decision of destiny is, let us say … prearranged, for a lack of a better word. Once the traveler's destiny has been decided, some minor control is allowed."

"But, if you or Gentle Raccoon were with me, I could visit them?"

"Yes. We are not going to prohibit you from visiting your parents. It just cannot be done any time the mood strikes you. He and I both have a life in our world. There will be times when neither one of us can leave."

Floating Flower looked to her parents for confirmation. Both nodded that they understood she would not be able to visit on a regular basis. Sadness creased Little Red Hawk's forehead, and tears trickled silently from the corners of Little Owl's eyes.

Devoid of her usual sparkle, gloom etched Floating Flower's features as tears welled in her eyes. "That's not fair. I cannot choose between the love for my parents and my love for Gentle Raccoon."

The baby howled in protest. Floating Flower looked down at the infant and cooed an apology. She had not realized she had squeezed the baby. Tears poured from her eyes as she realized she might never have Gentle Raccoon's children. Floating Flower could never leave her parents, her home. It was all she knew.

"I'm not asking you to choose between your parents and Matthew. It will be a very complicated situation." Spirit of the Mountain shook her head. "I am not saying you will never see your parents again, either. Are you prepared to deceive all you meet in my world? Because that is exactly what you will have to do."

Spirit of the Mountain leaned forward. "Would your love for my son be strong enough to endure the tribulations you may encounter in our world? You would not be able to tell anyone who you really are or when you were born."

Floating Flower blinked in confusion. "Why?"

"Your answers would be neither acceptable nor believable. My world would attempt to put you in a home for the unstable or force you to go to a psychiatrist because they would consider you imbalanced."

"Have they done that to you?" Little Owl asked.

"No. However, no one knows my personal history in my world, except my immediate family." Pausing, she looked at her old friend. "Sings to the Wind knows because she is from the same world."

"Not even my parents?" Floating Flower expressed surprise.

"No, but they do know much more than most who live in this world. However, I do believe Two Feathers and your father have some serious suspicions." She replied, smiling.

Little Red Hawk smiled back and made a sad attempt to appear innocent of such knowledge. The group of friends laughed at his comical attempt. Floating Flower penetrated him with a stare, daring him to speak the truth. She bit her lip when he shook his head no; the words would never pass his lips. Looking toward Two Feathers, she noticed he was intently staring at his moccasins.

Floating Feather was earnest in her response, "I will not break the code of silence. My heart and my soul belong to Gentle Raccoon. I will wait until you believe I am ready and will do what is necessary."

Spirit of the Mountain smiled. "That makes my heart sing, Floating Flower. When the time comes, I will be honored to welcome you as my daughter."

"Well, I must say that makes me feel a bit better myself," Gentle Raccoon said as he entered the room.

Spirit of the Mountain jumped up and gave her son a hug. "How long have you been listening, Brat?"

Laughing, he shook his head. "I just heard Devry's, Floating Flower's vow, and your reply. I am surprised to see you here. I thought you would be going to Standing Rock first."

"We arrived at Standing Rock to find Sitting Bull had been killed," Little Red Hawk replied as he watched Gentle Raccoon greet everyone. "Gall told us you were on your way here."

"He said you were at the cabin but were not among those who were arrested," Little Owl queried, her tone pumping Gentle Raccoon for information.

Leaning against the arm of the couch, Gentle Raccoon's voice shook as he told the tale of Sitting Bull's death. He expressed his suspicions regarding the actions of the government, the Indian agents, and the Special Police.

"It was odd. I was there walking beside Shave Head of the Special Police when it started. Someone pushed me out of the fracas. What amazes me is that there was no one around me. It was as if invisible hands pushed me out of the way to protect me from the bullets whizzing through the air."

"The Great Spirit was there to protect you," Sings to the Wind smiled.

"We heard that over a hundred were arrested," Little Red Hawk added.

"Yes, and more will be. I'm surprised they haven't come here to the reservation to arrest those who came for refuge."

Two Feathers cocked a brow. "How did you escape arrest?"

"Two main reasons: Gall and Indian Agent McLaughlin."

"Son, did you go there to warn Sitting Bull?"

Gentle Raccoon shook his head. "I went to speak to him about stopping the Ghost Dancers. I did not know they had ordered his arrest. If I had known …"

Guilt plunged a dagger in his heart. Humiliated, he felt the tears swell in his eyes. If he had just kept his mouth shut, would Sitting Bull still be alive? Was it his fault?

"I had told him that the people needed him. By stopping the Ghost Dancers, maybe he could have avoided getting arrested, prevented the people from getting hurt." His voice caught in a grip of anguish.

"Don't blame yourself!" the room exclaimed in unison.

"It is not your fault," Little Owl stressed. "You had no control over the decisions of the military or the Indian agent."

"You were doing what anyone would have done. Alerting a friend that they had gone too far," Floating Flower pleaded.

"It wasn't supposed to happen!" His voice bled guilt-ridden drips of pain. He looked at his mother and whispered, "He wasn't supposed to die."

"This had been planned for a long time. Anyone who rebels is asking for death. Sitting Bull would not stop the Ghost Dancers because that would have been against his principles, but he would have left the reservation to avoid further disruption," Two Feathers sputtered in anger.

"Yes, which is why he most likely packed up to leave," Spirit of the Mountain said quietly.

"He must have been under surveillance. Someone had to have been watching him. We packed everything at night when we could not be seen."

"Could someone have betrayed him to the Special Police?"

"Crow Foot, Sitting Bull, and I were the only ones who knew he planned to leave."

"The Special Police had to have been watching him then." Little Red Hawk nodded.

Gentle Raccoon asked Two Feathers. "What has Red Cloud said about all of this?"

"In the beginning, Red Cloud encouraged the Ghost Dancers. In the last few months, he has rallied against it. As more and more soldiers have come to the reservation, he worries for the welfare and safety of his people. He has invited Chief Spotted Elk to the reservation to help him establish peace between the people and the government."

Gentle Raccoon absorbed the fervor radiating from his friends. He rubbed his face in exhaustion and leaned back against the couch. What more could be said? He did not look forward to the treacherous days ahead.

Chapter Twenty-Five

The wind howled a soul-wrenching song as Gentle Raccoon stared at the fire. Spirit of the Mountain was quietly speaking with Two Feathers and Sings to the Wind about their visit with Red Cloud. The three of them had spent the morning discussing Lane Parker, the murders, and reminiscing about the old days.

Lane had hit a brick wall. The murders had stopped and evidence was nonexistent. Brandt had been the last victim. The murderer lay dormant, ever since Lane and Lydia had exchanged their vows. According to his mother, Lane had done a thorough search of Mrs. Enlow's house.

If it was Mrs. Enlow, she was not working alone. Who could it be? Who could possibly mastermind such a premeditated scheme? Gentle Raccoon bit his lip promising himself that he would help Lane when he returned to Tokata.

Two Feathers was discussing the movement of military forces in and around Pine Ridge. After listening to Red Cloud, Gentle Raccoon had decided to ride out and find Black Elk and encourage him to come to the reservation.

* * *

Red Cloud had fought in his younger years against the United States government. Many years ago, he had told his father, Standing Deer, that the only way for the Indian to survive was to fight the white man's way. Red Cloud heeded his own words and learned the way of the white man. He had surrendered his gun and became a warrior for the Lakota, a diplomat. He was a successful and influential official who used his power to fight for the rights of the Indian.

Red Cloud had restrained himself from picking up his rifle to fight against the government, even after Custer's massacre, and the loss of the sacred Black Hills. He used his power to fight for the Lakota on the reservations, making life difficult for the Indian agents.

Now, it had come down to the issues with the Ghost Dancers. Red Cloud withdrew his encouragement. Many criticized his actions but Gentle Raccoon understood his stand. One did not have to lose their Lakota heart when one accepted the ways of the white man. The combination could make a very powerful soul.

Would he be able to reach an understanding with Black Elk? He had to try. Gentle Raccoon took a deep breath. He could not lose another to the hatred and racism of this world.

Red Cloud had told him Black Elk had originally been against the Ghost Dance ceremony. Over time, the need for discovery enticed him to learn about the ceremony and to uncover what was inspiring the Lakota. Once Black Elk had started participating in the Ghost Dance, he had taken the beliefs to his heart.

A large group watched as the two men hugged and greeted each other jovially. Turning to the group, Black Elk introduced his old friend, Gentle Raccoon, to the men sitting in a circle around the fire. Black Elk said a prayer holding his pipe with both hands raised to the heavens. Reaching to his bag for tobacco, he carefully prepared his pipe and passed it among the circle of friends.

"Sit here, *kola*." Black Elk pointed to an open space next to him.

They spoke of cherished memories and childish pranks from days gone by. They reminisced fourteen years of friendship, bonding once again through the laughter, fondness, and tears. Black Elk spoke about his trip to Europe and his days with Buffalo Bill.

"It was exciting and it was unsettling. As we traveled across the country on the iron horse, each rest was a larger town surrounded by many buildings and many whites."

Black Elk described the homes and crush of people, and his amazement at the use of the power of lightning to illuminate the hotel rooms. The streets were so bright that when he looked to the skies after sunset, he could not see the stars. Many voices and loud noises surrounded them, and they could not hear the music of the night creatures. He could not smell the fresh clean air of the land.

Gentle Raccoon listened, enthralled by the colorful scenes unfolding before him.

"They treated us fairly but there was much selfishness in the people living in the city. We spent the winter months in New York City and we performed in exquisite regalia, enjoying the races, dances, and some of the recreated battles."

Black Elk's features creased with dismay and sadness. "They had white men in a prison with guards watching them as if they were wild animals. It reminded me of the reservations, where my people are prisoners of the white man. Gentle Raccoon, I do not understand," he shook his head, "I do not understand why the white man would put his own people in cages."

After Gentle Raccoon explained the white man's penal system, Black Elk grimaced. He opposed such a system, his upbringing making it difficult to comprehend the necessity of such inhumane treatment. He smiled and looked forward to another time and a rigorous, healthy debate between the Lakota's ways and the white man's beliefs.

"Many had returned to the Lakota Territory when they decided not to travel to Europe. However, I desired to see more of the world. I believed that if I traveled to Europe it would help me understand the white man's way and why he lived as he did.

"It frightened us when we traveled across the great waters of the Atlantic. For many weeks, all I could see was the ocean and feared we would never return. I worried that we would never see land again. Many of our people became ill and began to sing their death songs.

"A storm had blown the ship about and the wasicu laughed at our fears, but their laughter did not last long. The storm continued for many hours. The sailors worked fast, running down the passageways. Those on the deck had ropes tied around their waists."

Black Elk took a drink from his flask. "The men, they gave us these … I do not know what they are called … they were to be used if we had to leave the boat and go in the water …"

"Floatation devices," Gentle Raccoon prompted.

"Yes, I believe that is what they called them. I refused to put mine on. Instead, I dressed in my best clothes and sang my death song. If I were to die, I would die as a brave warrior.

"But, we did survive, and the sailors worked hard to repair damages from the storm. Many days passed before we saw land. I was on the deck when I heard someone call 'Land ho.' Another ship approached ours; many men boarded. They searched the boat. I do not know what they lost, but they did not find it.

"We did not leave the ship until the next day. We had performed for many crowds. One day, everyone was very excited. The Queen was coming to see the performance. We had to do our best. After the show, Queen Victoria invited us to her home. Later that day ... we learned it was an honor that she had chosen to speak to us."

Gentle Raccoon handed Black Elk the pipe. For a few moments, Black Elk became lost in his private thoughts.

"We got lost the day we were to return home and missed the ship. We knew the only way we would be able to come home would be to make more of the white man's money. We trekked through Europe working for different people, trying to make enough money for our voyage.

"One day, after many months of living in Europe, someone told us Buffalo Bill had returned to England. We went to England and found him. He has a generous heart, understood our desires to return home, to Pine Ridge and our families. He gave us money and bought our passage. We had a wonderful experience and many laughs in Europe, but it is so very good to be home. My heart ached to be with my family."

"Every path has its puddles." Gentle Raccoon grinned at the memories the group had shared.

"Indeed, and just as much fun to jump in them and scatter the droplets, soaking everyone around you," Black Elk laughed.

"What has been happening the last few months, Black Elk?" Gentle Raccoon asked.

A frown creased his face. "Too many dark clouds have come to the Lakota people while I was gone."

Black Elk explained how they had camped on Wounded Knee, White Clay, and Grass Creek. They had moved about to avoid the military soldiers stationed at Pine Ridge. They followed them wherever they camped, trying to stop the Ghost Dancers.

"Friends had come to tell us there would be a meeting with the Indian agent and soldiers. I had not gone to the meeting, but later, they informed me of the agreement. The agents, they claimed they did not want to prohibit the Ghost Dance. They requested that the Lakota not dance every day. The Ghost Dance ceremony could continue, but only once a month. They also informed us that we were required to find employment, make the white man's money.

"How, when we do not work the white man's way? We do not have the knowledge to live like the white man. I do not have the desire to learn. This is who I am."

Black Elk refilled the pipe and passed it to Gentle Raccoon. "The day after the meeting, Good Thunder and I received a warning of our impending arrest," Black Elk nodded toward the other warrior. "We rode to the Brule's camp, on Wounded Knee, and stayed with them. With them, we moved camp a few more times. Father Kraft found us on the White River and asked the warriors and families to return to Pine Ridge. We did not listen and had continued moving camp until American Horse and Fast Thunder arrived. They told us that we needed to return to Pine Ridge. Many of the Brules had refused and tried to keep the group from leaving. As we returned to Pine Ridge, we heard about Sitting Bull."

Gentle Raccoon passed the pipe to the next warrior. Black Elk and he stared into the fire, sharing a moment of silence.

"And here you are," Black Elk proclaimed.

"Are you still performing the Ghost Dance? I heard soldiers were shooting into the dancers."

"Yes, we are."

"In the morning, will you join us in the Ghost Dance, Gentle Raccoon?" Good Thunder asked.

Gentle Raccoon bit his lip as he considered the invitation. He was not convinced of the validity of the ceremony. From what he had heard, the Lakota believed it would be the end of the world for the white man. He could not accept that belief. He knew in his heart it would not be that way, so what was the ceremony for? Was it just a last fruitless effort grasping for hope? Did it have a greater meaning beyond the bitterness that had started it?

"I am not convinced that it is a true religious ceremony. Enlighten me."

"I had to see for myself," Black Elk intoned. "So should you, Gentle Raccoon." Black Elk understood his skepticism. "I too had found it hard to believe when I had first heard of the Ghost Dance ceremony. I had shrugged it off as foolish propaganda, the despair of those who dreamed of the return to the old ways.

"I became more curious as the ceremony swept through the Lakota Nation, as a storm cleans the air. Tales and stories from respected and reputable men blazed through the different tribes. The Wanekia could make animals talk and spirit visions for all to see. Yellow Shirt spoke of a vision he had shown the people. Everyone but one man had seen the same vision of green pastures and flowering trees. The grass had been deep and the buffalo plenty.

"Many had resisted, even after they heard about the first Ghost Dance that Kicking Bird had held on the Cheyenne, and then at Wounded Knee. Once they had gone to Wounded Knee they were amazed at the essence of joy they felt as they approached the Ghost Dancers."

The next morning Black Elk stood next to Gentle Raccoon. Before him in the center was a tree, sleeping in the winter months, with dead leaves scattered among its branches, painted red, as were other sacred objects offered to the Great Spirit.

Gentle Raccoon watched the ceremony unfold as the dancers approached, their faces painted red, some with a half-moon painted on the side. The men wore Ghost Shirts, the women ceremonial Ghost dresses.

The clothing for the dancers was red and decorated with the gifts of nature, the sleeves and necklines fringed with feathers. Animals, birds, the sun, and stars painted in detail, their tribute to the gifts of the Great Spirit. Everything used had come from and was a part of the land, a part of nature.

A Brule was chosen to lead the ceremony. He quietly spoke to those around him who had elected to dance. When he had completed his instruction, the dancers formed a circle holding hands as they walked around the sacred tree.

They sang sacred songs and chanted, "*Ate, Wau.*" Father, I come. "*Hunku, Wau.*" Mother, I come.

The songs and chanting stopped. For a few moments, silence enveloped the sacred grounds. Piercing cries of sorrow interrupted the serenity. It shredded the air, shattering the peacefulness of the moment. The Ghost Dancers screamed, howled, and cried. Their mournful sorrows, their grief, sent chills up Matthew's spine as they called the names of their lost relatives and loved ones. After bending down and grabbing a handful of dirt, they prayed as they threw the dirt in the air—the Mother Earth dusting their bodies. With hands clasped together, they raised them as one, never breaking the circle. The Ghost Dancers looked to the heavens as they cast their prayers to the Great Spirit.

The Brule chosen to lead the ceremony entered the center of the circle and prayed. He encouraged those experiencing the Ghost Dance for the first time to set their minds free, to allow the Great Spirit into their hearts and souls. He would not forsake them.

Circling the sacred tree, the Ghost Dancers increased their momentum as they rushed with clasped hands. They continued running and chanting until one by one they broke from the circle and fell, staggering away or collapsing unconscious. Warriors aided those who experienced a vision, to walk to the sacred tree, where they described to all what they had seen.

Stunned, Matthew watched the dancers. Most walked away disgruntled or disappointed. He resented the ascetic farce of what had happened before his eyes. If any government official from D.C. had seen this, they would laugh and throw up their hands wondering why they had bothered to feel threatened by the Ghost Dancers.

Not that Gentle Raccoon belittled the beliefs of the Ghost Dancers. If that is what they needed to keep their faith, then they should continue with the ceremony. The white man would never understand the need of the People. However, it was not for him.

He shook his head no. Looking at Black Elk, he carefully considered his words. "I see no threat for the Ghost Dancers to continue. It is not for me, my friend. I believe I will prepare to enter the sweat lodge tomorrow morning. Would you join me?"

Black Elk nodded in agreement.

Chapter Twenty-Six

Gentle Raccoon had not eaten since his decision to enter the sweat lodge. His stomach grumbled its objections as he gathered willow branches and sticks while he prayed for a shred of light in answer to his many questions. Silently praying, Black Elk prepared the pit where he would place the hot rocks.

Gentle Raccoon placed his father's pipe and knives on the altar in front of the opening to the sweat lodge. He crawled through the opening into the pitch darkness of the lodge and acknowledged Black Elk with a nod.

Removing his clothes, he sat cross-legged on a blanket near the pit. The fire pit represented the center of the universe. He closed his eyes, preparing himself for the ceremony. Rocking, he felt a kinship with Mother Earth. He prayed to the four corners of the world. He prayed to the Supreme Being.

He slowly relaxed, preparing for the meditation, praying in the tongue of the Lakota. Silently, he repeated the words from his Catholic faith, singing Lakota songs as well as songs he had learned in church. Starting at his feet, he moved slowly to relax the tension, as he made his way up to his temples.

Gentle Raccoon felt the chilled breeze of autumn and saw the leaves turn their bright colors as they fell from the trees. Snow covered the grounds, the branches remained bare, as they slept through the winter. As spring entered, the deep green buds of the trees appeared, the grasses grew, flowers bloomed, and the animals scurried upon the branches of the trees. Summer arrived and the vision was lush and full of life.

The warmth and radiance of the hot rocks in the pit comforted him. Warm as the morning sun, strong as the river, he felt the holiness of the Supreme Being. In a distant memory, wisps of a dream, he heard the song of the mockingbird. The music of Mother Earth joined the solitary voice and filled his senses with a symphony only nature could offer.

Gentle Raccoon lay on the blanket, pillowing his arms under his head and bending his legs, curled up as a newborn baby. He lay naked, taking nothing with him on his spiritual journey. He humbled himself to the Higher Power as he prepared himself for the nurturing and cleansing of his body, heart, and soul.

Thunder and wind rolled across the skies. Gentle Raccoon stood atop the Badlands overlooking the land of the Lakota. Ominous darkness shrouded him. He saw changing shadows as a dark and sullen gloom covered the earth before him. He watched as the hue slowly changed, as the gentle fingers of the One added color to the land. The sun blazed high in the sky before him. Blinded, he covered his eyes.

A deep, melodious voice spoke to him. *A new world will come, one of shining hope for all.*

Gentle Raccoon sailed to the sacred grounds in the Paha Sapa, the sacred Black Hills. He stood alone looking toward the heavens. Awed, he watched as round, colorful spectra drifted as snowflakes from the sky. Thousands of tiny shimmering balls swooped across his line of vision, creating a rainbow. They danced into, but never filled, the large gold caldron before him.

The flames flickered under the sparkling gold caldron. As the fire danced, the colors of the rainbow licked and opened to the gifts of the spectra. Glistening silver fingers from the flames caught those that strayed and gently guided them back into the caldron.

Above him, the sky burned with the colors of the rainbow as the caldron formed a dome of prismatic fluorescence. Falling on his knees in the presence of this gift to him, Gentle Raccoon watched as a large bald eagle ascended from the caldron. The head of the eagle had not yet turned fully white as the majestic bird bowed his head toward Gentle Raccoon.

It rose higher, and Gentle Raccoon saw that it clutched two flags, one in each claw. In one, the eagle held a Lakota flag, unlike the flag in his world. This flag was ecru with a large circle surrounding an eagle holding two spears. One of the spears was red, the other white. The flag's border matched the ecru background, the colors of the rainbow shimmering off its fringes.

The other claw clutched the American flag.

Gentle Raccoon stared, humbled at the sight before him. Skyward, the eagle circled him, the flags becoming its wings. It called to him … "One nation—united. *Mitakuye Oyasin*, we are all related."

Toward the heavens, the eagle flew … fading into the sun as Gentle Raccoon slowly returned from his vision.

He was reborn, enlightened with the hope and faith gifted to him by the Supreme Being. He would now have the strength to carry any burden. His spirit was set free, and the gladness of the Holy Spirit touched his soul. Serenity emanated from him as he gave himself into the hands of the Great Spirit. He hoped he would see his vision come to be in his lifetime.

The two friends prayed together, and once outside the sweat lodge, Gentle Raccoon described his vision to Black Elk. They sat quietly, discussing its meaning. Gentle Raccoon was confident in their conclusions. After all, it was the day before Christmas. Would this not be the season to reach the highest level of spiritual enlightenment?

As evening dangled, a crier informed the camp that Spotted Elk approached with almost four hundred people from his and Sitting Bull's band. They had been running from the soldiers and were starving and freezing. Spotted Elk was very sick; they were bringing him in on a travois. They could not keep running, and had agreed to allow the soldiers to escort them to Wounded Knee Creek. They would be arriving in a few days. There were less than one hundred warriors. The rest of the band consisted of women, children, and the elderly. The people rushed to gather extra food and gifts to offer the members of Spotted Elk's group.

Black Elk's mother approached with a package.

"Here you are, Gentle Raccoon."

"Thank you." Opening the package, he inhaled in elation. "It is exquisite."

"I have some packages to bring with you when you leave tonight to give your mother. Stop by the lodge before you leave?"

"I will. Thank you so much. It is beautiful."

Black Elk leaned over to see what was hidden in the package. His mother had made an ornamental hairbrush. The carved handle had wings outstretched, and beads of red, yellow, white, and black circled the outer edge.

He nudged Gentle Raccoon, mischief springing in his eyes. "Who is this for?"

"It is a Christmas present for the woman of my life—whom I can't touch for four more years."

Black Elk's eyes widened. "Four years! That is a long time to wait. I'm not sure I could wait that long."

His mother patted him on the shoulder. "You would if you had to." Kissing Gentle Raccoon and her son on their cheeks, she strolled toward her lodge.

Black Elk stared expectantly at his friend. With a deep sigh, Gentle Raccoon explained the love story.

His friend was silent for so long, Gentle Raccoon was not sure what to think.

"*Kola*, my friend, I wish you good fortune and love. If you have to wait four years to have the life partner you desire, then so be it. The magic moments you shared will be a cherished memory to warm you at night. Something to look forward to again."

Gentle Raccoon rolled his eyes at Black Elk.

Laughing, he responded. "It sounded good!"

"Four years of celibacy does not sound comforting to me at all. I like having sex. I like a lot of sex. There is just one major problem. Every time I look at an attractive woman, I see Floating Flower and I feel as if I am betraying her."

"What if Spirit of the Mountain is right, and this is a young girl's infatuation? Or possibly, her desire is inspired more from rebellion, wanting the forbidden? No promise has been made."

"My mother made many good points in her argument. You are correct. A promise of betrothal has not been made. However, she is everything a man could desire. Every day that I worked at the ranch, I could not wait to go home and be with her. My life was already a good life. With her, it was fantastical, mystical; everything around me had a clarity and sharpness that I had never noticed before. Then …" Gentle Raccoon inhaled deeply, "Then I found out her age. I thought my life had ended. It was as if a cannon had blown up in my face."

Black Elk nodded. "If it is meant to be … *aho.*"

Chapter Twenty-Seven

Floating Flower sat wrapped in a wool blanket on the seat in front of the cabin, staring in the direction from which Gentle Raccoon would approach. Smiling to herself, she felt a warm sensation stir her heart and fill her with happiness. It had not been very long ago that she believed she could not wait to hold him forever, and never let him go. Now her heart was willing to wait as long as the wind commanded ... four long years along a winding path that would lead to their shared eternity.

The breath of time would have him for a while. Would the winds bring him back to her? She would gladly sacrifice her life, her heart, and her home to be with him in his world. As she watched him the other afternoon, she could understand that it was not time for them to share a blanket. Floating Flower ached to have him back in her arms again. As he walked the winding path, would she lose him and never hear the words she longed for him to say? That he loved her and would cherish her forever?

Could she live without him? She had him and then someone had ripped him from her arms. She would never forget his face when he had learned her age. Since that day, he had avoided her. Sometimes she would see him smile. At others times, she saw sorrow in his eyes.

So many nights she had sat, waiting for him to come, keeping so many of her dreams deep inside. She sat alone in the dark, searching, and now he was here. He brightened her life, gave her confidence that her dreams would become reality. In four years, he would belong to her. She had to keep that hope and continue with her life.

When would she have the chance to say she loved him? It could not be wrong to love him, not when it felt so very right. The path in front of them would be long. The winds of time would soon lift them up and they would have their time together. She had to stop looking behind her and know that the here and now would be a long and hard path. Until the day they would unite as one, so much time would pass.

A lone rider approached. He rode as one with the mount and she knew instinctively that it was her man. Tying the horse to the post, he advanced toward her and smiled.

"Is the pleasure mine, knowing you have been waiting in this freezing cold weather for me?"

Floating Flower nodded, shy and embarrassed but full of gladness that he was here, safely standing in front of her.

Sitting down next to her, she opened the blanket and they sat cuddled together in the warmth.

"We have to talk, Devry."

"I know. I am prepared to listen to your words." Her voice shook as she braced herself for the words she did not want to hear.

"I have a path I must follow before I become a husband and father. I have a dream to help change the world. I am a dreamer, but I am also a warrior. Ignorance is our enemy and I shall fight it. I know I cannot fix all the wrongs in the world, but if I can help, then I will have passed on a legacy."

"It is an admirable goal. Do not call it a dream, for you can help many people."

"Do not worry. I will not allow myself to see this as a hopeless cause. I do not know how I am going to accomplish it yet, but I have ideas ... different ideas about spreading knowledge to all and squashing ignorance. I do not care how far the path takes me. It will be a lifelong task. When my time has come to face the Creator, I will know I fought for a good cause. Although some men will scorn me, I will face my Creator with battle scars and achieve the impossible. He will know I fought for the right causes with faith and courage."

She kissed his cheek. "I believe in you."

"My wife must have the same beliefs and join me in the fight."

Floating Flower nodded. The wind increased as the temperature dropped. The night air stung her feet, but she could not move, could not interrupt his words, now that he had finally started opening his heart to her.

"I cannot ask for your hand in marriage. Yet. The people I call friends and family have helped me become the man that I am. Through each passing page of my life, I want my wife to be there when times are hard, but we as a couple must make it through the bumps and storms. At the end of the day, I want to know that through it all, whatever the reasons, my wife will be there to share in all the pain and glory.

"Here in this world you are a woman; in my world, you are a child with much to learn. If we still love each other when the time comes and feel our love is strong enough to devote ourselves to being man and wife, then I shall make my offer to your father for your hand."

"As you wish, my love."

Kissing her on the forehead, he departed to tend the horse before he went inside the house.

Chapter Twenty-Eight

Christmas had come and gone, the cherished gifts shared. Gentle Raccoon and Spirit of the Mountain had returned to their world to spend the holiday with their family. Somehow, they had managed to return with bundles of blankets for some of the Indians on the reservation. Gentle Raccoon had just given his last three blankets to a family in need when he heard of the arrival of Chief Spotted Elk. The Seventh Cavalry with Major Whiteside leading the escort had brought them to Wounded Knee Creek.

Spotted Elk arrived in Major Whiteside's ambulance, tended by a doctor, a token of compassion for the chief. The major ordered tents and rations for those who did not have housing and needed to ease their hunger, in addition to blankets, clothing, and other necessities.

Gentle Raccoon watched as two traders passed by in a wagon, a barrel of whiskey and unmarked crates in the back, heading toward Wounded Knee. He clenched his jaw. Over five hundred drunken soldiers and officers did not bode well. Kicking his horse into a gallop, he raced to Two Feathers' cabin.

Whistling a warning of trouble, Gentle Raccoon dismounted as Two Feathers and his mother ran out the door. "We need to follow that wagon, there's trouble coming."

The three raced toward Wounded Knee. Two Feathers, Spirit of the Mountain, and Gentle Raccoon arrived to observe the soldiers niggling and harassing the Indians. Colonel Forsythe had commanded the soldiers to place Gatling and Hotchkiss guns on the hill, strategically aimed directly at the lodges. The menacing guns surrounded the Spotted Elk camp.

They watched stunned as soldiers, unsteady on their feet from the whiskey, entered Spotted Elk's lodge and struggled to haul him through the opening. The American flag and the flag of truce next to his lodge flapped in the cool breeze. Spotted Elk, known to the white soldiers as Big Foot, kicked and struggled as they dragged him across the ground. His weakness from pneumonia had left him feckless in his attempt to get away from the drunken soldiers.

"What the f ..."

"Matthew!" His mother admonished, though she had silently spoken the same words.

Spirit of the Mountain slid from her horse and ran past the piles of guns, knives, and bows and arrows that the soldiers had already confiscated. Bitter cries of revenge from the soldiers sliced the air. They would revenge the death of the Seventh Cavalry at Little Big Horn. Hoots of encouragement came from another group of soldiers enjoying the drama unfolding before them.

Grabbing one soldier, she knocked him on the ground and barreled her way toward Spotted Elk. "Leave him alone! Can't you see he is ill?"

Two Feathers approached the malicious group. A soldier turned to him and spit, "Get your white whore out of here."

Gentle Raccoon sizzled hatred as the soldiers laughed. While they were distracted, Spotted Elk's wife discreetly and silently helped him back to his lodge.

Behind Two Feathers a soldier added, "No reason why we can't take turns with the white whore."

"No reason why you can't die young," Gentle Raccoon spit venomously at the soldiers.

The soldier replied as he lifted his rifle toward Gentle Raccoon's heart. "Are you threatening us?"

"Are you threatening my mother?"

"Come." Spirit of the Mountain pleaded and pulled on his arm, not budging his strong bulk. "Come, this is not wise."

"Listen to your mommy, half breed."

Just as Gentle Raccoon jumped toward the soldier, four Lakotas caught him and dragged him away.

"What is wrong with you?" Spirit of the Mountain hissed. "Who cares what they think?"

Turning toward the soldier who had dragged Spotted Elk from his sick bed, she concentrated. The soldier flew back as if a wild horse had hit him. Jumping to his feet, he looked about to see who had knocked him down. No one was near him. Puzzled, he wiped the dirt from his uniform and strolled back to the barrel of whiskey.

Gentle Raccoon laughed. "God! I wish I had your gifts."

Smiling coyly, she quipped, "Gifts used wisely."

The next morning, in Two Feathers' cabin, Gentle Raccoon, Spirit of the Mountain, Floating Flower, and Sings to the Wind joined each other in breaking their fast. Floating Flower had just heard the news of what had happened the night before. Her face was mottled in displeasure.

"What?" Gentle Raccoon snapped.

"Did you not just tell me you had a world to change?" Floating Flower cried. "They would not have hesitated in putting a bullet through you. Do you think your death now would help you accomplish your goal? Your behavior was reckless."

"All they need is one little excuse, Gentle Raccoon," Sings to the Wind pleaded.

"We don't want to lose you," Floating Flower whispered.

Chapter Twenty-Nine

A bugle sounded, awakening the campsite on the cool morning of the 29th day of December, in the year 1890. The people gathered in the center to listen to the announcement. Warriors carried Spotted Elk from his lodge and seated him at the opening, assuring his comfort.

A soldier came forward and read the proclamation.

"... Spotted Elk and his followers shall receive escort to Pine Ridge, will be taken to Omaha by train, and placed in a military prison. By order of the United States, you are to surrender all your weapons."

The Lakota warriors warily surveyed the surrounding hills. Anticipating trouble, the soldiers were alert. The Gatling and Hotchkiss guns were poised as omens of what would be if they resisted. Without qualms, the warriors, one by one, placed their weapons in a pile in the center. Soldiers smiled glibly at the effortless surrender. Others, who had known the Lakota warriors, knew it had been too easy.

"Bring the men to the center of the camp."

Herded in a cluster, they stood cautious and watchful for any possible deception.

"Search the lodges and warriors for any hidden weapons!" The Lieutenant pointed to the left of Spotted Elk's lodge. "I want the women, children, and elderly on this side."

The soldiers carried out bundles of supplies and carelessly threw them to the ground, ripping them to shreds as they searched. Knives, axes, anything considered a weapon was confiscated and loaded into a wagon, ready to be taken to Headquarters. With the exception of a handful of carefully hidden weapons, the Indians were helplessly disarmed.

Yellow Bird started yelling his protests, stirring others to also voice their objections. In the middle of the uproar, he started dancing and singing Ghost Dance songs. Chanting in the Lakota language, he ridiculed the white soldiers, telling them that their weapons would not harm them.

Black Coyote, who was deaf and did not understand what was happening, began grappling with a soldier who had attempted to take his weapon. "No. This rifle is mine. I worked hard making white man's money so I could buy it."

Holding the rifle with both hands, he yanked it away from the young soldier. He raised it over his head in resentment, his thumb on the trigger. Several soldiers wrestled with him to confiscate it.

One of the soldiers watching the ordeal fired a shot. Before the reverberation of the bullet faded, another rifle discharged. The soldiers watched as an officer went down. Another officer raised his rifle and shot Spotted Elk.

The warriors raced with instinctual speed toward the pile of firearms and the wagons that held the weapons. They yelled to the women and children, "Take cover! Go! Go! Hide in the ravines!"

Soldiers and warriors lifted rifles and handguns and opened fire. The Hodgekiss guns boomed as bloodcurdling screams from men, women, and children permeated the air. Shrapnel tore deadly wounds in both the soldiers and Lakota.

The confined warriors and the soldiers guarding them in the center of the camp fell from the onslaught of bullets. Warriors, some on hands and knees, scrambled toward the pile of weapons. Knives not confiscated sliced and tore wounds with deadly precision. Fists, sticks, and rocks became deadly weapons.

Terror exploded and pounded innocent people. The world collapsed around their feet as many watched dead bodies fall from hatred. Smoke burned their eyes, blinding them, as they fought the white soldiers. The sight, sound, and smell of burning flesh filled their senses. Blood bubbled from the victims and seeped from the ground. Thunder from the cannons rumbled around them; the screams of children and women would haunt their memories for the rest of their days.

Instincts of self-preservation and survival scattered those who could run. Women grabbed any child within reach and ran toward the ravine. They rushed toward the trees, struggling to escape the mayhem. A handful of elders courageously surrounded the pregnant women, attempting to protect future generations.

A young mother crawled toward the opening of Spotted Elk's lodge. Bullets pelted her. The mother's arms cradled her infant, still drinking from her breast and oblivious to the lifelessness of the body that held him.

The roar of the cannons subsided, trickling to an eerie silence.

Soldiers beckoned to those in hiding to show themselves. "Come out! It is safe to return to the campsite."

Young children and toddlers warily came forward. Shots rang out as those who had exited their hiding places were killed where they stood.

* * *

"Cannons!" Sings to the Wind exclaimed, looking toward her husband, Two Feathers.

"Oh my God, no!" Spirit of the Mountain prayed.

Chaos slammed through Two Feathers' peaceful home as everyone scattered. Gentle Raccoon and Two Feathers ran to the storage room and returned with rifles, bows and arrows clasped in their hands. Rifle in hand, Spirit of the Mountain opened the door to the cabin. Floating Flower looked on in horror as her parents clung to each other, Little Red Hawk's rifle clenched in his hands.

"You're not going anywhere, Mother."

She looked at her son and laughed as she ran to her horse. "It's good to know you still have such a good sense of humor."

Two Feathers snorted, "Like you could stop her."

The four raced toward Wounded Knee Creek, weapons primed and ready. On the way, they encountered Black Elk and a group of Lakota heading in the same direction. Black Elk was dressed in his sacred shirt, his face painted red. A single eagle feather attached to his hair bounced as they joined in the ride together.

Gentle Raccoon noticed that Black Elk did not carry a gun. He reprimanded himself for not carrying an extra one. He had a sick feeling they would need it. As they rode as fast as the horses could carry them, more warriors joined the group. Approximately twenty riders now raced toward the unknown, fearing the worst.

A lone warrior rode toward them and they stopped as one to hear the news.

"They are murdering them! They are shooting them all down like target practice. Men, women, and children are being slaughtered without care. Those who have not been shot down are running this way."

At that announcement, the unknown warrior turned his horse and raced toward Pine Ridge.

They arrived at the top of the ridge. A few groups of women and children had already passed them. An elderly couple strained to climb the hill where the church stood. In the distance, they witnessed cavalrymen riding along the ravine, shooting at the Lakota trying to hide. They watched them shoot into the pine trees, riddling the women and children one by one.

The persistent pounding of the cannons was deafening. The screams clenched their hearts. Hiding behind the ridge, they made their plans. Black Elk said a prayer as the resounding blasts boomed.

Over the ridge they charged as one, yelling, "Courage, take courage!"

They raced toward the closest group of soldiers, who were guarding a small group of Lakota. Gentle Raccoon took out his revolver and shot at a soldier. Two Feathers and Red Hawk lifted their rifles in pure offensive maneuvers. Three of the cavalrymen who had seen Black Elk's group attack turned their guns toward them.

Spirit of the Mountain lifted her rifle. Without hesitation, she dropped a soldier off his horse. Direct and clean, the bullet hit the man between the eyes. The Lakotas detained by the three soldiers ran to the ravine.

Moving closer to the conflict, Black Elk abruptly turned his horse around. Dismounting, he picked up a baby that was lying on top of his lifeless mother, wrapped it in the covers that had fallen beside her, and hid the child.

Lakota warriors started converging from different areas of the reservation. Taking turns, they charged and pounded the white soldiers with waves of feral combat, thrusting into a gurge of attacks. Each new surge of warriors coming from different angles compelled the soldiers to retreat.

Grabbing their horses, the soldiers raced toward the center of the campsite where the major conflict was still transpiring.

Spirit of the Mountain and Gentle Raccoon rode along the ravine, following the retreating soldiers. They were appalled at the wounded and dead bodies of the women and children in the ravine. Rancor pulsed in their blood, revenge in their hearts. As the soldiers retreated, the group rapaciously shot at them.

Gentle Raccoon scanned the carnage before him. Body parts lay scattered, blown apart by the cannons and shrapnel. The earth beneath them was seeping, saturated with blood, making it slick and dangerous for the horses.

Black Elk called his name as they rode closer to the battlefield. He pointed to two young boys who had burrowed themselves in the ground, their rifles peeking like venomous snakes waiting for prey. The two children, approximately five or six years old, waved to them, the weight of a grown man's responsibility hardening their cherub features. They had been sniping at soldiers, quite successfully, as the lifeless bodies before them testified.

"Little boys should not have to live with this. They are brave little ones," Gentle Raccoon said to no one in particular.

The Lakota warriors fought with a ferocity that boiled deep in all men and women forced to defend their children and homes. They would not surrender after this invidious attack. Though outnumbered, the warriors would never succumb.

By evening, the soldiers had departed Wounded Knee Creek and the Lakota warriors apprehensively approached the campsite, searching for any who might still be alive or wounded.

Spirit of the Mountain rubbed her eyes as she grieved to see the bodies of the dead piled atop each other. An elder had cradled a small child, trying to use his own frail body as a shield, a feckless attempt against the onslaught of the Gatling and Hotchkiss guns; many were shot in the back as they ran for cover. She spied a pregnant woman on her side, her arm ripped off at the shoulder. The fetus … oh my God! She ran away from the body as she leaned near a pine tree to empty her stomach. Spirit of the Mountain closed her eyes, wishing the hideous vision to disappear. Shrapnel had hit the mutilated body of the fetus. The morbid picture burned in her mind.

She wiped her mouth and braced herself. Revenge, anger, and shame pulsed through her veins. Walking toward the church, she knelt down and helped a woman mortally wounded in the fight. A light snow had started to fall and was covering part of her body.

"Father Kraft … he is hurt. He has my daughter. Please help him," she croaked, and laid her head back on the ground.

Spirit of the Mountain held the woman's hand as her life slowly drained away. She might not have been able to do anything for the injured woman, but she could at least prevent her from dying alone. Saying a prayer, she walked away, scanning the area for the good priest.

She found him near the church holding a newborn child. A young man was trying to help him.

A young teen boy with Irish eyes stared at her, tears flowing down his cheeks. "He won't let me take the baby so I can stop the bleeding."

Father Kraft held his side with one hand and cradled the baby with the other. He was severely injured. The priest's eyes were filled with grief at the inhumanity of what had happened. Shaking her head, she realized that the soldiers had even left *him* to die.

A warrior approached and he and the boy helped Father Kraft into a wagon heading to Pine Ridge. The priest handed the baby to Spirit of the Mountain. Opening her coat, she tied the baby around her and fastened her coat to give the child more warmth. The snow started falling harder, the wind howled its warning. Battle-weary, the Lakota knew their search would be cut short. A snowstorm was blowing in fast.

The boy stood forlorn and stared at Spirit of the Mountain. She could see he had lost his spirit. "Come with me." Silently he followed her.

Joining the others, they frantically called to those who could hear them. "Reveal yourselves so we may help you."

Returning to Pine Ridge the warriors anticipated the peacefulness of home. As they entered one of the campsites, they could see that there had been a conflict at the Indian agency. Lodges stood abandoned; food lay on dying fires. The Lakota had abandoned their homes as quickly as possible. Black Elk and Red Crow separated from the group as they followed the tracks to find their families. The night would be a long and cold one. If the Lakota had abandoned their lodges, chances were they would not find shelter at the end of their path.

They used dark hulking shadows as guidelines, unsure if they would reach their destination. The blizzard was so fierce they could not see their own horses. The warriors were frustrated that they could not gather those who had died before the storm hit and prayed that the injured they had rescued would survive.

Exhausted from the physical battle and the emotional turmoil, they returned to the cabin. Instinct alone had guided them. When the frozen, weary friends arrived at the cabin door, a snowdrift prevented them from entering.

Gusts of wind pulsed freezing snow, blinding those who had dared to look out the window of the cabin. Dizzying streaks of white flashed and reflected the flickering firelight and candlelight in the chilly room. The fireplace struggled to keep the inhabitants warm and comfortable. Those who sat in front of it shivered, chilled and numb with fear.

The pile of food lay untouched on the sideboard. The day of death sat heavily upon them, churning and grinding away in their stomachs, burning their eyes in acrimonious memories. Their husbands and loved ones had not yet returned.

Beatrice, whose husband James had joined the Lakota in the battle, sat gazing wistfully at the baby on her lap. She had recently lost her newborn to sickness. When the storm had blown in, Sings to the Wind insisted she stay and not penetrate the disastrous storm that had blown in unexpectedly. They flinched with tension when they heard a banging and scratching near the door.

Sings to the Wind opened the door to find Little Red Hawk grasping James by the shoulder, preventing him from leaving. The white man's face was blistering and red from the irritation of the biting snow. "I have to go to my wife. You do not understand. She'll think I didn't make it."

"I am here, James," Beatrice called to him as she handed the baby to Little Owl. "Sings to the Wind suggested I wait here instead of fighting the storm."

They rushed into the house and grabbed blankets from the women to wipe the snow that had glued itself to their faces.

Hugs passed among the group; all were relieved that their loved ones had returned to the safety of their loving arms. No one questioned who the young Irish boy was; they made him warm and comfortable, accepting that he had joined their group. Spirit of the Mountain introduced him to the room, explaining how Michael had left the Home Guard and ended up at the church with Father Kraft.

They poured and distributed hot tea and strong coffee while the friends huddled in the room, the thought of food repugnant.

"Tea isn't enough. Is there any whiskey around?" James sighed.

Sings to the Wind opened the cabinet, grabbing the bottle and glasses. She hesitated at giving the Irish boy some whiskey.

Spirit of the Mountain piped, "Give him some, he deserves it."

Her body thawing and warming in the cozy room, Spirit of the Mountain opened her coat. The baby that was sleeping peacefully bellowed its objections. The story of the battle unfolded and the baby continued to cry.

Hunger vocalized in the cries of the infant painfully tightened and filled Beatrice. Mother's milk started pouring from her breasts, seeping through her dress. Her body had reacted instinctively to feed the hungry child.

Stunned and embarrassed, she jumped up. "I believe the child is hungry." Taking the baby, she excused herself and raced from the room.

After several minutes, she hunted in the chest of drawers for diapers. She had fallen in love with the babe immediately. The newborn, dry and full-bellied, cuddled against her heart and drifted into a peaceful slumber.

Beatrice returned to the main room of the cabin and calmly whispered to her husband. He nodded and spoke to Spirit of the Mountain. "Do you have plans for this child?"

"Not yet."

"We would like to raise her as our own," the couple replied.

Not knowing the couple well enough, she looked at Sings to the Wind, who smiled with a nod of assent.

"I don't have a problem with you taking the child, as long as you go through the proper authorities."

Tears streaked down the cheeks of both as they cried in happiness. It was a wonderful gift to receive after such a tragic day.

"I shall call her Bea. It is a tradition in our family to name all the first-born girls Beatrice."

Sings to the Wind and Spirit of the Mountain gaped at each other, stunned. The memory from almost twenty-five years ago came rushing back, when Spirit of the Mountain had purchased the bed, the bed that had brought them to this world … purchased from a woman named Bea, who had a mother … also named Bea.

Spirit of the Mountain stared at the infant she had carried through the storm. This infant's survival was a part of their destiny. Looking at Sings to the Wind, she could see their thoughts were the same. The math in their heads tallied; the birth order would be correct.

Chapter Thirty

The sun rose and peeked through the dark, heavy clouds. Scattered streaks of light caressed the snow that had blanketed Pine Ridge. Black Elk gathered a small war party to pursue the sound of more gunfire. Weaving their way westward, the group traveled through ravines and followed the ridge toward Wounded Knee, where the Lakota were fighting the soldiers.

Warriors sniped at the soldiers, from both sides of the creek, as they traveled toward the Mission. The war party joined the men and someone bellowed a war cry.

Gentle Raccoon had fired a few shots when Black Elk arrived with the war party. Black Elk knelt in prayer as he ceremoniously covered himself with the soil of Mother Earth. Returning to his mount, he cantered to the hill, stretching his arms as if he were in flight. He charged his horse toward the soldiers; reports of rapid gunfire besieged the warrior as he returned fire, angling his way back to the hill.

Seething bullets buzzed around him as he reached the crest unharmed. Black Elk dauntlessly surveyed the soldiers and slowly lowered his arms. Gentle Raccoon watched, mesmerized. A bullet found its way through the celestial protection and struck Black Elk, the impact convulsing his body. Wounded, Black Elk galloped down the hill back to the Lakotas. One of the other warriors staunched his wound and temporarily bandaged it, hoping they could reach a medicine man. Snow had started to fall.

Gentle Raccoon was careful with his shots. On both sides of the battlefield, nuns and priests tended the wounded and prayed over those who had died. The Lakota outnumbered the soldiers and expected the soldiers to call a retreat. Then, a roar of cheers bellowed from the soldiers across the field as reinforcements joined the battle and reversed the advantage.

Before the noon hour, the Lakota warriors reluctantly called a retreat. Gentle Raccoon rode back to Two Feathers' cabin. The snowstorm was relentlessly obscuring their sight, creating an inadvertent fortress that made it impossible for the warriors to defend themselves.

The blizzard pummeled South Dakota for three days, halting the battles. Residents of the reservation were now Mother Nature's prisoners, locked in their homes by walls of frozen snow; all attempts to get to the battlefield at Wounded Knee Creek were unsuccessful.

On the fourth day, Gentle Raccoon and Spirit of the Mountain rode toward Wounded Knee. They joined the Lakota who were gathering the bodies; thirty soldiers and three hundred Lakota from Spotted Elk's band, massacred. Their contorted bodies were frozen into ghastly positions. The Lakota, with soldiers assisting in the search, had found some members of Spotted Elk's band almost two miles from the original battleground.

Spirit of the Mountain knelt and prayed as she held Spotted Elk's hand. He had died propped against the seat they had given him. His features frozen in warning, interminable astonishment carved on his face.

Gentle Raccoon stood next to his mother, watching the soldiers struggle with the hard ground. The soldiers were piling the bodies on top of each other, dropping them into mass graves, no priest, no holy man to say prayers or perform a burial ceremony.

"Mom? I think I saw someone move." He rushed to the soldiers, sliding and slipping on the ground.

"I saw someone move! Stop, let me get him out."

Stunned and incredulous eyes pierced Gentle Raccoon. The soldiers grimaced, holding their shovels suspended in the air. They eyed him as if he were crazy.

"You've got to be kidding. There's no one alive in that pile." The officer who spoke raised his arm, and the soldiers proceeded to fill the grave with dirt and snow.

"Jesus!" He rushed to his mother as she was making her way to the grave. "Can't we do anything? I know I saw a hand reach out. I know I did."

"Stop!" Spirit of the Mountain yelled to the soldiers. "Let my son go down and get the one who is alive."

Soldiers stared open-mouthed at the officer in charge. Gentle Raccoon grabbed the temporary reprieve and jumped into the massive grave to search.

The officer growled, "There is no one alive in there."

One of the soldiers looked into the grave and saw Gentle Raccoon moving bodies ... searching. Nudging the soldier next to him, he filled his shovel and started throwing dirt onto him.

Spirit of the Mountain screeched and dove into the soldier, knocking him down. She yanked the shovel out of his hand and started hammering his face with her fists. Gentle Raccoon scrambled out of the grave as other soldiers tried unsuccessfully to pull his mother off. The moment he was clear of the grave, the officer cocked his gun and pointed it at Gentle Raccoon's head. The soldiers managed to subdue and restrain Spirit of the Mountain, a handgun at her throat, arms held securely behind her back.

Tears swelled, falling unbidden, as she scanned the mound where her son had seen movement. Someone was alive underneath those frozen bodies. She prayed for them, respecting their will to live. Whoever it was had managed to survive through three days of freezing weather, only to be dumped like garbage in a mass grave, buried alive.

"Leave," the officer demanded. "Now."

The soldier restraining Spirit of the Mountain released her arms. She turned and walked away, covering her face, repressing emotions too dangerous to release. Gentle Raccoon put his arm around his mother and smirked when he heard the soldier whine that she had broken his nose.

"We have to leave." She hissed, rubbing her wrists where red marks had already started marring her skin. "There is nothing else we can do now, son. We will return when they are gone."

Hours later mother and son returned. The Lakota who had returned with them prayed over the mass graves. Many had informed them that the priests had come and prayed for the spirits of the dead.

Gentle Raccoon felt unadulterated fury. "I am an American and I was proud to be one. Now …" He lifted his arms, sweeping gestures across the swath of destruction before them, "Look what they have done. I hate this country. I hate the ignorance of the white man."

"Please don't say that. This is a different world from ours. We had no control over this. I am just as angry and understand your resentment. Son, these soldiers were … are ignorant. They allowed their fear of the unknown to destroy them. They will have to look at themselves every day and live with what they have done. Do not carry the antagonism back with you to our world."

"I haven't felt this much anger since the World Trade Center."

She nodded. "Yes, and do you remember what you had said our government should do?"

He fisted his hands in memory. "Yes. I said we should take the rubble from the buildings and dump it on Afghanistan. We should use the country as a landfill. And when we were done clearing the debris, we should drop the bomb on whatever was left standing."

"You did not consider the innocent people that lived there."

"That's different."

"How?" She demanded. "How is it different?"

"We did not provoke war with them. The terrorists assaulted us. They attacked and killed people from all over the world."

"Not all Afghanis are terrorists."

"Our troops did not go over there and massacre innocent women and children. Even though some were injured or killed, it was not intentional." His eyes widened. "Have you changed your feelings about the war over there?"

She shook her head. "No. I have not changed my mind. However, I have struggled with prejudice against them. There are times when I find it hard to trust those that I see walking free in our world. I do not hate all Afghanis. However, I would be lying to you if I said I do not resent them."

"As far as I'm concerned, the soldiers who attacked the Lakota belong in the same category as the Japanese and the Afghanis. If the soldiers had besieged only the warriors, it would not be so shameful … if the terrorists had not murdered innocent people, I would not have so much rage."

His mother was silent for a few moments contemplating the words she wished to speak. "It is understandable that many still have volatile feelings toward the Japanese and the Afghanis. Any attack on our country is not something easily forgotten, or forgiven. This country is still learning and growing. I agree. It is a shameful and cowardly act. Only cowards attack defenseless men, women, and children."

"I feel so helpless. What can we do to help these people?"

"Which people?"

"Our people."

"The people in our world? Or those here in this one?"

Gentle Raccoon rolled his head, stretching and relieving the tension that had been beating him down for the last week. Snow from a drift swept up and swirled around them. They walked slowly to their horses. He helped his mother mount and they rode toward the cabin.

"I want to do both."

"Fight for their rights, Son. Fight against prejudice. The Lakota need to be educated in the white man's ways. Help the American citizens understand that the Lakota, or any Indian nation, deserves the same treatment as any other American citizen." Spirit of the Mountain bit her lip. "Our country is not perfect. Scream, shout, and criticize all you want. You have that right. As my son, I expect you to also have a solution. Help change this world. By doing so, you will help the future for the Indian."

"But I thought you weren't allowed to involve yourself and change the past."

"I'm not suggesting that, Gentle Raccoon."

"What do you think I should do?" A sparkle of hopefulness softened the anxious creases on his face.

"Follow your heart. Do what is right for you. What do you believe you should do?"

"I'm not sure."

Spirit of the Mountain bit her lip. "This is how I see it, as plainly and simply as I can put it to you. The past is done. It cannot be changed. What would happen to our world? What event would not happen because of your actions? There are good things that have happened in addition to the bad. Once the past has been changed, so has the future."

Rubbing her hands to warm them, she continued. "Sings to the Wind believed that she could change the past, and therefore change the future for the Indians. She manipulated the past by alerting the Lakota, attempting to avert the coming battle at the Little Big Horn. By doing so, the repercussions turned out to be worse than the initial past occurrence. Am I making sense to you?"

He nodded. "Yes, basically, what you are saying is that the battle was inevitable, but the outcome after she interfered ended up worse than it was initially supposed to be."

"Right. However, it had also changed the future. After she had attempted to change history, and I had returned home to our world, the Pine Ridge reservation was in a worse situation than when I had left. Buildings did not exist, schools were shacks, and repression was rampant. It was much worse after she tried to fix things."

"I'm surprised you still talk to her."

"Her heart was in the right place."

"But, she chose to stay here."

Spirit of the Mountain smiled. "Yes, she did. Sings to the Wind and Two Feathers do what they can to help the Lakota people. She is much more cautious now, careful about which battles she chooses to fight. *All* of her actions are an indirect battle for the Indian nation."

"What do you mean?"

"I'll give you one example. She is helping Christine, Little Owl, to fight for the woman's vote. She believes women are more compassionate. They would understand suppression better than men would. Once the women have the right to vote, she can push for the rights of the Indian nation."

"But women don't get the right to vote until 1920!"

"Some of the states gave women the right to vote before that. It was not a constitutional amendment until 1920. Once that was passed in 1924, the Indian became a citizen and received the right to vote."

"Does she know that?"

Spirit of the Mountain laughed. "Yes. Unfortunately, that is one of the things that has not changed. She refuses to cower."

"Sounds like someone I know quite well." He grinned as he nudged his mother.

"Yeup! And the chip riding next to me, too."

Chapter Thirty-One

Matthew stood on the hillside overlooking Tokata. Leaving their Lakota names back on the reservation, Christine, Andrew, Devry, Karen, and Matthew had returned the day before to a town oblivious to the true tragedy of the massacre. The people understood only what they read in the papers. His eyes filled with tears, his throat closed, and his heart thundered, exposing the raw pain he had buried the last few weeks.

The nightmare filled his eyes. *The babies, my God, the babies blown to pieces!* The old men and women, warriors who had defended their friends and family with honor, destroyed, killed like rabid animals. All destroyed! What was wrong with these people! Matthew resented their ignorance, the blind destruction of weakened people who could not defend themselves.

If I had known how it was going to end. His life would never be the same. He had actually believed he could do something good, but this had shown him how insignificant he really was. How arrogant and pompous, to actually believe he could have done something to fix the world, to change it and make it a better place.

With hands shaking, he fell to his knees, his heart crushed. He sobbed with deep wrenching cries. Matthew leaned forward, his forehead digging into the dirt as his soul shattered. Rocking, he allowed the tears to fall until he had none left to give Mother Earth. He rolled onto his back and stared at the clear, blue sky. His heart pounded and his jaw ached from the pain. He relished the throbbing pain. It made him appreciate that he lived and had survived the battle, for a reason.

Having the Lakota in his life was a precious gift. He was glad he did not know how it would end. He wished he could have stopped the tragedy … he would never regret the chance he was given to live with and love the proud people of the Lakota nation.

As he lay upon the earth, his mind unwound the intricate details and his body relaxed. An eagle circled above him, calling to the heavens. Smiling at the message from the Creator, Matthew knew where his path would lead.

He had work to do.

The hot steam from the water and the bubbles was hypnotic. Karen stretched in the luxurious bathtub and sighed. How wonderful it was to have hot water again. It was her first chance to be alone and it was glorious.

She raised her hand and stared at it. She had been in the water so long it had puckered. Her eyesight blurred, she saw Spotted Elk's hand clasped in hers. The vision at Wounded Knee and all that had happened that fateful day invaded her senses. Tears slowly trickled down her face. Leaning back against the edge of the tub, she wept. Heart-piercing, soul-sanctifying tears drenched her face, neck, and chest.

She could recall the storm clouds rolling over the skies as they fought the white soldiers. Deep inside, Karen had feared that day would come. And come it did, in a way she never anticipated. She wanted the bitterness and hatred of the world to go away. Deceit and cunning had left the Lakota unprepared for the tragic death of innocents.

"Why?" she asked the heavens.

Allowing hatred to fill her would destroy everything she stood for. She could not let this make her bitter. She had to put her trust in the Creator. Where were the colorful balloons that she carried in her mind, the child-like optimism of hope, faith, and happiness? Would she be able to dance again as she held onto them? The doors of faith had slammed shut on the Lakota. Would she be able to help them see that there was still a chance?

Karen mourned the inane deaths and the hostility she had been allowing to consume her. She wanted to surrender but she could not. There had to be a way to see the sun shine again. She could still see the slaughtered bodies and carnage of the women and children piled in mounds, scattered along the ravine, the mud and snow slicked with their blood as if Mother Earth herself had bled.

The Lakota's dream had died at Wounded Knee. A great nation, now broken and scattered by the winds of change. Their dream to return to the old ways ripped from their hearts, destroyed by the storm of hatred, ignorance, and fear. Their desire for justice and liberty, the pursuit of happiness, now lay beyond their reach. Ironic, since theirs *was* the American dream.

She could not continue to cry herself to sleep. She had to leave the sorrow behind and allow the love of the world to permeate and saturate her being. She refused to relinquish the good that was there, a beacon shining for her to grasp and hold closely to her heart.

Calming herself, Karen reached for the hope that dangled precariously within her grasp. It was in the skies, in the smiles of the loved ones that surrounded her. She longed for the sunlight of those who did see that happiness was available to all people. She would parade in the rain, because the sun would shine again.

Karen dressed, serene in the knowledge she had not lost hope. Determined, she shut the door to her room and searched for Matthew. She had to reassure herself that he had not lost his faith; that he still held onto his dreams.

Karen found him sitting alone, a blanket covering his legs and the fire blazing. The room was stifling with the heat. He looked toward her as she entered.

"I just can't seem to get warm enough."

"Are you okay? I mean, considering everything that has happened?"

"Yes, I'm fine. Don't worry about me."

"A mother's prerogative."

Smiling, he looked at his mother. *Does she know how much I respect her? That she is my hero? That even now, as old as I am, she still sits upon a pedestal? If I could be half the person she is, I would be happy. I would feel that I had succeeded in life.*

"I know where my path lies now."

She nodded and poured herself a cup of green tea. Sitting back in the chair, she waited patiently for him to continue.

"There are people here who will continue the fight for the Lakota. My place is in our world. I have work to do and a goal to reach. Many would consider it an impossible dream. But, I believe America is the best chance we have. It is a country of immigrants, a rainbow of diversity. I will start with the children; spread the rainbow of culture that is our country. I shall learn about different cultures and teach the children, and anyone else who wants to learn."

"It is an admirable quest. A worthy cause, my son."

"America has come so far. I do not want to be among those who hold racism and prejudice in their heart."

"I never believed that you had."

"It shames me but I must admit that I have. This experience has changed me. Could it have been prevented, if people had only opened themselves to different cultures and beliefs? We are the People. This country has ideals that can become reality. If we can get rid of ignorance, the world can live in peace."

Karen hugged Matthew, pride filled her heart, and tears threatened to spill. "I am proud of you, Son."

"Now, on a more personal note, I have an idea that I would like to throw at you."

During dinner, the opportunity had not arisen. They had discussed Red Cloud's meeting at the reservation. A telegram had come that day informing Andrew of what had been decided.

Red Cloud asked the insurgent warriors to cease their fighting. The winter had been a long and hard one. It was time to stop and take care of family and survival. It was time to make peace. He would protect those who agreed to peace.

Black Elk had come down from the Badlands and returned to the reservation. The battles had ended.

Later that evening, Matthew poured champagne around the table. Curious eyes followed him as he returned to his seat. Standing ceremoniously, he looked at everyone, those he respected and loved, who sat at the table. They had been through both rough seas and calm waters together. Through it all, they had stayed good friends, the kind who knew all your faults and still loved you just the same.

Lifting his glass to them, he proclaimed, "To everlasting love and friendship."

Cheers of concurrence followed with sips of the champagne.

"I have a request, and will humbly accept your decisions." Sitting down, he played with the napkin next to his glass.

Clearing his throat, he apologized. "Sorry, I'm a bit nervous."

His mother smiled, encouraging him to continue.

Matthew stared into Devry's eyes as he spoke. "Andrew and Christine, I would like to request that you allow Devry to accompany me and my mother to our world. It would not be a permanent situation but a trial, to see if she can live and accept our lifestyles before a decision to wed is made."

Christine's eyes widened. Andrew's unreadable eyes watched Matthew and Devry's reactions. He caught unfettered hope flaring in their eyes.

"For how long?" Christine asked, surprised that her husband had not asked the question.

"Not long, no more than a month at a time. We can improvise and work with it," Karen replied.

"Where would she stay?"

"With me, of course. It would not be wise for her to stay at Matthew's apartment. There is no one there to chaperone them. He lives alone."

"I don't have a problem with it as a trial. Actually, it would be wise to test the waters to see how it will go," Andrew stated.

Christine nodded her agreement. "When will you be returning home?"

"Monday," Matthew answered.

"After The Widow's party on Sunday." Karen shook her head and smiled. "Silly me, she is no longer a widow. After Lydia's party on Sunday, we will prepare for our departure."

Andrew turned to his daughter. "Devry, you have not uttered a word. Have you no say in this?"

A spurt of happiness tickled her features as she laughed. "I was afraid to say anything. I was too busy holding my breath and praying that you would consent."

Laughing, Andrew raised his glass and decreed, "To future endeavors."

Chapter Thirty-Two

Lydia Parker waddled about the room, holding the jar of honey Domina had brought her. Steeped in happiness, she was showing off the nursery and the fine craftsmanship of her husband, who had insisted on making the cradle himself.

Though she was only twenty weeks along, she had ballooned so quickly it appeared as if she were in the last trimester. Everyone said she was going to have twins. The way the baby (or babies) moved about, she complained she had a team of horses inside. Lane had moaned at the pronouncement, but she had spied him in the barn making another cradle.

Karen was looking out the window at the rear garden and grounds. "What a beautiful view you picked. If you put the rocking chair near the window, you'll have an excellent place for yourself while you feed the baby."

"Oh, yes it is!" Domina exclaimed, looking out the window. "What happened to the row of oleanders, Lydia? They are gone. I thought you loved those."

Lydia sighed. "I did, but they were not growing very well in this climate, so I gave up on them."

Karen twitched an eyebrow, stared at the honey and then at Lydia. She had never seen such beautiful and well-tended plants as those in Lydia's gardens. If she recalled, the oleanders flowered better in Lydia's garden than they did in her own yard in Florida. It did not make sense that Lydia would have them removed …

"When did you take them out?" Domina asked, disappointment coloring the words. "It looks so barren there now."

"I had Lane pull them out about a month ago. I have not decided yet … what I want to put in their place. Shall we join the gentlemen? I am famished!"

"Domina," Karen bit her lip, "how close were your bees to the oleanders?"

Domina's eyes widened. "Oh my, the bees are on the opposite end of our property, far away from the oleander. I have a field of wild flowers for the bees, Karen." Domina added, "Our family has kept bees for generations. Oleanders are beautiful, however, any decent beekeeper would know to keep their bees away from the plant."

Karen slowly turned to Lydia, who met her penetrating stare with a slight smile.

The ladies entered the sitting room and joined the gentlemen, deep in a political discussion.

"I don't think the government needs any more land. They've taken enough as it is," Andrew growled.

"This is not about taking land. It is about preserving natural wildlife. If they do not do something about it now, people will destroy the land, move on to more fertile land, and then destroy that, too," Lane emphasized.

"What are you gentlemen disagreeing about now?" Domina asked.

"The Forest Reserve Act they are going to sign into law."

"So they take land away from the Indian and sell it, or they take land and then make a law that creates a National Forest or a National Reserve out of it. It doesn't make sense to me."

Matthew lifted his hand. "Andrew, can I be presumptuous and ask how you became a landowner?"

Andrew smiled. "It's all your mother's fault. She told me about the Dawes Act."

"I don't understand. What's the Dawes Act?" Lane queried.

"It gave the government the right to take Indian land and sell it for private ownership," Andrew explained. "What it also did was give the Indian who accepted the land grant one hundred sixty acres of property and full citizenship."

Matthew added. "It not only satisfied those who were greedy and wanted Indian Territory; it squelched the humanitarians in D.C. who were causing a ruckus over the deceptive takeover of Indian tribal lands."

"Correct."

"So why do you object to the National Forests and Reserves?" Lane asked

"Why take land away that the Indian was living on, then make it a public Reserve where the white man doesn't know how to live on the land anyway? If they wanted to preserve the land for its natural wildlife, why destroy the buffalo and the Indian's way of life?"

"Well Andrew, at least it won't be destroyed by greedy white hands. It'll be preserved as nature intended."

Juan laughed. "Until the government decides it wants it for other purposes."

"I believe the law is being passed so the government can't take it for themselves."

"Until someone discovers gold," Andrew added dryly.

"Oh, did you hear the rumors about gold near Cripple Creek, Colorado?" Catherine piped, now fully recovered from her ordeal.

"I hope they are prepared for the rush of miners."

"They will be swamped with thousands of people. Towns built overnight, gunfights, rapes, and murders will be common."

"And those same towns destroyed and deserted once the gold is gone," Karen added.

"More ghost towns. That is just what we need. I had my fill of lawbreakers when I was a Pinkerton man."

"Those who want to succeed stay and find a way."

"And those who don't have true grit leave and go somewhere else."

"I imagine you did get tired of it, Lane," Domina remarked. "However, you still came to our town to help anyway. How is the hunt for the murderer going?"

Lane shook his head. "Not well. There has not been an unusual or questionable death in months. Not that that is a bad thing, but I have not found any evidence to help convict anyone. I am not giving up. Sooner or later, the murderer will strike again and I will be there waiting."

"He is bound to make a mistake. The murderer isn't exactly going to shout out his guilt either," Matthew pointed out.

"Since we've married, the town has become the peaceful paradise it was when I first came here," Lydia noted.

"It doesn't make sense," Lane continued. "Someone has to know who was murdering all those men. Yet, no one has come forward. Why would they protect a murderer?"

"Maybe whoever was doing it left town?" Matthew surmised. "Has anyone moved since the murders stopped?"

"Possibly the murderer knew he was about to be exposed and stopped to evade capture?" Andrew proposed, staring out the window.

"Interesting suggestion, but not normal for a serial murderer. They would move to another town or state, continue their spree somewhere else."

"Has anyone moved away?" Karen asked, as she watched Andrew avoid eye contact. "Did you see if there were any murders in other towns that were similar to the ones here?"

"No one has moved lately." Lane blew out a frustrated breath. "I've got telegrams and letters sent to all the sheriffs in the state and the surrounding territories asking to alert me if they come across anything like the murders here."

"Nothing?"

Lane shook his head. "Absolutely nothing."

"I fear he will never be caught. The murderer is free, walking around our town as one of our own." Catherine pushed a strand of hair away from her eye.

"I'm afraid this will be one of those unsolved mysteries," Lydia frowned. She walked over to the cabinet and brought out a bottle of port. Devry noticed her carrying the bottle to the table and grabbed glasses for the group.

"Like the Boston Strangler," Matthew observed, and his mother cringed.

She whispered in his ear. "Wrong century; that happened in the 1960s."

Matthew blushed as everyone in the room looked at him blankly.

Devry added, "Or Jack the Ripper."

"Suspected but never caught," Lane grumbled.

Chapter Thirty-Three

Monday morning arrived with the hot sun blazing through the window and a mockingbird chirping its many tunes. Devry threw the comforter off. She was hot and sweating. Anna must have stoked the fire, heating the room as if it were summer. Stretching like a Cheshire cat, she opened her eyes and screamed.

Jumping out of bed, she quickly scanned the room. *Where am I? How did I get here? What an odd place!* Devry rubbed her eyes and when she reopened them, she expected to see her bedroom. However, it was *not* her bedroom. Running to the window in a panic, she stared out at the oddly shaped houses and strange carriages on the streets. Devry squealed when the door flew open.

Karen stood before her, strange clothing draped over her arm. "What is it? What happened?"

Devry whimpered as she looked around the room. Karen wore men's clothing, dressed in the oddest outfit she had ever seen.

"I'm sorry. I just went to the kitchen to let the cat out and send Jen to buy you a few clothes. You were sleeping so soundly I did not think you would awaken yet. I had every intention of being here in the room when you woke."

"W – w – where's Matthew?"

Karen looked at her watch. "He'll be here soon. He had to wait for us to return before he went to sleep."

"I know the two of you explained that I would be in a different world … but," she shook her head. "I guess I really did not quite understand."

"It took me a while, too. Here, I have clothing for you." Laying each item on the bed, she explained. "These are called jeans, a T-shirt, bra, and underpants."

Devry lifted the lace underpants with two fingers, suspending them in the air.

"They do not cover much, do they? I take it I wear them under the jeans?"

Karen nodded.

"And this?" she queried, picking up the bra with a puzzled face.

"That is a bra or brassiere, depending on what part of the country you live in. You use it in place of a corset."

Devry's eyes widened while Karen laughed at her incredulous expression.

"It is much more comfortable. Honest, you will never want to wear a corset again. I will leave you to dress. If you have a problem, call out. I'll be in the kitchen making coffee."

Devry nodded her head as Karen shut the door. Turning about the room, she looked at all the odd and unusual items. Lavish ornamental furnishings dominated the room. The large bed had four posts and was set up for a canopy. The bureau and mirror were similar, made from the same wood but not carved with angels and other symbols. Next to the bed, she saw a table with a lamp and an odd box with numbers on it.

The walls had electric switches on them, similar to the switch plates at home. The lamp on the table next to the box was electric. She could see the cord. Devry reached over and touched the base of the lamp. She jumped. The light turned on!

Her heart beat rapidly. She felt a slight breeze even though the window was closed. Looking up, she spied a large fan circling overhead. It was creating a pleasant indoor breeze. Devry took a deep breath. She had only seen such elaborate ceiling fans in pictures. *Is this what I want, to be in Matthew's world?* Taking another deep breath, she repeatedly told herself she could do it. With that, she fumbled with the unfamiliar clothing until she managed to look presentable.

Looking in the mirror, she stared at the odd image before her. The T-shirt had a painting of a whale on it and words that said … turning her head, she twisted the shirt to read it. *Sea World. Maybe that is the name of this country.*

Shutting the door as she left the room, Devry called out to Karen and followed her voice to the kitchen. They sat and enjoyed the morning coffee and biscuits. For over an hour, Karen explained her world, which Devry soon discovered, was Florida. Sea World was a park she might see in the near future.

Jen came barreling in with armfuls of packages and various bags. Karen was making introductions just as Matthew stepped into the room. Jen dropped the bags and packages on the floor as she leapt into her brother's arms. Devry had never heard anyone talk so fast! Matthew spit his answers out with each ricochet of questions.

After a few more minutes chatting about the last few months, Matthew drained his coffee cup and bid them good-bye.

Stunned and hurt that Matthew would leave so soon after he arrived, Devry asked, "Where are you going?"

"I have to go talk to my boss. Let him know I'm back from my sabbatical, so he can put me on the schedule."

She watched him rush out the door and looked quizzically at Karen. "What's a boss?"

Karen smiled and explained. She could see Jen was starting to prepare an onslaught of questions for Devry. She was surprisingly quiet during most of the morning, listening intently to the conversation. She watched Jen squint her eyes with suspicion when Devry mentioned her ceremony into womanhood.

"How old are you?"

Devry smiled. "Fourteen."

Jen's mouth dropped open in shock. "What? No one told me you were fourteen. Isn't that a tad bit young, even for your world? That is disgusting. What in the world is he thinking?"

She jumped up to run after her brother.

"Stop!" Karen called out. "Just wait until you hear everything."

Listening intently to the drama that unfolded before her, understanding dawned and Jen finally sympathized with Matthew and Devry. She knew her brother well enough to know that this situation must have upset him.

"What did he do when he found out?"

"He avoided me and refused to speak to me."

"He was not happy." Karen sighed, hurting for her son. "He did not take it well, at all."

At least Matthew had found someone, even if he could not have her yet. She looked over to her daughter. Her Indian name fit her well; *Kimimala*, butterfly. Jen just bounced from one 'I'm in love' to the next, never having a relationship last more than three months. Devry told Jen and Karen about the "kissing test" suggesting that Jen should try it. Jen's quick retort had the three laughing and giggling the rest of the morning.

Karen left to meet her husband John for lunch. The two girls, who quickly became fast friends, grabbed the packages and bags and went to the spare room where Devry had awoken that morning. The first thing Devry noticed when they went into the room was the elegant hand-embroidered canopy. *Matthew must have put that up because Karen was with me the whole time. How odd that he would do that.*

"That wasn't there before."

"Matthew put it up after he arrived back from South Dakota."

"Why?"

"It stops the bed from allowing us to travel. My mother keeps the canopy up unless she is using the bed. Come on; let's try on some of these new clothes. They are going to look really cool on you."

Devry stared at herself in the full-length mirror. She cleared her throat, shaking her head in denial at the vision. The jeans were snug and formed tightly around her thighs, flaring at the bottom. The lavender shirt was sleeveless and dipped in a V-shape on the front. Turning around, she looked at her backside.

"Oh, my stars! Is this clothing normal for this world?"

"You look fine and it is conservative compared to some of the clothing that is available."

Devry bit her lip and inhaled deeply.

"Here, try this skirt. I bought it knowing it would match the shirt you have on."

Devry took the lavender and blue daisy print skirt. She stared at her reflection in the mirror.

"This is appalling! You can see my calves and ankles." She wrinkled her nose. "It looks odd with these socks."

Jen laughed. "This is so cool. I have not had this much fun in such a long time. Take off the socks and put these sandals on."

"Oh, no. I cannot show my feet and toes. That is completely unacceptable."

"Give yourself time. Soon enough you will be wearing shorts."

"Shorts?"

"I'll show you at the mall."

Trying on the garments took a while, but the girls enjoyed the bantering of their growing friendship. They put away the ones that fit and set aside the clothing to return.

Jen smiled conspiratorially and winked. "Ready for more cool magic?"

The two hopped into the Jeep Wrangler, where Jen showed her how to attach the seat belt, and off they went to the mall. They rode past open areas where horses and cows grazed. After a time, they turned onto a wide road. Devry was amazed, her mouth hanging open the whole trip. Wide-eyed, she pointed. "What is that? It is huge!"

"That is an 18-wheeler, a truck. It is used to transport many things, for example food supplies, clothing; basically any kind of delivery needed for a business."

She could not believe the magnitude of everything that whizzed by her. *Imagine! Not needing horses for transportation. There were so many of those trucks and automobiles on the road.*

She was amazed at all the houses; all bunched together with hundreds of rooftops, as far as the eye could see.

Pointing out the window, "That must be a very affluent rancher or farmer to have all those homes for his workers."

Jen creased her forehead. "What do you mean?"

"All those houses."

"No, those are all privately owned homes."

"Privately owned? They all look the same! Doesn't your world allow people to have a choice on what they want their house to look like?"

"Well, of course they do. Those houses are in what we call deed-restricted neighborhoods. They have certain rules that they must follow to own a home in that particular area."

"Doesn't sound like much of a choice to me."

Jen laughed. "Now you sound like John, my stepfather. He doesn't care for homeowners associations, either."

"I don't blame him."

Jen reached over and touched a button. Strange music filled the air. Devry eyed it warily. Before she had a chance to ask about it, they arrived at a restaurant owned by a Scot. She watched as Jen spoke to a box with pictures of food behind it. Arriving at a window, a smiling boy handed them bags and containers.

"These are hamburgers and French fries. This," handing her the soda, "is what you would refer to as a fountain drink."

Smiling, she bit into what Jen called French fries.

"This is amazing. What an interesting world, a Scot or Irishman selling French food. Ha! You speak into a box and go to a window and have the food in minutes after you request it."

Devry licked her lips as she chewed her sandwich. Sighing at the delicious taste of the meat in her mouth, she grinned at Jen.

"This is … what did you say before … chilly?"

Jen laughed. "Cool. The word is cool, not chilly."

"I shall remember. Cool. This is cool."

They pulled into a large parking lot and Devry whispered. "Does everyone have automobiles?"

"Feels that way, but no. Not everyone."

Armed with a credit card, Devry and Jen entered the mall. Throngs of people rushed about intent on their own business.

"There are so many people, how does one greet them all without constantly nodding?"

"This is not Tokata. Do not greet or acknowledge anyone we have not introduced you to. It isn't safe."

"But, that is rude."

"It is not safe."

Devry slowed her steps looking toward the ceiling. "Where is the orchestra? How does the music come from the ceiling? I was about to ask you about the music, earlier in the automobile, but I was distracted."

"It is called a radio. It sends music over the air waves, like a telegraph, only you hear music."

Devry nodded, staring at a window display with jewelry glittering in the light.

They accomplished a great deal in the two hours they were at the mall: clothes, make-up, jewelry, and hair supplies … they bought it all. Devry had everything she would possibly need for the month she would be visiting. She had just gotten her ears pierced, when she nudged Jen on the arm.

"Look at that boy," she whispered. "His hair is blue! How does he make his hair point like that?"

"Hair spray and hair gel. We have some at home." Jen raised her eyebrow. "Would you like to dye your hair blue?"

Giggling, they left the mall, hands full of packages.

Saturday came and the group arrived at Sea World. Devry was amazed at the animals and talked incessantly about the seals, Clyde and Seymore. They saw the show three times.

Jen and Devry squealed in delight as they fed the dolphins. At the underwater viewing area, Devry stood mesmerized as she watched the dolphins play. All enjoyed the seals, the killer whales, and the manatees.

She dug in her heels when they tried to convince her to ride on what they called a roller coaster. She did not think she would like it at all. Devry refused to try the other ride, also. She waited patiently while Karen and John put coins in the machine so she could spray Matthew and Jen as they went down the big hill and splashed into the water.

Matthew and Devry's friendship grew strong. As each day progressed, both knew in their hearts that their marriage would come in time. Devry completely understood why it was in Matthew's best interest to wait.

She had visited the fire station with Jen. The men greeted her as if she were a small child. They did not see a grown woman, ready for marriage. And like a child, she stared wide-eyed, exploring the fire trucks and firehouse, cementing their opinions. Matthew introduced her to his co-workers as a distant relative, a cousin on holiday enjoying the Florida sun.

The month flew by. Devry adjusted to their magical world without difficulty. She and Jen had become as close as sisters. Matthew arrived at his mother's, tired and frustrated. Wildfires were being set and the firefighters were forced to go in too many directions. They spent a quiet evening at home. He walked Devry to her room. Tomorrow, she would not awaken in this world, but would return home with the sunrise. She did not want to leave, but she also missed her family and looked forward to seeing them again.

"Don't be sad. We will see each other again," Matthew whispered as he held her close.

"I know. I am going to miss you."

"I'm going to miss you, too."

He kissed her on the forehead. Devry closed her eyes and wished he would kiss her lips, just once more.

Matthew saw the need and desire and succumbed to impulse. Slowly, he touched and tasted her sweet lips. A sigh of satisfaction passed her lips as she turned off the light. He looked once more at the woman of his dreams. Smiling, he shut the door. Leaning his forehead against the closed door, he shut his eyes tightly and whispered ...

"I love you."

Milestones

1890 Congress establishes the Oklahoma Territory, taking Indian territory from the Eastern tribes.

Congress establishes Yosemite National Park to preserve the Sequoia forests.

1892 Under the Dawes Act, approximately two million acres in Montana is opened to white settlers.

1901 Congress offers U.S. citizenship to Native Americans if they agree to give up their tribal affiliations.

1909 The Dawes Act continues to open land to white settlers—700,000 acres in Washington, Idaho, and Montana.

1924 Native Americans receive the right to vote under The Indian Citizenship Act. Many western states try to prohibit their voting.

1934 The Dawes Act is repealed.

About the Author

Pamela Ackerson was born and raised in Newport, Rhode Island where history is a way of life. She now lives in Central Florida, a place that flaunts imagination and fantasy.

For years she wrote poems and short stories and was determined that one day she would write a book. Encouraged by her family and friends, she started writing *Home of the Braves*, the first novel of her trilogy.

Her love of history and the Native American people encouraged the combination of reality and fiction. The idea that you could travel anywhere you wanted came from her own dreams and inspired the use of the antique bed as transportation to experience the wonders of history.

Pam is currently working hard on the third book of the trilogy. Will Matthew and Devry realize their greatest dream? Or, will the modern world steal her away? Will it be Jen's turn to use the bed?

Printed in the United States
43791LVS00003B/1-51